Taking the Tumble

by

Eve Dew Crook

Taking the Tumble

Cover Art by *Diana Carlile*

The Wild Rose Press, Inc.
PO Box 708
Adams Basin, NY 14410-0708
Visit us at www.thewildrosepress.com

Publishing History
First Crimson Rose Edition, 2013
Print ISBN 978-1-61217-974-2
Digital ISBN 978-1-61217-975-9

Published in the United States of America

"But, Mac, are you quite sure about the job offer?" Cyn asked. "It's such a big responsibility…and your father?"

"Big M's agreed. He believes I know what I'm doing." Mac looked pleased to say the words. "Suppose we try it for six months, at a salary commensurate with the position. And did I mention benefits? Health insurance, pension, sick days, dental plan…the works."

"The works, you say? Just what other benefits do you have in mind?"

"Your own corner office, big desk, couch."

"Any other fringe benefits?"

"Making out with the boss?"

She giggled. "I'll want that written into the contract."

"Deal!" Pressing her close, he ran his fingers down her spine. "I'm sure I can accommodate whatever you want. This is definitely a job with perks."

Cyn clung to him, wriggled her hips, then pulled away. "Come inside. My driveway is no place to make such a momentous decision. You can keep me company while I consider it—from several different positions."

Oh, yeah…. He nudged her toward the front door.

As Mac stepped over the threshold, he turned back, glanced around. This was not the moment for a chill to creep up the back of his neck. "Dammit," he muttered. "What's wrong now?" The icy feeling shocked him, momentarily wiping out his euphoria.

Someone was watching.

Dedication

To the best of friends, Phyllis and Marilyn,
whose encouragement and support
made this book possible—
and to the special, important men in my life,
Ken and Randy.

Chapter 1

It was the perfect put-down. The sassy retort was there, right on the tip of her tongue when she needed it. Cyn turned to face the intimidating man behind her. "I'm not falling for you."

Her brain must be working double time. One day back, and school was already sharpening her wits. Eager as she was to make the right first impression, this opportunity was too good to pass up. Cyn looked into the professor's eyes and grinned.

A gasp sounded in back, then a hiss. "Smartass."

Her elation died, but she ignored the remark, focusing on the professor. He didn't return her smile. As she stared, eyes bright from holding back tears, someone clapped, then stopped abruptly. She resisted the urge to turn and see who was on her side. Waiting was all she could do.

The classroom grew so silent Cyn could hear the Third Avenue bus rumble by.

The professor surveyed each student standing in the circle. His gaze returned to Cyn, weary patience dripping from his tone. "I'm trying to conduct an experiment in trust. Which part of that statement don't you understand? The students have all fallen backwards, and I've caught each and every one. You're the last." He swept back the graying lock of hair that had fallen to his forehead. "Double meanings can work in the right place. We'll be looking for them when we study subtext. But for now, let's try again."

Cyn didn't budge—the prof couldn't know how fast her heart was beating. "I can't fall backwards," she said. "Never could. I'm backwardly challenged."

Raising a thick black eyebrow, the professor watched her a moment longer. She locked her knees to stop their trembling. Why had she picked today to brush her unruly mop into a ponytail? To make herself look younger, of course, so she'd fit in. All she'd accomplished was to expose herself to embarrassment. *Dammit*, her ears were burning! They felt redder than her hair.

Oh, hell. No one had pushed her into the registrar's office. No one had held the pen while she signed up for this crazy communications course. Thank goodness all her other subjects were online. She wouldn't have to face embarrassing moments doing the assignments at home.

It took weeks of waffling before she'd decided to return to grad school after the divorce. So what if ten years had passed since she'd last smelled chalk? This was the right move. With the freelance proofreading her old editor had offered, she had enough in the bank to keep her solvent for a year. It should suffice to get an advanced degree and then move on.

Not on, but *up*, Cyn corrected herself, repeating the word like a mantra. A little blip like failing to fall backwards into the professor's arms wouldn't stop her...but it might slow her down. She bit her lip, hoped he hadn't taken offense. If he disliked her, an entire semester in his class would be the pits.

But she couldn't back down. This was the twenty-first century. Fear of falling had to be allowed.

A half hour ago she had walked into this faded classroom, watching the dust motes float in the air where sunlight streamed through sooty windowpanes. Tax money certainly hadn't been wasted on this building. On the white board in front of the room, MARZIN had been written in bold black letters. No first name. No title. Yet it was clear who the dark-haired, blown-dry hunk slouching beside the board was. His shirtsleeves were rolled up, red tie loose, button-down collar open. The only thing missing was the day's growth of beard. Wasn't he a little old for this pose?

He straightened, waited till everyone was seated. "You may not have known it when you signed on," the professor said, "but this is an experimental class in communications." His voice was soft but commanded attention. The students leaned forward, straining to hear.

"An important element in developing friendly relations is trust, and we'll begin by testing that statement. You're all going to fall backwards, one at a time, trusting me to catch you. Leave your belongings on your desks and come to the front of the room." He gathered the fifteen students in a circle and stood behind them, tapping shoulders. One at a time they went down like ten pins, landing on his chest and held up by strong arms. Now here she was, the last to "perform." *Damn damn damn.* She'd never wanted to be the center of attention.

Cyn turned to look at her fellow sufferers. On her left, a tall, skinny redhead with straight hair reaching past her shoulder stared balefully at her curls. Wasn't it always the way? She wished her hair was straight and silky, yet Cyn could have sworn the look she got from her neighbor was envy. The girl's eyes glazed over, as if she were looking right through her. For a microsecond, Cyn felt her body vanish. The spot where she had been standing was empty. How weird!

Her imagination was overactive today. Shrugging off the eerie sensation, Cyn turned back to the world she knew. On her right, a blond-haired man with a tennis player's build caught her eye. His sympathetic smile sent a glow of warmth through her. Cyn's knees stopped trembling. Her ponytail bounced as she nodded and smiled back.

The startled look he returned was puzzling. Could he have felt that warmth, too? He looked about her age—maybe she wasn't alone among these teens and twenties. What an intriguing development....

Cyn took in the sharp planes of his face, his well-shaped lips. Not bad. When they returned to their seats, she'd take a closer look. He couldn't help her now.

Across the circle, she glimpsed an Asian girl switching her weight from one foot to the other, a black guy gazing out the window, another who looked Spanish and attentive, and a bored muscleman-biker type. Then came a heavy, freckled girl and a brown-skinned guy with a bushy mustache—the class was a regular UN.

She ended her perusal when the professor spoke to her once more. "Try again," he coaxed. Swiveling to face him, Cyn shook her head so hard, a wiry curl slipped out of the ponytail. *I should be able to do this*, she thought. *I'll be safe—Marzin won't let me fall. What's wrong with me?*

But she couldn't get past lifting her toes and

rocking back on her heels. Couldn't take the final step and let go—backwards. She wanted to kick herself.

The professor studied her once more, sighed long and loud, then turned away. "Okay, class," he said. "Resume your seats." He leaned on his desk, his eyes darting around the room. "You may as well prepare yourselves. More experiments of the kind you've just *endured* will follow."

A groan rose from the back. He ignored it. "Here's your reading list," he said, pulling a batch of papers from his bulging briefcase. We're a small group, so we'll be using pen and paper for assignments. Electronic devices won't be necessary, but if you wish, you may record my words of wisdom." He surrounded this last line with a mocking grin that surprised Cyn. Maybe the guy had a sense of humor, after all.

Prof Marzin handed the stack to the Asian girl in the front row, and she jumped up to pass around the papers. Cyn admired the ivory chopsticks with ladybugs at the tips she'd stuck in her hair. Pity the sequined glasses didn't go with them.

At the thought, she mentally slapped the back of her hand. Stop judging! You're in Manhattan, Cynwyd Westland. The cosmopolitan melting pot. Everything is different here, including this conglomeration of students. So one of them likes flash around her eyes. Her choice. This isn't the suburbs...and aren't you glad?

You're in for a joy ride if you've got the guts, her inner self whispered. *New faces, new friends, new ways of looking at the world—remember that.* Cyn sat up straighter, ignoring the Daddy voice trying to override, ordering her to lose the distractions and concentrate on getting her M.A. degree.

The professor's tone had grown impatient. "We've had enough excitement for today. Between now and the next class, I want everyone to think about the different ways we communicate with each other. Although we converse, a great deal of information is passed without words. How?

"Let your minds roam. Stretch your imaginations— your powers of reasoning." He paused, then added, "Don't dwell on what's expected of you for the rest of the semester. You'll find out soon enough."

Stuffing the leftover sheets back into his briefcase, he directed his gaze at each student—paused briefly when he caught Cyn's eyes—then grabbed his jacket from the back of his chair and dismissed the class.

For a moment Cyn remained in her seat, stunned by his swift exit. She glanced at the clock. Half of the session was still to come. The prof must have a hot date.

Noise erupted in the room. She looked around the milling bodies for the man with the warm smile but didn't see him among the students hurrying out the door. A ripple of disappointment passed through her before she returned pen and notepad to her brand new briefcase and followed the gaggle out. She'd be back on Tuesday—and so would he.

Once on the street, Cyn reached into her purse for her cell phone. "Hi," she said when her friend Audrey answered. "I want you to know—I'm backwardly challenged."

"You made that up, Cyn. Why aren't you in class?"

"The Prof let us out early. I'll explain all, soon as I get there. Make coffee."

She walked to the parking garage and retrieved her

car. With fingers clutching the steering wheel, Cyn headed home via the Midtown Tunnel. The yawning opening always spooked her—all those tons of water overhead. What if the roof sprang a leak? She knew the idea was farfetched, but her buttons were really being pushed today. She had to calm down. Her imagination had already gotten away from her once.

Concentrate on something else. The blond man with the tennis player's build slipped into her mind, but before she could recall the delicious feeling his smile had left her with, the memory of her embarrassing moment returned and captured her thoughts. With a sigh, she began to sing aloud, mimicking the lilt of her Welsh forebears. "Cynwyd-Backwardly-Challenged-Westland, look you," she warbled, blocking out everything else. Her foot tapped the brake, keeping the rhythm as she inched forward.

At last, sunlight broke through the darkness; she'd reached the tunnel exit. Easing her grip on the wheel, Cyn surveyed the road ahead. Bumper to bumper traffic still—Long Island formed a concrete ribbon stretching out to the ocean. It's going to sink one of these days, she thought. All those cars will weigh it down.

Her imagination took over. The Island tilted, its lighthouse at Montauk Point dipping into the sea first, like the prow of the Titanic. Cars rolled off into the surf, piling on top of each other. Images flickered of the long skinny island slipping under the water beach by beach—East Hampton, Southampton, Freeport—while beach balls bounced on car roofs and striped umbrellas bobbed in the waves.

Giggling at her imaginary scenario, Cyn almost forgot that dreadful moment when she'd stood paralyzed, unable to fall. But when she neared her friend's home, the memory drifted back.

Just one snicker from Audrey when I describe what happened, and I'll keep my catastrophes to myself. Why did I let her talk me into returning to school?

Pulling into the driveway, she turned off the ignition and sat gnawing on a knuckle. She had to compose herself. It was time for a little T.L.C.

****

Mac arrived back at the office to find a line of people waiting for him. Three of the magazines were going to press the next day.

"*New Fuels* has a hole in the ion story," a young guy with floppy yellow hair yelled the loudest.

"You know the routine," Mac said patiently. "Add subheads."

"*Flying Car* ran over," broke in a young woman, her glasses tucked into a thick mop of brown curls.

"How much?"

"Four lines."

"Read it over. Kill the widows. Look you guys, gals. You know I'm going to be out of the office two afternoons a week for the next four months. What's the rule?"

"WLT-LET," they said in unison.

"Yep. Work late tonight, leave early tomorrow. This always happens the day before press time. Live with it. You're all highly trained, and you know what to do." Mac dropped his gaze to a four-page insert an older, balding man had shoved into his hand. "For *E-Book Markets*?"

At the man's nod, Mac gritted his teeth. "They're always late. Can you still fit it in between the first and

8

second folios?"

The man looked at his watch. "Possibly."

Mac gripped his shoulder. "You will, Charlie. I can always count on you." He turned to the others. "Get going, gang. You know your jobs. Leave copies in my office and then get the hell out of here."

With a good-natured grumble the crowd departed, clearing the door to Mac's office.

Shaking his head, he sat down at his desk and reached automatically for a cigarette. Hand in mid-air he swore, then swiveled around to the tiny refrigerator mounted on a bench against the wall. He was grabbing a beer when his door opened.

"Hi, Dad," he said, back still to the door.

"How did you know it was me?"

"Things may be more informal here than when you were publisher, but I still expect my staff to knock. You never know who I might have on my desk." He grinned. "Want a beer?"

"I can use it," his father said, glancing at the desk and chuckling. "It was hot on the golf course. I just stopped by to ask how your first class went."

"Have a seat...if you can find one." Mac pushed aside some papers and scrutinized his father, noting the bright green T-shirt with the tiny logo beneath his open sports jacket. Took in the rosy face, the trim body in gray slacks hiding the barely-there signs of a paunch. "You're looking well."

His father sat down. "Fresh air, good food, and I didn't use the golf cart."

"You're not overdoing it?"

"No, exercise is good. Stop sounding like your mother. How did it go?"

"You couldn't wait till I got home? You know I'm coming to dinner tonight."

His father looked at Mac, his lips shaping that same beguiling smile. "Even after three years, it's not easy to give up this place."

"You never change, Big M." Mac shook his head but didn't quite hide a grin. "That mini heart attack hasn't slowed you down."

"I should hope not. So I'll ask again. How did it go? Did you meet anyone interesting?"

"None of those movers and shakers you mentioned when you talked me into taking the course were there," he said. "And if their grown-up kids attended, I couldn't tell on the first day. The professor ended the class early, and we all hightailed it out of there. I was a little anxious myself, with press day tomorrow on three of the prints and two of the 'zines."

Finishing his beer, Big M stood up. "You've got them well in hand. It's a tight ship, I can see. Later, then."

His father left and Mac shrugged, the grin still hovering. The guy couldn't let go. No matter that he had retired after the heart scare and turned everything over to Mac. No matter that he'd accepted Mac's e-versions of all six magazines and saw the company's revenue doubled. A son was still a son, and Mac knew he had been a trial as a teenager. Rebellion was in his DNA, but his dad conveniently forgot that. No doubt that troublesome teen still lingered in the back of Big M's mind.

Recalling the afternoon, Mac looked down and saw he had been doodling on his yellow pad. A sketch had appeared of a female leaning back on her heels, arms out to brace herself. Her curvy figure came easily to his pen. So…agreeable. He drew her face with her eyes scrunched shut, full lips pinched tight. A bushy ponytail appeared to bounce on her back, adding a comical touch. Comical, but charming. Yes, he'd credit himself with hitting the right note.

As he eyed the cartoon, Mac recalled the odd sensation that had left him glowing when she'd returned his smile. Hers was a knockout. He knew his effect on people, but feeling the reverse was a shock.

Well, four months of classes—time enough to figure out what it meant. If he didn't want to be late for dinner, he'd better get his mind off those curves. Slipping the pad into his desk, he looked over the sketch one last time, then slammed the drawer shut and rolled up his sleeves.

****

Audrey was already pouring two mugs of coffee when Cyn reached the kitchen. Steam hissed from a shiny cappuccino machine. She sniffed with pleasure, recalling their college days, the dorm reeking of cheap ground beans perking all night on a hot plate while they crammed for exams.

Cyn watched Audrey carry the steaming mugs topped with foamy milk to the table. Her friend's silky brown hair swirled around her shoulders, the way it did in shampoo commercials. "Some people have lucky genes," she grouched, the old joke between them bringing out Audrey's smile.

"So, what was your cryptic phone call about?"

Cyn didn't answer.

"What aren't you telling me? Come on, spill it."

"One day back in school, and I've already failed!"

Cyn choked on the words. So much for composure. "You wouldn't believe how humiliated I feel!"

Audrey waited.

Dragging her fingers through her thick hair, Cyn pulled one of the coppery strands from the ponytail and wrapped it around her finger. Opened her mouth but couldn't get the explanation out. "Where's Merry?" she asked instead.

"Mom took her to get new sneakers. Don't change the subject. School wasn't quite what you expected?"

"Not exactly. In fact, not at all. Maybe going back was a mistake?"

"Nonsense." Her friend snorted. "You were always a good student. It'll come back to you, like riding a bicycle. Or a horse? Whatever." She waved her hand in the air. "And you'll be able to concentrate now, without your hormones getting in the way."

"I'm not so sure about that." An image of the tennis guy flashed through Cyn's mind. She colored, but before Audrey could poke her nose there, she hid her blush with a frown. "Studying isn't the problem. We haven't even been given a course outline yet, so I've no idea what's expected of me."

"Then why are you in such a state? Why did you call to say you were backwardly...what was it, handicapped?"

"Not handicapped—backwardly challenged. It's less demeaning."

"Whatever. There you go again, hiding behind words. No wonder you went into publishing."

"I guess I'd better begin at the beginning." Setting aside her coffee, Cyn described the class, the professor, the experiment. She shuddered when she mentioned her fear of falling backward. "He wants us to start out by trusting him, but look what he's done to me." Her voice rose. "I'm a shadow of the woman I was before I entered that ghastly room."

Audrey leaned over and pinched her arm. "You feel pretty solid to me. Enough with the dramatics. What was the teacher like?"

"Mature but sexy. A know-it-all. Sympathetic but snide."

"All at the same time?"

"Well you asked for my impression."

"Hmmm. You're usually pretty good at reading people. Is that all?"

"No-o. From my considerable years of experience, I'm tempted to add—phony."

"That's a quick take. Sure you aren't projecting your embarrassment? You're assuming a lot for the first day."

Cyn's shoulders slumped. "I guess so. I've got to stop being so quick to judge people, just like Daddy. But falling backward hardly belongs in a communications class."

"Do you think everyone felt the same way?"

"I did get some sympathy. There was this blond guy next to me..."

"Oh? Tell me more."

Cyn pushed away that fleeting memory. "Nothing worth telling. I hope the professor's not using us as guinea pigs...." Her words faltered. "Something's not right in that class. I can feel it."

"You're reading too much into a simple experiment. What did he say when you couldn't, uh, perform?"

"He teased me a little. Hinted that he'd have to work on me."

"Well, you certainly came to his notice. Maybe that's good."

"But I have to fit in!" Cyn's voice rose again. "I've been out of school for ten years. That's enough to cope with."

Reaching out, Audrey squeezed her friend's hand. "You've got to get it out of your head that age makes a difference. Look at it as a challenge. The whole class is in the learning experience together."

"I know, I know. That's what education is all about."

"Can I quote you on that?"

"Be my guest." Cyn drummed her fingers on the table.

"Hey, don't stop there. What happened next?"

"He finally let us resume our seats, told us to stretch our minds—try to think of ways to communicate trust. Then he let us out early. Never even called the roll."

"Odd. Isn't he required to?"

"I suppose. I'll find out next Tuesday."

"That's my old roomie talking! I never doubted you had the moxie to return and face him."

"Thanks, Daddy."

Cyn looked up quickly, caught the hurt look on Audrey's face. "I'm sorry," she said.

"I'm not your daddy, Cyn. I'm your cheering section."

"Same thing. Push, push, push." She tried to make her voice light but wasn't sure she succeeded. The hurt look was still there. "Girl, you're my backup," she hurried to say. "Best in the world. Sometimes I spout words without thinking."

"Only sometimes?" This time Audrey grinned. "It's okay. I know where you're coming from, but you've got to stop letting your dad control the way you think."

"I know, but I'm glad he's too far away to learn about today." Reaching over, she hugged her BFF.

The front door slammed. "Hey, Mom!" A bubbling, blue-eyed child came bounding into the room and twirled. "I got the sneakers that light up. See? I'm a flasher."

Cyn and Audrey looked at each other and grinned.

"Well, I guess it's time for me to head home." Cyn rose. "Tune in next week for the schoolroom sequel." She winked, raised her voice. "The fighters are in their corners. And there's the bell for Round Two!"

Chapter 2

With a goodbye kiss for Merry, Cyn drove the half block to her own driveway, parked, and unlocked the door. Dropping her keys on the hall table, she stepped into the living room, her gaze lingering on its cozy yet chic elegance. Roger had left the decorating decisions to her. Once he was gone, and the huge TV screen moved to the den, she realized how much the house reflected her personality alone. Hard to believe he'd ever lived here.

Turning on the hi-fi, Cyn let the rich sound of *Scheherazade* fill the silence. She was getting used to the quiet. It left her time to gather her thoughts, to look back and try to fathom the reasons why her life turned out as it did.

The answers centered on the house. When Roger had been an intern at a hospital in Queens, most of their furniture had come from yard sales. They ate on a card table lit by a candle stuck into a Chianti bottle. Cyn shook her head, remembering. A romantic cliché, right out of the movies. She'd been so young....

As Roger got busier and busier, their income rose but their intimacy faded. He was seldom around, so she found a new passion in making their home unique. It was compensation for the loss of affection; she understood that now. At the time she told herself only that a plastic surgeon could afford the very best. He deserved a home that stood as a symbol of his success. Still, the raffia-covered wine bottle with its brightly colored streaks of wax running down the side still sat on a high shelf in the back of her closet. One of these days she'd put it in the trash.

As the music rose to a crescendo, Cyn gazed at her cherry wood tables and chairs. They'd been on display at the American Crafts Museum, and she'd bought them on the spot, loving their sleek, modern look. The satiny wood contrasted with the nubby texture of blues and greens on her plump chairs, an ideal match for the swirling shades in the hand-woven rug beneath her coffee table. She had fallen in love with that rug. It was horribly expensive, but it was the one perfect thing in her life, surpassing even the dreamlike painting on the far wall of a young girl standing in a field of bluebells. She'd picked up the painting at an art auction, a gift for Roger's thirtieth birthday. When he'd moved out and left it behind, she didn't trouble to hide her delight. Out went the TV and in came the painting.

The house became hers in the divorce settlement. Surrounded by her treasures, she hadn't insisted on more. It was a relief to be free. As long as Roger paid off the mortgage, good riddance. She could take care of herself. Where had depending on men gotten her? First Daddy had left, and then it was Roger's turn.

She was strong. She didn't need bossy guys making decisions for her. Still, this afternoon's episode had rattled her. Failure wasn't an option—not now.

Was using her savings to return to school the right decision? When she'd worked out her budget she hadn't included parking fees in Manhattan. Highway robbery, Daddy would call them. But she'd never make it to class on time if she had to cruise around looking for a vacant spot on the street. Pity she hadn't figured out a way to include garage fees in the divorce settlement.

Snorting at her sour attempt at a joke, Cyn walked into the kitchen. She gathered eggs, feta cheese, onions and parsley, popped a croissant into the toaster-oven, poured a glass of wine from an open bottle of chardonnay, and set about making an omelet for dinner.

An hour later, as she settled down with Laurie King's latest novel about Sherlock Holmes and Mary Russell, the phone rang. Glancing at caller I.D., she sighed and stuck the bookmark between the pages.

"Hi, Mama. How's everything?"

"Cynwyd, the toilet in the front hall bathroom is stuffed up."

"So, call a plumber."

"I'm afraid it's going to overflow. That stupid cleaning woman must have thrown something into it."

"The plumber's name is in the little address book, Mama. Under P. And Esperanza isn't stupid. She just doesn't speak English very well. She keeps your apartment clean, and she's a terrific cook."

"Her food is too spicy. I keep telling her so, but she doesn't understand."

"If you'd step into the kitchen and point out things to her, I'm sure she'd get the message."

"I'm worried about the toilet. If water leaks into the hall, the oriental carpet will be ruined."

"Call the plumber, Mama. I can't help you. I have to do my homework. Did you remember that I started school today?"

"I forgot. But you were always an A student, you won't have any problems. I wish you'd come and take care of a few things your father never got around to doing. The toaster isn't working right, and the dryer gives a groan every time it goes around the drum."

"That's what repairmen are for."

"But—"

"Daddy left you plenty of money to take care of all those things. If you don't like living alone, why don't you ask your sister to move in?" Cyn could feel her mother's shudder right through the phone.

"Cadi will reduce me to speaking Welsh, you know she will. And I refuse. I'm an American!"

"American women are independent." Cyn forced herself to stop there. A headache started up as she felt the old arguments rise. She had to stand firm.

"What are you studying?" her mother surprised her by asking.

"Right now I'm listing all the ways people communicate."...*and manipulate each other.* It was all she could do not to say the last words aloud.

"Well, I'll try to communicate with a plumber."

Was her mother being sarcastic? Cyn refused to react. "Good. And get Esperanza to sign up for an ESL class. I left that information with you last Sunday."

"Yes, yes. Try to come this Sunday, too."

"I can't promise, but I'll call. Good night, Mama." She pressed the button for disconnect and stared unseeingly at the field of bluebells.

Talk about living in the now. Three years have passed, yet Mama still acts like Daddy stepped out for a smoke.

With a sigh, Cyn wished she could disconnect the phone. Her mother's calls were all variations on a theme. The heart attacks that turned out to be indigestion. The frantic calls when appliances broke down. The whining about maids—either they broke things, or they stole from her. And now toilet floods.

What next? Cyn closed her eyes, trying to wipe out the memories. Her cell phone slipped from her fingers and slid under the couch. Too much trouble to pick it up.

****

A sleek, silver Porsche pulled up beside Cyn's Camry as she parked in the underground garage the following week. The tennis guy with the streaked blond hair and smoky eyes got out and smiled. She liked his mouth, the corners turned up ever so slightly. Would he remember her?

"Hi. Going to Marzin's class?" he asked.

"You recognize me? I guess I was rather noticeable," she added, avoiding his glance as she started to blush.

"Hey, you have a right to your feelings. Don't let the authority figure push you around."

His confident tone killed her shyness. "Sure." She thrust a fist in the air. "Up with the classes!"

"That's the attitude." His smile grew warmer. "Did you just drive through the Tunnel?"

"Yeah, fighting my nemesis again. The Tunnel and I are sworn enemies."

He laughed. "I thought that was you I was driving behind. Recognized the hair."

Cyn's pulse speeded up. There went that vibe again. Something special about this guy. As they stepped out of the garage, a glint of sunlight caught on the slim gold pen in his jacket pocket.

She stared at it, trying to cover her reaction.

"Unfortunately, taking the Tunnel is the easiest way to get here from Roslyn."

"True. I live on the Island too. Oyster Bay."

"Isn't that where Teddy Roosevelt's home is?"

"Yes, Sagamore Hill—quite a contrast to this garden spot." He waved his arm to encompass the large square they were crossing.

Cyn glanced around at the cigarette butts, candy wrappers, and assorted debris that littered the curb and settled around scrawny tree trunks. She sighed. "This park must have been pretty and green, once."

"Back in Father Knickerbocker's day, maybe..."

Surprised, she slowed her steps. "I haven't heard that nickname for New York City since I was in grade school."

"Not surprising. Symbol goes back to the Dutch settlers. Chubby guy in a curly wig and rolled-up pants. Then along came the Big Apple, but he's not gone. Just got shortened to the Knicks."

"The basketball team?"

"You got it," he grinned. "I'm into cartoons and history." Before he could say more, they had reached the Communications building.

Cyn scrunched her nose as they pushed through the metal doors and entered the classroom. "It still smells of chalk in here—must have permeated the wood in these old buildings."

"Yeah, takes me back, too. Say..." He didn't finish, as the class quieted. Professor Marzin had walked in.

Cyn didn't even know this attractive guy's name. No time to ask him. The prof's hand shot up, calling for attention like the street guard at a school crossing. "We begin a new experiment today." Again, he spoke so softly the class shifted, necks craning, to hear. "One about identities. There's a lot of talk about stolen identities these days, but we're going to look at the situation from a different angle. We're going to give away our identities."

The room grew silent.

"To achieve this, we'll explore how we see ourselves—from the outside. We'll find out how our names affect our actions, our developing personas. How they help make us what we come to be." He paused to let his words sink in.

"Is everyone here?" Restless squirming as he counted heads, then nodded. "Okay, class, you may have noticed that I didn't take attendance last week. Now, I want this to be spontaneous. I'm going to give you only two minutes to think about it. Everyone choose a new first name—a name you'll use for the entire semester. Keep your real name a secret. Pick one that you feel suits the inner and outer you—not only as you are, but also as you'd like to be.

"I have my class roster here." Stopping to zip open his briefcase, he held up a black spiral notebook. "It has only last names. As I call you alphabetically, I want you to respond with the new first name you've chosen."

For a moment, no one moved. A few eyes closed. Then heads started to turn, each person looking at another's bewildered face. There was a rustle of movement, but only puzzled mutterings broke the silence.

"Ready?" the professor asked. The sardonic smile was back. "What do you think my name should be?"

"How about Mephistopheles?" a male voice

growled from the back of the room. Nervous titters followed. Marzin laughed aloud.

"I see you're getting into the spirit of the thing. Well, since it's my choice, I'm selecting—Rocky."

Grins appeared on a lot of faces. A snort, quickly stifled, came from the back. In the front row the Asian girl with the ladybug hair picks opened her notebook, but the professor stopped her.

"No jotting down the names. We're entering a non-linear world. I want you to let your impressions rush in together—from all your five senses, not just sight and sound. How will your new name feel, smell, taste on your tongue? Give in to your first impulse when you reply."

His glance swept the room. "Okay, we're set." A peek at his notebook and Marzin called out, "Alvarez?" A tanned young man with wavy black hair sat by the window. Hesitantly, he raised his hand. Prof Rocky lifted his eyebrows in query.

"Antonio," the young man said, "like in Banderas."

Chuckles filled the room, along with wolf calls. "Yeah!" He turned to the guy behind him, and they smacked palms in a high five.

The professor wrote it down and moved on to the next name.

Silently, Cyn thanked her father for being a Westland. She'd reclaimed her birth name after the divorce, and it gave her time to react to the ones the others chose. She had decided on her new name in a flash, unsure of her reason but knowing instinctively it was the one she wanted. Hearing other far-out choices reassured her.

The slender redhead with the ghostly pallor chose

Pandora. Oh boy, Cyn thought, in Greek myths she's the world's first woman. Didn't Pandora open a forbidden box and let out all the troubles in the world? Quite a power trip. Goes right along with making people disappear. I'll bet that devil of a prof has fun analyzing her choice.

She grinned at the man with the gold pen, and he smiled back. His turn was next. "Merlin," he announced in a deep, confident voice. Cyn peered more closely at him. Yes, those golden streaks in his hair, those smoky gray eyes—they fit a sorcerer. For a moment, she pictured him in a swirling black cape embroidered with the planets. Holding a wand... She flushed. Better not go there.

Her turn came next, the last on the roster. Licking her lips, Cyn stared at the teacher, daring him to question. Taking a deep breath, she blurted out her choice.

"Cleopatra."

Chapter 3

Out of the hospital and back in school again. Joy unlimited...yuk. And what a class! I've moved from one set of crazies to another. Still, the prof is good looking. Possibilities there. He should be paying more attention to me, not to that upstart with the curly hair. Who the hell does she think she is, monopolizing Marzin? She's old enough to know better. Like Ma would say, someone should teach her some manners.

Maybe me?

****

The minute Cyn showed up at Audrey's house a week later, Merry dragged her into the kitchen. Audrey was standing on a stepstool, reaching into a high cupboard. "Mommie," the five-year-old called. "Looka what Auntie Cyn brought me—a Pat-a doll!"

Audrey looked down at the excited child yanking at her jeans. "Hold it a minute, sweetie. These wine glasses will break if I drop them."

"Okay." Merry ran out, waving the doll. "I'm gonna show Nana first."

"Another present from 'Auntie Cyn'?" Audrey shook her head as she climbed down. "You know you're spoiling her."

Cyn shrugged, her lips hinting at a smile. "Kids don't spoil that easily. There's no date stamped on their lid."

"Think so? Just wait till you have your own."

"I'm not holding my breath." Grabbing the wine bottle from the counter, she followed Audrey into the living room.

"You give up too easily."

It was an old refrain, and Cyn didn't rise to the bait. She was lucky her first brush at marriage hadn't involved a child. That would have really added to her guilt.

"So, what's new?"

"Well, Mama's being a pain again, this time about a stuffed toilet. Same old, same old."

Nodding to commiserate, Audrey waited.

"I've also endured class number two." Cyn sat down and filled the stemmed glasses with the ruby merlot. "We've chosen new names for ourselves. For the entire semester, no one is going to know our real ones. Even the prof chose an alias. Would you believe, Rocky?"

"Interesting choice," Audrey mused. "Prof Rocky...ah, so. It has a ring to it." She raised her glass, sipped. "And what name did you choose?"

"You know, I'm more into ancient lives than those of movie stars. Egypt popped into my mind first." Cyn hesitated. "How do you like Queen Nefertiti?"

Her friend sputtered, choking on a swallow of wine. "That's a mouthful."

"Yeah," Cyn laughed. "I did toy with the idea of Queen Nefertiti—that bust of her in the museum is so elegant. I wouldn't mind people making a connection between her profile and mine. But if the class ever got around to nicknames I'd be shortened to Nefer, which sounds like a constipated German, or Titi, which has even worse associations."

"Oh, I don't know about that." Audrey burst out laughing. "So what name did you choose?"

"Well, I liked the idea of being an Egyptian queen..."

"You didn't...?" She paused. "You did? You chose Cleopatra?" Audrey whooped. "Well, hallelujah."

"Mm-hmm." Cyn winked.

"I'd say your nerve is back. Is that what Merry meant before she bounced out of here? You brought her a 'Cleo-Pat-a' doll?"

"I couldn't resist. They had one in the museum gift shop. Long dark curls like Merry's, and a beaded turquoise collar to match her eyes. She loves it."

"I'm sure she does." With a snicker, Audrey shook her head. "Just don't bring her the asp next time."

"I don't know...there was a bin full of wiggly rubber snakes in the shop."

"Enough, *Auntie* Cleo-pat-a. You chose a good name to blend in with the crowd."

"Yeah." Cyn nodded, eyes twinkling. "Isn't it?"

"And you won't have to change your initials."

"Good point. They won't give me away when I carry this fancy briefcase the gang at work gave me when I left. You were behind that, weren't you?" Cyn said as Audrey refilled their glasses. "Making sure they used my old initials?"

"Absolutely. They asked my advice, and I wanted to crush any lingering memories of the divorce. But the party was their idea. Wasn't it great?"

Cyn nodded, her head swaying to the mariachi music playing softly in the background. "Divorce parties beat wedding banquets by a mile. Only your good friends are there, and you don't have to keep smiling."

"And you can stuff yourself with pizza and beer, instead of chicken *cordon bleu* and gooey wedding cake. Think of how many calories you save!"

"That's a plus!" Cyn chuckled, then grew earnest. "You knew I'd been going around in a daze ever since Roger the Rat moved out. The party helped me snap out of it. Made the starting over and going back to school decision real."

"It's real all right, Miss Backwardly Challenged." Grinning, Audrey clicked her glass with Cyn's. "So what else happened in this week's class?"

"We got an assignment. Our revered prof told us to take two sheets of paper, but write on one side only. On the first sheet we'd describe our outward selves—how others see us. The second was for our inner selves—how we see ourselves right now, before we've experienced any reactions to our class name change. He promised to hand our papers back at the end of the semester so that we could redo the assignment from, and I quote, 'our new perspective.'"

"Wow! What a challenge. He expects the new name to make a radical change in each student. Give you all a fresh start...and four months in which to grow."

"Exactly. The idea's exciting, but a bit scary."

"How do you mean?"

"Abandoning our comfort zone is the scary part. I think everyone felt it. We can't lean on our achievements—our career or marriage or happy single state, whatever. We'll be giving up those expectations of ourselves, and that means we won't be able to guess how others will react to us. Without that support, we'll be taking chances."

"I think I understand. You'll no longer be the surgeon's wife, the magazine editor, the champion swimmer…."

"Oh, big joke. That last is your expertise. I won't even have my reputation as a gourmet cook to lean on."

Audrey's eyes flared, and they both broke out laughing.

"I can still see that fancy dessert you were going to bake. What was it?"

"Baba au Rhum. The French cookbook didn't tell me how to make yeast rise, and Mama certainly never taught me." She caught Audrey's chuckle, grinned. "Good thing I had Ben and Jerry in the freezer. I can keep that embarrassing meal a secret now, but no one will know I went through a phase as an adventurous cook, either. Nothing left to boast about."

"Come on. Did you ever fancy your chef's skills to be your finest accomplishment?"

"Well, no."

"Okay, moving on. I see the hazards of starting over, but what about the exciting bit?"

"Hard to explain." Cyn paused. "We'll be meeting people naked, so to speak. No protective coloring. The results could be…invigorating."

"Stimulate new responses you mean, not the old automatic ones?"

"Exactly."

"I'm intrigued. Wish I were taking that class with you."

"Hey, if you're that motivated, you could do the assignments at home. I'll bring you weekly reports."

"Hmm. Maybe I will. Sounds like fun."

"What name would you choose for yourself? Answer quickly now. First one that comes to mind."

"Well, since I'll be joining you down the rabbit hole, I can keep my own initials if I go for Alice!"

****

Cyn had laughed when she first heard the assignment, but no one joined her. *Doesn't anyone else find describing ourselves for a communications class just a tad—hilarious?* She looked around. Even Merlin was tapping his gold pen thoughtfully against his teeth, his gray eyes more fog than storm as he gazed straight ahead.

Well, she intended to have some fun with her answers. She began writing down her ideas as fast as she could. If Rocky were frustrated trying to decipher her scribbles, it would serve him right.

"Cynwyd Westland, a.k.a. Cleopatra. Outer Self: 5 feet 7 inches, 128 pounds—except after Thanksgiving turkey and pecan pumpkin pie. Age: 32—not your average student. Hair: burnished copper, thick and wiry—too curly, really. Eyes: a polished Granny Smith green. Torso…" she bit her lip. *Better not get too romance novelish.* "…acceptable. Long legs. Feet that love stiletto boots for special occasions." *Does that give me a hint of dominatrix? Yeah!* It couldn't be farther from the truth, but only she knew that.

Cyn stopped, shook out her fingers and flapped her wrist, missing her computer. Glancing out the window, she noted clouds starting to gather. One was slowly changing from a blob into a shark. Scowling at the fickle autumn weather, she began again.

"Clothes—professional: dark pin-striped suits, but

bright colors for blouses to bring out the highlights in my hair. Jeans and tees on weekends—informal chic. For dress-up—slinky skirts, silk scarves, and loopy earrings."

That should do it. From top to toe, the me everyone sees. Let the prof make of it what he will.

Turning the paper face down, Cyn picked up page two. How to describe her inner self? There wasn't enough time. No way! She couldn't arrange her thoughts, her feelings, much less condense them to one page.

She bit her knuckle, worrying about her answer. Ever since the divorce, her self-image had veered wildly. Guilt and unworthiness overtook her first, but these emotions were soon followed by anger, justification, then back to the circle of guilt again.

She had to organize her mind, yet that's just what Marzin didn't want her to do. "Be spontaneous," he'd said. "Be impulsive. Assess your good and bad points. Jot down your thoughts as they pop into your head."

She didn't want to reveal all to the professor. He had no right to ask. There were things she wouldn't...couldn't...talk about. No way would she tell him about her childhood; that would be whining. As for her early marriage....

For a moment Cyn shut her eyes, pain throbbing behind them as she recalled the stupid mistakes she'd made that ended in divorce. The signs were there from the start, but she hadn't wanted to see them. She'd ignored all the clues. How could a Phi Beta Kappa have been so dense?

They should take away my key. Defrock me. Better yet, I'll pin it on Merry's Pat-a doll. "Probably has more brains," she mumbled.

Merlin turned around and looked at her. She shrugged, turned away.

With a grimace, Cyn began to write. She'd give Rocky a sentence or two. Let him know she was efficient at work and had a sense of humor. She could admit to a flair for the dramatic…over the top after a glass or two of wine. Was that saying enough?

She paused, thought, went on. "Ambitious but not obsessed. Interested in people but tries, maybe too hard, not to be superficial, not to have phony relation…" *oops, end of page. Can't write on the back.*

Squeezing in a hyphen and scribbling "ships" sideways in the margin, Cyn retracted the point of her pen and dropped it in her purse. With a glance at the clock, she read over her paper once, refusing to change a word. The prof wasn't looking for revisions. Folding the two sheets together, she dropped them on Marzin's desk and scooted out of the room.

Cyn left the building, still disturbed by all that concentrated introspection. The overcast sky seemed to be holding in the heat. A week or two more and the weather wouldn't be so hot and sticky. She began to walk.

Coming upon a gourmet deli, she entered and took a stool at the counter. "Coffee and a corned beef sandwich," she ordered, staring into the mirror behind the bar while waiting for the food to arrive. She didn't look like a Cleopatra. It wasn't just her coloring—there probably were some copper-haired, green-eyed Egyptians. What was missing was the royal demeanor.

Straightening her shoulders, Cyn raised her chin, narrowed her eyes and flared her nostrils, trying for an imperial look. As she made faces at herself in the mirror, another face came into view beside hers. Streaked blond hair, straight nose, square chin beneath a kissable mouth. And eyes like the sky on a foggy day. In the smoky mirror, he appeared surrounded by a mystical aura.

"Cleopatra?" a voice questioned.

Caught! Well, it could have been worse. Her blush faded.

"Merlin," Cyn smiled, "we meet again."

"May I join you?"

"Please do." She didn't turn around, just continued to talk to the face in the mirror. His thigh touched hers as he sat down on the next stool, and a tiny shiver fluttered between her shoulder blades. There was something about this man...

It was that mouth. She couldn't stop staring.

As the seconds passed in silence, Merlin turned his head and looked directly at her profile. "Have I cast a spell on you, Cleopatra? Cat god Bastet got your tongue?"

Chuckling, Cyn turned to him. "That remark broke the mirror's spell. What's your real name, Merlin?"

He eyed her appraisingly. "You wouldn't want me to break my promise to Prof Rocky now, would you? Just because it's after class? Ask me in four months."

"Oh ho, a stickler to the rules. Okay, I'll remain Cleopatra."

"It's not the rules I care about, it's the challenge. As long as I'm involved, I'm curious to see the results of this experiment."

"I can accept that. I'm curious, too."

His glance dropped to the case at her feet. "I see

initials on your briefcase—CFW. What does the F stand for?"

"Ftatateeta, of course."

He grinned. "Cleopatra's handmaiden. I should have known."

His quick smile softened the chiseled lines of Merlin's face. In a twinkling, it changed from austere to appealing. His eyes grew warm, the bar lights adding glints of gold to their silver gray. Cyn blinked.

"Is it legit if I ask you why you signed up for this class, Merlin? You told me it's been a long time since you were in school, too."

He looked down at her hands as if searching for a ring, then back into her laughing eyes. "Perfectly kosher question. Partly, I decided that improving my communication skills would benefit my work."

"And the other part."

"You could say I was coerced."

She waited for him to continue, but he said no more. Too early in their friendship to push. Instead, she said, "What kind of work do you do?"

"Don't know if that question is permitted either, but it can't hurt to get an advanced degree. Why are you here?"

The counterman interrupted, placing the corned beef sandwich in front of Cyn. "Anything for you, sir?"

Merlin didn't take his eyes off Cleopatra. "Coffee, black. And one of those muffins you've got over there under the dome."

"Bran or lemon?"

"Fine."

Cyn laughed. "I take it you're not very interested in food."

"Everything in its place. Right now you have all my attention."

She grew warm at his words. Biting into her sandwich, Cyn took her time deciding how much to tell him. She chewed, swallowed. "I'm starting a new life," she said. "Post-divorce. Returning to school seemed a good idea, and the communications field fascinates me, even though I quit my editorial job so that my new start could be really fresh. But this class may convince me that print is too old-fashioned."

"You mean linear thinking has had its day?"

Cyn groaned. "I'm not sure I believe it. I enjoy reading too much to give it up. But Rocky can be very persuasive."

"I don't think he'll change my mind," Merlin said, "for lots of reasons. But I'm open to new ideas...and new starts."

She wanted to ask more, but the suggestive look in his eyes made Cyn gulp down her next bite. *The man is a sorcerer...*

"Er, how did you do on today's assignment?" Now he'd caught her blushing twice. She was too old for this. It had been so long since the last time she'd flirted.

He shrugged. "I don't find it easy to write about myself." He turned back to watch her in the mirror. "Disguise is more in my line. The professor will find the facts I gave him dull reading."

She looked at his reflection, swallowed another bite. He'd made that remark with a straight face! She couldn't leave the statement alone.

"I doubt that. It's only a first impression, Merlin, but you don't strike me as dull."

"No? What adjective would you use, Cleo?" He

grinned at her again.

"Fishing for compliments?"

"Who says the adjective would be complimentary?"

Cyn turned back to her coffee, drinking slowly to gather her wits. "A sorcerer is mysterious... intriguing...puzzling, perhaps," she responded, "but never dull."

Now his gray eyes gleamed. "And I have to live up to my name, of course."

"Naturally. It leaves room for interesting speculation."

This time he laughed aloud. "I can see your royal training has stood you well, Cleopatra. So diplomatic. But getting back to your question, I don't plan to let Prof Rocky get his hooks in me."

Cyn frowned. "What do you mean?"

"Just that a little knowledge can be a dangerous thing. I'm not a trusting soul when it comes to personal revelations."

She was quiet for a moment. "He does like to manipulate us. I didn't lie, but I'll admit I left out things that were none of his business. I may not be able to fall backward, but"—she crossed her fingers—"basically, my life's an open book."

He glanced at her hand. She caught a quick grin, but it was gone when he looked back at her.

"Every life has its secrets," he said softly.

Turning, she stared directly at him. "Yes, secretive is another adjective I would put in your description," she said, then smiled. "It only adds to your charm."

Reaching for the hand that wasn't holding the sandwich, Merlin ran his fingers lightly up to her wrist.

"Despite all your protestations, I think secretive works for you, too, Cleopatra."

She hoped he didn't feel her pulse jump at his touch. Slowly, Cyn slid her hand out from under his large one, sensing its strength even though he held hers so casually. She grabbed her napkin and wiped her lips.

"Well, I guess we have four months to ferret out secrets about each other. And to figure out what Rocky's up to."

As they slid off their stools, gray eyes peered once more into green ones in the mirror. "I'm looking forward to it."

Merlin's deep voice, low and warm now, slithered into Cyn's head like Irish cream. "I may have been coerced into taking this class, but I've finally found something positive to say about higher education." He winked and Cyn laughed.

Outside, the lowering clouds had covered what was left of the sun. "Let me walk you to your car," Merlin said, squinting as he looked upward. "It's growing dark, and that cloud looks ready to dump its load. Are you parked in the same garage?"

"Mm hmm." She took his arm.

"No problem, then. My car's there, too." They hurried on in silence, almost reaching their destination when the first drops of rain began to fall. At the same moment, Cyn's cell phone rang. She glanced at the caller I.D., rolled her eyes, and tapped it open.

"Hello, Mama."

"Cynwyd, I have some Terrible News!"

Chapter 4

Frowning at the frantic note in her mother's voice, Cyn looked up. A fat raindrop landed on her nose. "Mama, you've caught me in the rain. I won't be able to hear you inside the garage, but I'm getting wet. I'll call you back as soon as I get home."

"No, no, don't hang up!" her mother wailed. "I've just heard from your father. He wants a divorce!"

Cyn bit her lip. She watched Merlin standing beside her in the rain. "Mama, I've got to go or I'll catch pneumonia. Daddy isn't still on the phone, is he?"

"No, indeed. It's all here in black and white. In the letter he wrote."

"Then it'll keep a little while longer. I'll call you back as soon as I'm home and out of these wet clothes." She hung up before her mother could say more.

"Trouble?" Merlin asked her. His gold-streaked hair was turning brown in the rain. He wiped the droplets from his lashes.

"I…I don't know what to say," Cyn replied as they stepped into the garage. "My parents have been separated for several years, but Dad just wrote my mother that he wants a divorce."

"Will that affect you? I can see that it makes the reality more permanent, but you say he's been gone for quite a while…."

"Surprising how it hurts," she mumbled. "I'll have

to think about it." As they reached her car, she turned to face him. "I'm sorry to cut you off so abruptly, Merlin, but I've got to rush home."

"Understood," he said gently. "Is there anything I can do to help?"

Her lips parted in a wan smile. "No, but thanks for the offer."

"I *will* see you in class next time?"

"Absolutely. I'll not let this latest aggravation sway me from my path. The divorce has been a long time coming...just as mine was. I suppose I never wanted to face the fallout before." She looked away, fighting her longing to lean against his broad chest, feel his strong arms around her. Silly, she hardly knew the man. Turning back, she caught his concerned expression, sensed that he shared her desire. Yet he resisted the impulse, just as she did.

With a wry grin, Merlin took her hand and squeezed it tightly for a moment. Then he took the keys from her. Had he caught the slight tremor in her fingers?

He unlocked the car door, held it open. "Are you sure you're up to the drive home?" he asked.

It was the right thing to say. Standing straighter, she grabbed her keys and glared at him. "Of course I am. Do you doubt it?"

"No. Forgive me for being overly solicitous. Faulty upbringing."

Her face cleared, and she chuckled. "No harm done. Your question has strengthened my resolve. I'll see you next week."

"Count on it." The smile he gave her was one to cherish.

****

Stripping off her damp clothes, Cyn gathered the bundle and threw everything except her shoes into the dryer. She set the timer for twenty minutes—long enough to get the clothes dry, while the machine's loud signal would remind her to end the phone call. She mustn't let her mother pull her any further into this mess.

Picking up her cell, she hit the speed dial. "Hello Mama."

"Cynwyd. It's about time you called."

"Traffic slows to a crawl when it rains. So what did Daddy write?"

"What do you expect? 'We've both had three years to assess our relationship.' He finally feels certain that separating permanently is the right move—to insure our future happiness. 'Our,' he said. What a hypocrite!"

"Did he tell you why he wants the divorce now?"

"No, only that the time is right. But he isn't fooling me. There is only one reason he would ask for a divorce now. He wants to marry that hussy on his committee—the soil expert."

"The PhD from Israel?"

"Yes. I was suspicious of the bitch when I saw them together on TV two years ago. Do you remember? His agricultural committee had returned to the States to report to the UN. PBS covered it live."

"I watched it too, and you're imagining things. The committee is making great progress toward increasing crop production in the underdeveloped countries of the Middle East and Africa. Her part of the report struck me as being intelligent and forceful."

"Domineering, you mean. Did you see the way he

hovered around her? As if a woman like that needed his protection!"

"Perhaps he got tired of being looked at as nothing but a protector."

"Just what are you implying?"

"I mean exactly what I said. Why do you think he walked out on us, Mama?"

There was silence on the other end of the line. Then Cyn heard her mother's muffled sobs. "Look, there's no point in crying about it now. You two weren't suited. Daddy was one of your throng of admirers, judging from the stories Aunt Cadi told me. I still don't know why you chose him. Your father paid for quite an elaborate debut in London. A number of men with titles loftier than PhD were after you."

"After my father's coal mines, you mean. I know I had lots of suitors, but it wasn't easy to discern whom to trust."

"Well, I know Daddy worshipped your beauty. And I do mean worship. He wasn't interested in coal mines. I've seen the wedding photographs—you were nineteen then and really something."

"I'm *still* really something," her mother sounded petulant.

"Of course you are," Cyn soothed. "It's time you realized it and tried to find someone new, instead of clinging to Daddy like a barnacle."

"Cynwyd! What a horrible thing to say."

"Oh, come now, Mama, you're too intelligent not to realize that you treated him like a servant. He was always waiting on you. I guess he got tired of waiting."

"You're playing with words again, Cynwyd. I don't know what you're talking about."

"So, were there other reasons why he left?"

"It's none of your business."

"Then stop making it my business. You're a big girl, Mother, and I have to hang up now. The dryer's signal is piercing my eardrums. Between you and it, my head feels like it's about to explode."

"Well, I'm not going to make this easy for him."

Cyn caught her mother's last words as she tapped the End button. Frowning, she ran her tongue along her teeth. What mischief was she up to now?

****

"So, school has dropped two good-looking men into your life." Audrey leaned back, fuzzy pink slippers sliding off as she put her feet onto the coffee table. "A dark man and a light one. A devil and a sorcerer. Fast work for only three classes."

Cyn licked her lips. "Well…."

"I was right. Going back to school was just the ticket. You've got sparkle again. *'I'll Take Manhattan'*…" She hummed the old tune.

Kicking off her shoes, Cyn put her feet up, too. She pulled the clip from her ponytail and slouched down, hair spreading out in a curly mass on the back of the couch. "That's silly. I don't *have* these men."

"But they are in your life?"

"Well, put that way, I guess so."

"And you do react to them?"

"Sure. I'm in a new and exciting environment. All my senses are alert. I'm intrigued by one because I don't know what he's up to, and by the other because I don't know who he really is."

"But they're both hotties."

"That, too."

"I should have your dilemma," Audrey said with a sigh.

Cyn reached out and crooked her little pinky around her friend's, happy to hear Audrey thinking about men again. It had been four years since Jonathan died.

"It's good to be back in school, Aud. I owe you for pushing me into it."

"My pleasure. Hey, maybe you'll introduce me to some of these fascinating people you keep telling me about. Once you sort out who you want, I can do wonders with leftovers."

"It's an idea. I'll see what I can do. Of course, I can't invite any of them out..."

"Why not? I can always dredge up a bottle of wine and some nibblies."

"Yes, but they'd be bound to find out my real name."

"Uh oh. Never thought of that. Well, maybe we can meet them on neutral ground. Who do you have in mind that's interesting?"

"Just guys, or both sexes?"

"One of each."

"Well, ladies first. There's that redhead I mentioned, the one with the straight hair hanging down her back—Pandora. The name fits her. I get the itchy feeling she's just waiting to open that box of troubles. Never volunteers, but when she's asked a question, her answers are always bizarre."

"Oh? How's that?"

"They're quirky. Confrontational. Pandora knows how to stir things up. She's seems so quiet or, rather, still. As if she's holding her breath, expecting an earthquake or at least a tremor. It's a cover-up, I think, but not for shyness."

"Could be stimulating."

"Mm-hmm, but disturbing, too. I had a queer reaction to her when we met the first day of class. She was standing beside me in the circle, and when I looked into her eyes, she made me disappear."

"Huh?"

"I can't explain it. My imagination, I'm sure. It was just a momentary feeling, but I felt compelled to fade away."

"Really, Cyn? That's one for the books."

"I know, I know. She let slip that she's attended those far-out weekend seminars where you get no sleep and they play with your mind. It's left her with an oddball outlook on life, maybe taught her a few tricks. I don't think she realizes what she's doing. The prof asked her a personal question in the last class, but instead of replying, she snarled that all men were cannibals and accused him of lighting the bonfire. I thought he'd bust a rib."

"Wow! That's quite a visual."

"Yeah. I'm sure everyone pictured him in nothing but a loincloth, dancing with glee around a huge cauldron while Pandora stood chest deep in the stew. I even imagined her red hair floating on top, ringing round the dumplings."

"God, what a vision," Audrey sputtered. "I don't know her, yet I can see it. Was the prof carrying a spear?"

"In a manner of speaking." Cyn joined Audrey in laughter. "I dreamed about it that night—only I was in the cauldron, and I was drowning." She shuddered.

"Well, if you gotta go, I hope the soup tasted good!"

Cyn poked her elbow into Audrey's stomach. "Go on, make fun of my fear of drowning." But her friend's remark had banished the nightmare.

"I've tried to know her better, but she pushes away any overtures. The more she keeps me guessing, the more intrigued I am. You know how I love to solve puzzles."

"She seems to have gotten under your skin, ha ha."

"Hey, I'm the one who plays with words."

"Not exclusively, girlfriend. Anyway, what about the guys in your class."

Cyn's eyes twinkled. "I've saved the best for last. There's this guy, Antonio. I've had a secret crush on Banderas ever since I saw the movie *Zorro*. Remember him in the lead? Except for his height, this guy could be his double."

"I do recall doing a little pitta-pat over that one." Audrey finger-tapped a quick dance on her chest. "Sounds like this Antonio would make a tasty leftover."

Nodding, Cyn licked her lips. "He's only about five feet nine or ten, but that should suit your perfectly proportioned five three."

"Hah, I should have your look. I'd rather be statuesque."

"Yeah, like one of those abstract statues at MOMA."

Audrey looked puzzled.

"You know, Museum of Modern Art. Tall female figure with pinhead, bumps, and bulges."

"Now, now. Don't start putting yourself down again. We've been through that phase."

"Sorry—it's just a souvenir remaining from the divorce. You know I never used to be that way."

"I know."

"Roger always made me feel awkward."

"Yeah, but Roger the Rat is toast. Burned toast."

"To a crisp." They laughed. "I'll try to head Tony your way," Cyn said. "You'll love the way he talks, with just a slight Latin intonation. Sounds so warm and sexy."

Audrey smiled into her wine glass. "I'm a sucker for warm and sexy."

"You know, the Eighth Street Crafts Fair is on in a couple of weeks—jewelry and pottery and such. Why don't we go see it that Saturday morning? The school's right around the corner. We might run into some of my classmates there."

"Super idea! Be sure you drop hints in class that we're going. I'll get my mom to sit with Merry."

"She won't mind a whole day?"

"She'll love it. Mom's got Merry helping her with the laundry, and you've gotta grin watching those plump little hands trying to fold the clothes when they come out of the dryer. Lately, she's taken to rocking her dolls to sleep in my underwear."

"Enterprising," Cyn giggled.

"You don't know the half of it. Last night I found one of my bras stretched across two dresser knobs, with a tiny doll in each cup. Merry'd been watching a pirate cartoon and told me she was rocking her babies to sleep in 'hammicks.'"

"Forget kindergarten. That child is ready for high school!" Cyn sipped her wine. "Okay, I'll drop some hints next class about our attending the fair. I've a feeling the guys will jump at the chance to bump into us." Laughing, they smacked hands.

"What's going on in class now?" Audrey asked.

"We're studying how the mind receives its impressions through the senses. A lot has changed in the last fifty years."

"Really? I don't think our brain has evolved much. Just read the headlines. We've acquired a lot of knowledge, but we're still doing the same dumb things. Our senses haven't altered."

"True, we still have the usual five, but we're receiving the information in new ways. Much more comes through our hearing, and we aren't given enough time to think about the consequences before the subject changes. Rocky says the politicians and ad men are experts at using this info overload to manipulate us. We're pawns in their hands."

"I'll buy that," Audrey grinned. "There's more time spent on TV commercials than on programs these days."

"And TV's only one source. In class today, the prof quoted from a book by a guy named Robert Coover. We're living in—hang onto your head," Cyn warned as she grabbed her notebook and read aloud, "omnidirectional cyberspace, in which time is spread out in a kind of geography."

"I beg your pardon?"

"Yes, my reaction, too. The world is too much with us." Cyn strummed an imaginary guitar. "Listen up, folks, look you," she adopted her singsong Welsh lilt, "while I state my case for omnidirectional cyberspace."

Audrey whooped. "I'll have to stop and think about each word in that quote. Maybe tomorrow. Or the next day. Whatever."

"If I think about it too much, my brain will seize." Cyn shook her head. "Say, maybe that's why I felt like I was disappearing the first day. I was walking into another dimension!"

"Sent by the pale-faced girl with the long hair? What was she—an alien?"

"Get real." She winked as Audrey chuckled. "Life used to be simpler."

"I suppose so, but duller, too. I think it's fun to be hooked up to the world."

"I wonder. People in class were talking about 'the hive mind.' If that's what we're turning into, it's scary. I don't want to be one of those drone bees, just there to serve the queen."

"You *are* the Queen, Cleopatra," Audrey teased.

"Well, in that case…." They laughed.

Audrey refilled their glasses. "Has Rocky 'worked' on you some more?"

"He flirts with all the females, loves to cross swords with Pandora, but I get teased a lot. He says I have to learn to be backwardly mobile."

Audrey snorted.

Standing up, Cyn stretched. "I'm going to raid your freezer."

"Help yourself. All that heavy thinking has given me the munchies."

Cyn took out a 3-cheese pizza and popped it into the microwave. "I'll get back to you on Rocky. Still haven't figured him out."

"What about the sorcerer?" Audrey asked as she returned from the kitchen.

"I haven't had a chance to talk to Merlin since he

walked me to my car after we met in the deli, but it's the strangest thing. I keep seeing his face as I glimpsed it in the tinted mirror. That hazy look is clearer in my mind than his real features."

"Curiouser and curiouser. I know—you're seeing him in omnidirectional cyberspace!"

"Now, now..." The two broke into giggles.

"You're certainly learning a lot about new forms of communication."

"We're studying body language too, and that's fascinating. We each had to think of a 'tell' as they call it in gambling. You know, like blinking when you're about to lie. I realized I'd picked up a family trait. When I'm really worried, I bite my knuckle."

"Yes, I noticed that."

"Really? You never told me."

"That would spoil the fun!"

"What about you? Give me a 'tell.'"

"Let me think. When I'm trying to hide my nervousness, I touch my throat."

"I've caught that. Then you try to hide the gesture by pushing back your hair."

They looked at each other and laughed. "We're giving ourselves away," Cyn said. "Good thing we're best friends. You know, learning all this is fun, but I can't help wondering where it's all leading."

"Down the rabbit hole, I told you. There's the beep for the pizza."

Chapter 5

The days grew brisk. The scraggly trees in the square turned gold and rust. Soon the falling leaves would hide the crushed cans and empty wrappers. There was something sad about the falling leaves, Cyn thought as she crossed the park. A line from a favorite poem came to mind—"Bare ruined choirs where late the sweet birds sang." She sighed, thinking once more of her father and his request for a divorce. She hadn't mentioned the matter to Audrey. Not even to her best friend, who knew her story so well. It was still too painful to talk about—as if a curtain were dropping down on a portion of her life. What did the second act have in store? More men who couldn't be trusted?

Oh, she was getting maudlin. She'd been falling into that state too often since her mother's phone call. What she needed was a drink to lift her spirits, and she knew just where to find the companions to share it with. Cyn headed for the gourmet deli.

Rocky's students had taken over a long table in the back for after-class socializing. She enjoyed meeting her new friends there, loved the leap her insides took whenever she heard a certain name called and realized they were asking for her. *She* was Cleopatra. That camaraderie was what she needed now.

One afternoon she got involved in a beer-tasting contest. With a kerchief over her eyes, she recognized the different tastes of Lowenbrau and Modelo Negro. "It's the Old World versus the New," she teased as she pulled the scarf down, dislodging a curly strand from her ponytail. "Everyone knows that."

"Smarty pants!" one of the guys shouted as she ran her tongue over her lips to catch the beer foam.

Merlin watched. She saw his pupils widen as he followed the gesture.

"Here's your prize." Antonio presented her with a T-shirt displaying a beer can with arms and legs playing the drums. "Souvenir from our local *bodega*," he told her. "Rock Me Tecate."

"Olé!" someone called out.

Laughing, Cleo draped it over her chest. She was one of the gang, and it was a great feeling. As she tossed the shirt over her shoulder, serape style, Merlin whispered, "You're not that macho, *chica*... You may know your beers but I see you still drink from a glass."

His voice tickled her ear. Turning, she deliberately brushed the wayward curl across his lips. "Would you expect less from an Egyptian queen?"

"Touché." His eyes darkened. "Your hair smells…exotic." Leaning closer, he took a deep breath. "Mmm, enchanted herbs. I'll bet you learned all about herbs and hops and beer in ancient Egypt."

His teasing retort fell flat. Until that moment, Cyn had forgotten her ex and his beer-drinking cronies. They had taught her all about beer in the early days of her marriage, when the bunch stilled in med school—before they became arrogant doctors and switched to dirty martinis. Before her marriage became stifling...

"Hey," Merlin looked contrite as he noticed her

expression. "Did I upset you?"

How does he know? This is one super sensitive sorcerer. "It's nothing," she said hurriedly. "Just a passing thought. Let's drink to sorcerers—and magic wands."

Merlin looked deep into her eyes. "I'll drink to that any time."

Another contest was in the works today—which of them could shell and eat the most peanuts in a half hour? She'd stay on the sidelines for this one.

****

The following weekend Cyn and Audrey, already practicing to call themselves Cleo and Alice, got an early start for the Eighth Street Fair. The weather had turned unexpectedly warm for late October. Merry held her grandmother's skirt as she waved goodbye with her Cleopatra doll. "Don't forget, Auntie Cyn," she called out, "you promised me a new dress for my doll. A princess dress!"

Cyn blew kisses. "I'll look real hard for one." Still waving, she joined Audrey in the car.

The air was fresh and breezy. Once on the highway, the two friends didn't stop talking. They were halfway through the Midtown Tunnel before Cyn remembered to tense up. Big improvement, she told herself when daylight appeared on the other side.

They parked in a garage near the square. "From here on, we think of ourselves only as Cleo and Alice," Cyn reminded Audrey. "Don't forget."

"Same goes."

By the time they reached the fair, the streets were already crowded. Jazzy music rose above the traffic noise. The spicy aroma of kielbasa and frying onions hung in the air.

"What a day! Looks like half the city decided to come on down," Cleo said. "Let's stop at this jewelry booth. They have cool earrings."

They picked up several, held them to their ear lobes. "I'm going to take these triple hoops," Alice decided. "Clever the way the wires are twisted."

"They look good on you—sexy. I'm buying these dangling ones with the snakes wrapped around each other. They fit my Egyptian persona." As she slipped them on, she heard a familiar voice.

"Cleo! *¿Qué tal?*" Antonio came loping toward them.

"Tony, hi! Meet my friend, Alice. She followed me down the rabbit hole today."

Antonio smiled, speculation in his warm glance. As the three began to talk, a hand touched Cleo's shoulder. It was barely a touch, yet she shivered in anticipation. "Hi, Merlin," she said, then turned around.

"How did you—" He stopped before finishing the question. A strange look crossed his face. Then he smiled. "You're psychic, right?"

"I'm discovering all sorts of new talents since returning to school." She peered at Merlin closely, searching for the reality behind the mirror image she remembered. This time she clearly saw the strong jaw, the sharp cheekbones, and cleft chin. The eyes were still that mysterious smoky gray. And the lips.... She imagined tracing their outline with her tongue, then slipping it inside. For an instant, the sensation made her tingle.

Good lord. What kinds of crazy ideas were flitting through her mind on this Indian-summer morning, outdoors among friends? What kind of sensual magic was this sorcerer calling forth? Shaking her head to clear it, she moved away from his touch. "Merlin, meet my friend Alice. She's the one I told you about—she's following our class at home."

Merlin's eyes gleamed as Alice looked him up and down, then nodded toward Cleo in approval.

The four began to walk slowly, Tony and Alice in the lead. Behind them a slender figure in cutoff jeans and embroidered vest followed a little behind, hidden in the crowd. Her long red hair swung in the breeze. At the look in her eyes, people unconsciously stepped away from her.

Strolling past another jewelry booth, Merlin stopped. "Look, Cleo." He picked up a necklace of carved turquoise beads and held them up to her. "Scarabs. Very Egyptian."

"You're right." She slid the cool beads through her fingers. "I love them!"

"Let me get them for you."

She touched his arm, stopping him as he reached for his wallet. "No, Merlin, they're too expensive. We're just classmates. Thanks for spotting them, but I can't let you pay for them." She opened her purse and took out her credit card.

"Wear them now," he said, lifting her ponytail and closing the clasp around her neck. "They look regal on you." As he let her hair down, his fingers brushed the soft skin of her nape.

A shiver ran down her spine. "Have you cast a spell on them?"

"Absolutely. Every time you wear them, you'll think of me." For a moment they were both quiet, staring into each other's eyes. Then Cleo tucked her arm in his. "Come on. Let's look around some more."

It was a great day for wandering, for feeling anonymous and free in the large crowd. Once her mother spoiled the mood, calling to complain that she'd chipped a tooth. "Does it hurt?" Cleo asked. "These things happen when you get older, Mama. Tell it to the dentist." She paused to listen. "I can't drive you, I'm not home. Take a taxi. I'm sure you'll manage."

It took a few minutes to regain her happy state, but Cleo's buoyancy returned when she found a booth selling handmade doll clothes from around the world. The princess outfit Merry wanted became a Mexican fiesta costume. Imagining the child's squeals of delight wiped out the nagging memory of the phone call.

Carryall bags with the fair's slogan were being given away. The women's were filled with Christmas gifts by the time the four grew hungry. "We're in gourmet heaven down here," Merlin said. "What shall it be? Dim sum in Chinatown, or sausage and peppers in Little Italy?"

"If you like small dishes and lots of variety, I know of a great tapas bar," Antonio put in. "Very Spanish."

"Ooh, yes," Alice murmured and patted her stomach. "*Muy bueno*."

As they left the fair, Cleo turned. Was someone watching them? Her glance raked the people milling about the booths, but she recognized no one. Shrugging, she blew off the weird feeling and hurried after the others.

The foursome sauntered over to Tenth Avenue, ordered scrumptious little tapas plates and a large pitcher of sangria. The smoked duck, garlicky white beans, Serrano ham, and Manchego cheese were gobbled up and washed down with the fruity wine. "Wonderful…spicy…great taste. This sauce is incredible." The compliments flew. Merlin topped them off with, "Food for love," and they all raised their glasses.

A shimmering flan capped the meal. It's amazing, Cyn thought as she licked the caramel from her spoon, how loose and comfortable I feel. No one but Aud— oops, Alice—knows my real name. Rumpelstiltskin was right. Names carry a lot of baggage.

At last the check came. Cleo reached into her wallet, then gave a startled gasp. She looked frantically at the others. "My credit card isn't here!"

"Where did you last see it?" Alice asked. "Do you remember which booth you were at?"

"No! I paid for some things in cash. I'm not sure where I used the card."

Quickly, Merlin picked up the tab and handed the waiter a wad of bills. "I'll take care of this and you can all pay me back later. We'd better get back to the fair before all the booths close down."

The four hurried out of the restaurant, half-running the few blocks to the stalls. Many were shut, the rest in the process of being dismantled as they arrived. They retraced their steps, but no one had found a lost credit card.

Giving up finally, they sank exhausted onto a park bench. Nearby a group of gray-haired Italian men were playing bocce, the heavy balls rolling toward their goal.

Cleo listened to them smacking together. The grating noise made her head pound. "What now?" she said, her shoulders slumping. "I suppose I'd better get on the phone..."

"Yes, call the credit card company right away. I think you'll only be liable for fifty bucks, if that," Merlin offered encouragingly. "Use your cell phone now. There hasn't been time for much damage to be done."

"I can't!" Cleo moaned. "I don't have my card number with me. I'll have to wait till I get home and take it off an old bill." She bit her knuckle. "I'm sunk if I lose my credit rating."

"Cleo, chill." Alice gazed anxiously at her. "You'll make yourself ill worrying."

"Put it out of your mind for now," Merlin patted her hand. "You've done what you can."

"Just think, gang," Cleo drew out the words over the pounding in her head, "here I am going around with a fake name, and out there someone could be forging my real name." Her laugh was bitter.

"Let's hurry, Cy-Cleo," Alice interrupted, almost giving the game away. "I've got to get back, too. My mother is babysitting Merry," she explained, "and I promised I'd be home for dinner."

They rose from the bench. Stepping close, Merlin lifted Cleo's chin. "Don't look so despondent. I'll help you out with this. I know someone who's been through it."

She turned to face him. "You do?"

"Yes."

She shook her head, ponytail bobbing. Reaching out, he removed the clip and spread her hair onto her shoulders. He ran his fingers up her scalp and rubbed gently. "I mean it, Cleo. I'll look into what can be done in case there's any trouble. Just don't forget to call the bank first thing. There's bound to be an automatic answering service for this problem."

She moved her head under his fingers, soothed by his touch. It felt so good. "I'll be grateful for whatever you can find out. Can we talk on our cell phones? We don't have to exchange names for that, do we?"

"No, we're on our honor. If I find out anything, I'll call you." They traded phone numbers, saw Alice and Tony were doing the same, and winked.

As they quickened their steps to the garage, Merlin played with the scarabs around Cleo's neck, under her hair. "I love these shiny blue beads," he murmured in her ear. "Someday I hope to see you wearing them, and nothing else."

Her pulse, already fast as she felt the tickle of his breath, began to race. She turned to him quickly, hunting for a smart answer, but he put a finger to her lips. "I won't move too fast," he promised, searching her eyes. "We have time to get to know each other. But when the semester's over, Cleopatra, it'll be Christmas. That's the present I want."

It was too much. He was reading her mind. "I don't think Santa is Egyptian," she called out as she and Alice got into the car. But in her heart she wasn't so sure.

Chapter 6

Pandora flicked the credit card over and over between her fingers. She gazed into the distance, ignoring the fluttering pennants, the colorful costumes, the jostling and chatter of the fair. A gust of wind sprang up, and one of the pennants flew into her eyes. She brushed it aside, the movement bringing her back to that moment of panic she had experienced the first day of class. The sun streaking through the dusty window blinds had landed on Cleo's face, and her hair had lit up, the curls bleaching from a copper color to a dark blonde.

The image of a tight golden curl splashed with red flew into Pandora's consciousness. It was lying in a beam of sunlight. The dirty curl on the bare wooden floor grew and grew until it filled her mind, just like in the dreams she'd been having. Nothing remained when she awoke beyond the fleeting vision of the curl, lying in the red puddle.

Pandora shook her head vigorously, shutting out the image. She didn't know where it had come from, or when. Her head ached when she tried to recall. Better to focus again on the credit card. She looked down, saw it resting in her palm. How does a person react to having her true identity stolen when she's just getting accustomed to a false one?

Should she take this card to Professor Marzin? It

would make a great ploy in his little cat and mouse identity game. She'd picked up on Rocky's keen interest in his experiment, and yesterday's stroll through his empty office had confirmed it. A folder on his desk protruded between two frayed books on the social aspects of language. She'd pulled out the folder and glanced at the tab. "Case Studies: the Impact of Identity on Personality and Behavior." Dull title but a dead giveaway. The students were his lab rats—she knew it!

The papers he'd collected were in there, along with notes he'd written on them. She'd just begun to read his loopy handwriting when she heard voices in the hall.

Peeking out into the corridor, Pandora saw the professor. Though his back was to her as he listened to an irate student, she could tell from his rigid stance that Rocky was getting riled. He'd turn around any second. No time to lose.

She'd slipped out the door and glided away on her soft ballet slippers. At the corner, she'd glanced back. The student was still arguing. That was close! Pulling a tissue from her pocket, she wiped the moisture from her grinning face. In the spy lingo she loved, she'd gathered important "intel."

Yesterday she didn't know what she would do with the information. Today, the credit card gave her ideas.... She'd use the card to entice the professor into offering her an assistant's job. Hint at being his accomplice. Work a deal. Surely, creating even more identity anxiety for one of his subjects would add another layer to his experiment.

Identity anxiety.... Pandora mulled over the words. Sounds good. Rocky will buy it.

The fair was starting to close down, but the department stores were open. She'd pick up a few items, put them on Cleo's card. That'd give the Queen a jolt.

Pandora studied the piece of plastic. In the tiny picture I.D., the two of them looked alike. She could get away with her impersonation as long as she hid her straight hair under the cap. Softening her expression, she opened her eyes wider to match the photo, then examined the signature. So...the real name of Rocky's favorite was Cynwyd. How foreign that sounded! It got your attention. The prof was right; names could reveal all sorts of things about a person.

Her own revealed too much. Prudence was *hateful!* It gave away her background. Her upbringing had to be worlds apart from Cleo's. That time when she'd thrown up, all the kids had called her Puker Pru. She'd thought she'd die! Her head pounded at the memory...it never went away.

Pandora gritted her teeth. It was all Ma's fault. Image after image flashed through her mind. Her brain became a slide show of stern religious pictures hanging on the walls of the small apartment in Brooklyn. Each unforgiving icon reeked of punishment.

She felt the bitterness start and took a deep breath, squelching it. Hadn't she outgrown the fear and the anger? Talked it out at the hospital? Shoved away the resentment? She'd taught herself to keep everything under control—even stopped taking those nasty pills that dulled her brain. No one knew about that.

From her book bag, Pandora pulled out an oversized Yankees baseball cap, twisted her hair into a braid and tucked it under. She'd overheard the group deciding to eat down in the Village. The subway ride to Bloomies was uptown—slim chance of bumping into Cleo there.

Now was her opportunity. She'd pick up some overpriced makeup, maybe a bottle of expensive perfume. Then she'd try on shoes. Yes, shoes were good. Something sexy, with stiletto heels. The kind to make Ma cringe if she ever saw them. But she never would.

Surely, she could get away with a few purchases. It would make her day. Grinning at the thought, Pandora swiped an appliquéd bookmark from a stall counter and left the fair.

Chapter 7

"Don't tell Merry about the dolly outfit I found," Cyn called as she dropped Audrey off. "I want to surprise her."

"Sure thing. Come for breakfast tomorrow. I'll make waffles."

"Can't resist that offer!" She tried for enthusiasm, but her anxiety about the lost card showed.

Her friend caught Cyn's uneasy response. "Don't sweat it, girl. It's not life threatening. You'll straighten it out, and Merlin will be a big help. That shoulder of his is panting to be leaned on."

The remark brought forth a chuckle. Cyn waved and continued down the block to her house. Unlocking the door, she flung the giveaway bag with her purchases on the hall table and hurried to her desk. A see-through green envelope held all her credit card statements.

Account number in hand she called the bank, drumming her nails on the desktop as electronic voices kept her waiting. All those automated responses were going to drive her nuts. How long would it take to hear the reassuring tones of a human being?

Memories of "identity theft" cases she'd read about filled her mind. There'd been the pint-sized woman who'd received dress bills from a store catering to the "full figure," and the traveling salesman who had been charged for a room-sized plasma TV. One family had discovered all their savings withdrawn from their bank account when they'd been flooded with returned checks for insufficient funds. Oh, God!

Cyn groaned, recalling the hassles people confronted to get their credit ratings restored. Mortgages didn't get approved, purchases were denied, travel plans were shot to hell. She couldn't face that!

Her head began to throb. She'd heard of a gang who used credit card info to produce drivers' licenses for I.D.s. With a hysterical giggle, she wondered if the picture substituted under her name would be any more awful than the real one taken of her. With her odd name, the next Cynwyd Westland could be anyone from an old crone to a bag lady. Or even a guy!

At last her call reached the proper customer service rep at the bank, and she gave the woman the necessary information. "Yes, I lost it today," she repeated. "I used it this morning for several purchases at the Eighth Street Crafts Fair. Do you want their names? Hold on."

Putting down the phone, she dumped her packages from the shopping bag and sorted through the sales slips at the bottom. "Only three," she reported—earrings from Carol's Cunning Crafts, a scarab necklace from Worldwide Treasures, and doll's clothing from Dorothy's Dollhouse. I paid for everything else with cash."

Cyn paused to listen. "That's it? A new card will be mailed on Monday? Thank you." With a sigh of relief, she hung up. She could hardly wait to tell Merlin.

Taking a bottle of vanilla Stoli from the cabinet, Cyn mixed herself a vodka and tonic. As she slid onto a kitchen stool and sipped, she noticed her fingers holding the glass were red. How tightly they had squeezed the wedge of lime, crushing it as if it were the thief's throat! She hadn't realized how angry she was, mostly at herself. How careless she had been. She could hear her father's voice. "You've lost one glove too many, Cynwyd. Your allowance won't cover another pair, so you'll go without."

"Cold hands, warm heart!" had been her insolent response, but not loud enough to reach his ears.

Daddy had always been strict with her, quite the opposite from the way he treated Mama. She knew he loved her, but his warmth flowed in only one direction. Mama certainly seemed to need it all. Maybe that's why they never had any more children. There was only so much affection to go around.

Cyn gulped down her drink. Rolling the ice cubes around in her now empty glass, she stared into space. Was Daddy really going to marry again? Maybe she'd get a baby sister or brother…oh, how she'd wanted one when she was growing up. Now, it was too late to make a difference. Cutting off that thought, she yanked at one of her curls. When would Merlin call? How long would it take him to get the information she needed?

Her fingers began tapping again. She knew she was fussing too much, but worrying was her pattern. Or was it only a habit? Could she change? That stupid class was making her question all sorts of things.

She needed a warm bath to calm her nerves. Picking up the cell phone, Cyn carried it into the blue tiled bathroom and placed it on the sink next to the tub. From a shelf by the window she reached for one of her cherished possessions, an art glass bottle in swirling blues and greens. Holding its teardrop stopper in one hand, she sprinkled camellia-scented foam bath into the slowly filling tub.

Ritual completed, she stripped and lowered herself gently into the water, savoring its soothing heat. The tingling bubbles were invigorating. As she ran the sponge in lazy circles around her stomach and breasts, her thoughts revolved, too—back to that buff guy who had been so quick to offer aid. Could Merlin really help her? Who *was* he? What was his real name? What did he do? Yes, she got the vibes—he could handle anything. He was so relaxed, so confident. It was supportive, but it was irritating, too. She sighed. What a mood she was in. Didn't know what she wanted.

Well, she'd go with her intuition…for now. She would trust him. If anything went wrong, Merlin would fix it.

Cyn stroked herself with the big old-fashioned sponge, her breasts bobbing up and down as she submerged them before rising slightly to let the water slide off her pink nipples with a lovely tickling sensation. Picturing Merlin's lean but powerful frame, his aristocratic face and knowing silver-gray eyes, Cyn twisted in the tub. A thrill ran up her wet nakedness from her groin to her tingling breasts. Her nipples hardened as his seductive voice whispered in her mind. *For Christmas I want to see you wearing the turquoise beads and nothing else...*

She'd left on the beads when she'd undressed, and now she played with them, sliding them through her fingers as she pictured Merlin watching her. Would he just watch, she wondered, if he were standing beside the tub right now? Would his eyes glow with appreciation? Or would he pull her up and press her to him, not caring that he soaked himself? Or, even better, would he undress and climb in with her, soaping her skin as his hands caressed her everywhere?

A soft moan escaped. It had been a long time. She slid lower in the water, her fingers sliding down...but she'd indulged enough. It was too soon to let her mind wander down that path. Besides, she was through with depending on a man—wasn't she? She'd begun to reshape her life, and she damn well wasn't going to let a little blip like a lost credit card derail her. *I will not lean on a man again*...Cyn repeated the sentence three times, her new mantra. She might—and that was a big might—be developing feelings for Merlin, but they had to be built on a stronger foundation. She had learned that lesson the hard way. It took time.

Sitting up straight, Cyn leaned over and pressed the lever to drain the water from the tub. She toweled herself dry, wrapped her body in a fluffy white robe and put her cell phone in the pocket. Mixing another drink with a little less vodka, she cut a hunk of cheddar, set it on a plate with crackers, and sat down at the card table in a corner of her living room. She'd never disposed of it when the new furniture arrived, kept it for jigsaw puzzles. Roger had found the pastime childish, but she'd held firm. "If it works," she'd insisted, "don't knock it."

Daddy had bought her the first puzzle when she'd had the chicken pox. He'd put a big plastic tray on her lap, covered it with a green felt cloth, dumped the pieces onto it. He'd pointed to the picture on the box's cover—she could still recall the cute puppies romping on a sunny lawn. "Fit the pieces together," he'd told her, "and that picture will appear. You can do it yourself. Concentrate, and it will keep you from scratching." He'd leaned over and found a corner piece, linked it to another. "This way, see?" Then he'd patted her head and left.

Years later, she'd explained to her college roommate how working on a puzzle relaxed her before final exams. After graduation, she'd eased the tension of her first job interview by arranging puzzle pieces on her smartphone. "It engages my mind, takes me out of myself," she'd told her ex. He finally "got it," but had it been worth the effort? No matter how she'd tried to fool herself, Roger had never understood her. After awhile he didn't even pretend to.

Perhaps she had finally found someone who could....

Until Merlin called, she'd be unable to concentrate on reading or even on a dumb TV program. An old quote from comedian Ernie Kovaks was making the rounds on the web. "TV is a medium because it's neither rare nor well done." How clever!

Puzzles were better therapy. The circus scene in this one was cut into a thousand pieces. She would finish filling in the acrobat in the spangly pink costume balancing atop the prancing white horse.

Cyn stared at the puzzle piece in her hand. Wasn't the white stallion a symbol of male potency? Oh, not again! Since class started she saw double meanings everywhere. Draining the last few drops of melted ice from her drink, Cyn placed her cell phone on the edge of the table. Merlin would call soon, and she longed to hear his voice. Her fingers grew busy searching for shapes, while her mind lingered on broad shoulders and silver-gray eyes.

Chapter 8

On Tuesday morning, Pandora walked briskly down the school corridor. In front of the professor's door she hesitated, debating with herself. Was she taking too big a chance? She could be expelled for this. It could be misconstrued, labeled dishonest. Which of course it was—but not really.

She shifted from foot to foot. *No, it'll be okay. Rocky will be tempted. I know my mark. We understand each other.* Not bothering to knock, she pushed the door open. This was his office hour after all.

Marzin was on the phone. He waved Pandora to the only chair not covered with books and papers, holding up a finger as he continued talking.

Instead of sitting, she wandered around the office examining everything—an Andy Warhol poster of Marilyn Monroe scotch-taped to the wall, a pre-Columbian jaguar figurine about to slide off a pile of magazines on a shelf. His tweed jacket with the leather patches on the elbows had been tossed onto a coat rack, and one sleeve dangled to the floor. On his desk, the class folder was sticking out between the same two books.

The room looked just as it had the other day when she'd sneaked in. Pandora shoved at a big dictionary that looked ready to topple off a bookcase, and a dust cloud rose. She sneezed.

Marzin gazed at her as he continued talking, rolling his eyes and pointing to the chair again. She sat down and waited. He was taking in the tight black jeans that hugged her ass like a second skin. When his eyes moved up to her pumpkin orange T-shirt, she pulled a strand of red hair to the front so that it caught on the heavy chain of the silver ankh hanging between her breasts. She watched closely. *Yes!* He winced as the bright red met the brilliant orange. Inwardly, she gloated. She'd counted on the clash of colors to create an edgy feeling. It was a power trip.

"Very well, I'll get back to you on that article," Rocky said into the phone. He placed it back in its cradle and turned to Pandora. "Right on time, I see."

"I haven't yet reached the status where I can afford to be late."

The professor's mouth quirked. "Such worldly knowledge in a young woman."

"Don't patronize me," Pandora snapped.

Rocky smiled. "Have your classmates given you a nickname? Do they call you Pandy?"

"Do I look the Pandy type?"

"I overheard someone trying out Pan-do-re-mi."

Heat crept up her neck into her cheeks. Added to her shirt and hair, the blotches would be over the top. Spoil the effect. Grabbing tightly to the arms of her chair, she took a deep breath. "Don't pander to me either, Rocky. Pandora stays as it is—three syllables."

"Well, it is a cut above Prudence, I'll give you that."

She stuck out her tongue at him, and he laughed. "Why are you here, Pandora?"

"I have something that may be of value to you in

70

your research." Deliberately, she stared at the revealing folder.

He followed her glance, his eyes narrowing. "Ah..." It was as if he knew she had sneaked into his office and peeked. Her pulse jumped, but she kept her face expressionless.

He sat back, steepling his fingers at the point of his chin. "And what might that something of value be?"

He's buying it! "Will you answer a question, first?"

One eyebrow went up. "About what?"

"Your research." She hesitated, then continued. "Am I right in assuming that you're writing a book on the reactions of a study group—students—who have feigned a new identity?"

"It isn't feigned in the classroom, it's real. And outside as well, if they find the experience intriguing enough to pursue elsewhere."

"But they're not using the name they were born with. It's a fake identity."

"I'll give you that for now. What's your point?"

Inwardly, she sighed with relief. He hadn't bitten her head off. "How about adding another twist by taking away their real identity at the same time? At least with one test subject, for comparison?"

"What are you driving at?"

Pandora reached into her back pants pocket, caught the card between her thumb and forefinger, and pulled it out—slowly. He was watching her every move. She handed him Cleopatra's credit card.

Marzin examined it suspiciously. "How did you get this?"

"It was, uh, left behind in a booth at last weekend's craft fair. I lost her in the crowd before I could return it." She grinned. "I didn't try too hard."

"Why not?" Rocky glared.

"You want me to spell it out? I thought you might find a different use for it."

Crossing her legs, Pandora sat absolutely still, guessing at the possibilities that raced through his mind. "Cleo hasn't had time to get used to her new name. Would misplacing her real one be a double whammy? Elicit a more emotional reaction to the experiment?" She could almost see the wheels in his brain spinning.

Finally, Marzin shook his head. "It's tempting, but I can't do it." He handed back the credit card. "We have to return it. Cleopatra must be quite upset. Right now she's dealing not only with the name changes in class, but with returning to her birth name after years of using her husband's. She's recently divorced, you know. Those changes will provide enough tension."

Pandora raised her eyebrows. Rocky protective? She didn't believe it. Something else was going on. Taking the card between her fingers, she flipped it back and forth. She continued to study his face, saying nothing.

"It was a clever idea to think of me and my project," Rocky admitted. "Too bad I'm scrupulous." He started to pat Pandora's knee, but stopped abruptly an inch above touching.

She sucked in her cheeks to hide her smile. Men were so easy. "Are you really that honest, professor?"

Marzin scowled.

She knew her scornful tone came close to insubordination. Before he could chastise her, Pandora rose and flung the long strands of fiery hair behind her shoulders, letting them sway. She straightened, her breasts thrusting forward as the ankh started to slide. His eyes followed the movement.

How she enjoyed frustrating the prof. He was aware that she saw through him, but what could he do about it? And he hadn't taken the credit card away from her. Was he playing a game, too, giving her enough rope to see what she would do? Well, so what? It kept his attention on her.

Cleo could use a few worries; it would even out the playing field. The Queen had Merlin—or so she thought. That could be worked on. The game was far from over.

Meanwhile, Rocky was hers. He had a larcenous soul, just as she had. Scruples, hah! That was another name for cowardice. She'd go forward with her plan.

"Have you any need for an office assistant?" Pandora asked as she slipped the card back into her jeans. "I could use a small stipend."

She watched him follow the card sliding into her pocket. Could he see the rectangle? Ignore the lining and imagine it against her bare skin…above her thong? When he swallowed, she stared at him insolently.

"I've already mentioned the position to Cleo," Marzin growled. "She's had a lot of office experience." He turned away, began reading.

Pandora's face paled, then flushed with rage. *No, dammit, Cleopatra can't have both men.*

The image of the curl flashed through her mind again. This time, it was attached to a head. A sprawled figure. Colored dots littered the floor. Candy? And there was noise, too. Papa and Ma were arguing…shouting. She stuffed her mouth with the pretty candies and covered her ears.

The figure on the floor became clearer. It started out as Faith, then faded into Cleopatra. It was Cleo. It was!

It's not fair. She's making Papa scream at Ma. She can't have everyone. Not Merlin and Papa! No, no, it isn't Papa. She's mixing me up. Those candies are hurting my tummy. I'm going to throw up. What is she doing to me? She's got that stupid curly hair. The professor is mine!

Marzin was looking at her strangely. She had to pull herself together.

Mentally giving Rocky the finger, Pandora marched out the door. Through the pounding in her head, a new plot was already hatching.

Chapter 9

Mac was still in his office at eleven p.m. He had just put two more magazines to bed. Only the light slipping through the transom illuminated the room, and he sat in the dark, tired but relaxed, letting his thoughts wander. He had always known that Morgan Senior planned to turn over the trade magazine empire he had built to his son, but he hadn't been ready for the responsibility when he graduated from Harvard. Instead, he'd flown to Hawaii that summer and surfed in every kind of wind and weather, challenging the elements. Had he really believed he could escape his fate? So young.... So foolish. His sudden marriage and even quicker divorce had only delayed, not prevented the inevitable.

That damned marriage. He'd really been suckered into it. Hard lesson to learn, but Miss Calculating Tiffany had been the blonde to teach it. Cost him a B&B on Maui, to say nothing of the emotional expense. She'd been quite a manipulator. He may have been prodded along by too many mai tai's to celebrate his twenty-first birthday, but she'd taught him to keep far, far away from such entanglements again.

Swallowing another mouthful of beer, he continued to brood. Six months after returning to the mainland he'd been back at the office, working his way up, step by step. Editorial, advertising, accounting—even circulation. Editorial was stimulating, but numbers crunching a bore. Now, if he could have drawn the ads instead of figuring out their costs…. Mac laughed softly.

He sobered, then, remembering that harrowing day when the lead story on new apps for cell phones had come in late, with a page missing. Big Morgan had blazed with anger, then clutched at his chest and slid to the floor. Thank God the collapse hadn't triggered a major heart attack, but Dad had retired after three days in the hospital, given a good push from Mom.

Mac had applauded the decision, even though he was appalled by the result. Imagine him, the publisher of a half dozen science and engineering magazines. It still freaked him out.

At first he'd liked being "The Boss." Of course he tried his damnedest to outshine Morgan Sr., but in his own shirtsleeves and sneakers style. As soon as he was in charge, he'd begun turning the mags into e-zines. He kept the print runs going, too—new designs for space shuttles, alternate fuels to replace oil—the lot. Corporate advertising paid well for the niche audiences, and the revenue kept rolling in.

For a while he'd tried out the fast track, but the playboy life wasn't for him. So he'd cut out the clubs, the yacht races, the flying to Cannes for the weekend, and concentrated on filling his dad's shoes.

But now the challenge was gone.

Finishing his beer, Mac opened another, his moody thoughts drifting to his secret dream—to publish a graphic novel. He would use some of the artistic talent he'd inherited from his mother, write the text and draw the panels himself. Barely conscious of scribbling, Mac drew a quick sketch of his hero—the handsome, clumsy oaf who depended on his lizard sidekick for the big decisions. He knew the character so well he could draw it in the semi-darkness. It was his sly joke. He would solve the world's problems in his own bumbling way. If he ever dug himself out of this shitload of work, Mac promised himself he'd do it. But for now....

He tore the page off his memo pad and trashed it.

Closing his eyes, Mac leaned back in his chair. He'd been so distracted of late, he'd missed his father's trap to lure him back to school. On a scorching day last August, his father had come into the office, caught him mopping the sweat from his neck.

"You need to be more involved in the new communications techniques," Morgan Sr. had sprung on him. "The computer isn't the answer to everything. Your innovations have worked well these last few years—I like the e-zines—but that's all mechanics."

"Electronics." Mac ran his fingers through his hair.

"Whatever. You need to do more on the editorial level."

"How the hell am I supposed to do that?" A last minute ad placement in *Beyond Space* had kept him hopping, and he was curt, but his father paid no heed.

"You need to make new friends, people who aren't buried in their computers. Go back to school. An advanced degree will get you in with the movers and shakers."

"I don't think they're in school, Dad."

"No, but their kids are. You need to mix more. Meet persons with varied interests. Get your foot in the door on an intellectual level."

"Are you sure you're feeling well?"

"I'm worried about you. Too much work makes Mac a dull boy. You should be involved with others, Morgan, and your mother wants a grandchild."

"Uh oh. So she's behind this. Tell her not to hold her breath."

"Look. Try one class, see how you like it. Get out of the office. You're running a smooth ship now. It'll function without you one or two afternoons a week. Do it for your mother."

Mac was a sucker for that argument. Anything for Mom. Anything, that is, except for settling down. Before he could come up with new arguments, he'd reluctantly enrolled in Professor Marzin's communications class. And by now he could admit that he wasn't sorry. He hadn't run into any movers, but he'd met one person who shook him up.

He wasn't about to tell his father that.

But enough dwelling on the past. Mac heard the light knock on his door. The old man had been at the theater and stopped in at the office afterwards. "Merlin" wanted his advice for Cleopatra. "Come on in, Dad."

"Mac, is that you sitting there in the dark?"

"Yeah, just taking a few minutes to relax and think."

"Got a problem?"

"No. All's running smoothly with the 'zines. I want to ask your advice for a friend. This girl I know lost her credit card." He got up and accompanied his father out the door. "Didn't Uncle Jay have some trouble when his wallet was stolen? Was there anything to be done besides informing the bank that issued the card?"

In the hall's bright light Mac watched his father home in on his first words. "Is this girl someone special?"

"What has that got to do with my question?"

"Nothing. But it's good to have all the facts before—" As his father continued to probe, Mac interrupted.

"Look," he said. "I met Cleo in the class I'm taking. Don't know her that well yet, but I like her and want to help her. Right now she's getting over a divorce. She's not up to a new relationship and, frankly, neither am I. If anything more is going to come of it, I'll let you know. When *I'm* ready, so quit poking around."

His father blinked at Mac's vehemence, but backed down. "Tiffany really left her mark on you, didn't she?" Mac grimaced. "Well, the girl in your class has taken the correct first step. Should anything illegal crop up, our lawyer knows how to deal with the consequences. Why don't you call Jerry and ask him?"

"I will. Thanks." The status quo restored, Mac relaxed. "How's your golf game these days?"

"I'm hanging in there, trying to get your mother to join me. The exercise will do her good."

"Still stuck in her studio all day?"

"Yes. I'm glad she's not gallivanting around shopping all the time, but she needs to get away from the paint fumes. Breathe in some fresh air."

"Now you're a convert." Mac smirked. "You were a *wee bit* excessive about being in the office every day...remember? It took a mini heart attack to get you out."

"It's not the same." They reached the elevator. "Ah, we're here. I'm for home. Don't stay too late."

"Right."

"About that insert for *Quarks and Questions*—"

"—I've already dealt with it," Mac interrupted.

"Well, good. I'll see you tomorrow, then."

Not if I can help it, but Mac didn't say it aloud. Six booming years later, three as boss, and his father still wanted a hand in. Sometimes subterfuge was necessary.

The confrontation had left him more tired than ever. It had been an exhausting week, and he felt himself beginning to nod. He'd better get home before the cleaning crew mopped him off the floor.

****

"Hello?"

"Hi, Cleo, it's Merlin."

"I recognized your voice."

He felt her smile through the lilt in her words. "Sorry I couldn't get back to you sooner, but I was unable to reach my father until last night. He suggested I discuss your problem with our company lawyer. I doubt that it's necessary, but I'll have Jerry's take on it for you after class tomorrow. Meet me at the deli?"

"That'll be fine."

"Meantime, you did call the bank?"

"Oh, yes. It took forever, but I finally got through. They've canceled that card and are issuing me a new one."

"Good. Then everything is okay?"

"I could still get into trouble, though. I've heard of cases...."

"Yeah, me too, but it's unlikely. Try not to worry about it."

"Thieves could use the card to get my address."

"Anyone can find that on the web. Nothing's private any more. Just lock your doors and windows."

"Now you're scaring me."

"It's a precaution. One you should take living alone. Nothing to do with the missing card."

"You're right. I do check every night—ever since the divorce. I've never had a problem."

"Well, don't let up now. Do it, then relax and forget about it."

"Easier said than done."

She sounded wistful. He could hear her breathing, a little fast. "Want me to come over and protect you?" Merlin asked.

"You know the rules." Cleo laughed. "Of course, you're too honorable to read the name on my mailbox, but we'd better wait."

"Well, it was worth a try."

"Merlin...there is something else."

He caught the hesitation in her voice. "What's up?"

"I got a strange e-mail today...anonymous."

"About the credit card?"

"I don't think so—at least, I didn't see any connection."

"What did it say?"

"Not much. It was all in caps. 'POACHING IS ILLEGAL. KEEP OFF THE GRASS.'"

"Huh?"

"Yeah, I've been trying to figure out what it means. I can't make any connections to the poaching bit, but back when Roger, my ex, was in med school, we hung out with a crowd that smoked a lot of weed. It's not something I'm comfortable talking about now."

"You're not running for office," Merlin assured her. "No one cares about that any more."

"I hope someone isn't trying to cause trouble. I'll

be looking for another job, soon."

"It's just a joke—some kids playing around. Listen, if you're really upset I could come over."

"No, thanks. I won't be silly about this. It doesn't fit my new persona."

"You still sound edgy to me, Cleo."

"Well, I did get a late night phone call with no one speaking, but it was probably my mother having second thoughts. It must have dawned on her that I couldn't be expected to fix something at that hour."

"I don't like it...." He paused. "It could be someone else."

"Who? It's the kind of thing Mama would do."

"So you say. I'm beginning to wish that classes were over."

"Then you could come here and protect me?"

"Mmm."

"I share your feelings, but I'm enjoying the class, too. I heard a rumor that we're in for psychodrama next. Strange way to communicate, but it sounds fascinating."

"Rocky will give it his own twist, I'm sure. Okay, then. See you tomorrow. Keep those scarab beads warm for me."

He heard her chuckling as he ended the call.

Chapter 10

Excitement hummed through the classroom when Prof Rocky mentioned psychodrama. "Today we'll have a chance to get to know ourselves better," he began. "I've assigned roles for each of you in our little plays. Be sure you take your new names into consideration as we act out the parts. Don't forget to respond as your new persona would. Are there any questions?"

Several hands rose, the Asian girl waving hers frantically.

"Yes, Butterfly?"

Hearing the name, Merlin and Cleo looked at each other and smiled.

"How are you going to grade us?" Butterfly asked timidly. "We're not drama majors."

"Haven't I told the class?" Rocky looked around the room. "This is not a course where grades are applicable. Everyone who does the work will receive an A."

After a startled silence, applause broke out. One of the few not clapping, Pandora narrowed her eyes. Prof Rocky glanced at her but turned away and looked again at Butterfly. "Is that answer satisfactory?"

"Yes, indeed," she whispered.

He smiled, omitting his usual "Speak up."

"Now, class, we're going to perform three short

plays, each with five characters. The plot will focus on the characters' reactions to a problem. How would this person handle the situation? Let's be spontaneous. After each act, we'll judge how integrated the characters are with their personas. I hope some truths will emerge."

By now the other raised hands had dropped, so he continued. "The first play will deal with family dynamics. Merlin will take the part of the father, Pandora the mother, Gwyneth the daughter, Antonio the son, and Napoleon, in the back row, the psychologist/narrator.

"Here's the problem. Dad wants the son in the family business. Son wants to be a dancer. Daughter wants to be an actress. Mother, an old-fashioned, religious woman, is troubled—you might even say horrified—at both her children's ambitions. And let's throw some recreational drugs into the pot…uh, mix." His eyes twinkled.

Pot? Cyn looked startled. *Rocky…e-mail…? No, it couldn't be. Just a coincidence.*

"What the family business is, who's smoking the illegal stuff, how each person reacts to the situation, I leave to you, the actors. Respond as the character you're playing. Got the idea? I'll stop and redirect as needed, giving the psycho-narrator a chance to comment."

Marzin looked around the room. "Everybody into this, now? Okay, the five of you to the front. Two minutes for conferring and we'll begin." He sat down at his desk, tipped his chair back and leaned against the wall.

"Wow!" Cleo whispered to Merlin. "Here's your chance to rise and shine."

"I'm no actor, never even made it into a school play. I think the teachers expected me to mess up on purpose." Merlin grinned. "In fourth grade, I was the class clown." Then he frowned. "I don't know if I like this. Too much could be revealed. I'm not sure Rocky knows what he's doing."

"Yeah," Cleo muttered. "I hope nobody gets hurt." She watched him stride to the front of the room, oblivious to the admiring female gazes that followed his movements.

With a nod from Marzin, the narrator spoke. "In zis dysfunctional tale of family dynamics," Napoleon said in a fake Viennese accent, "ve vill shstart vid ze fodder."

Rocky hushed the laughter. "Play the game."

After a moment, Merlin said, "My son, you know I'm the CEO of a huge insurance company. My golden parachute will keep the family in splendor, but I want an actuary in the family. In my office. Times are tough, and I need a spy in the organization."

Antonio couldn't restrain a giggle. "But Dad," he whined, looking up at Merlin from a slouch, "I'm not the type, I couldn't be a spy. And I can't add." He gave a theatrical shudder. "Haven't you always said we should follow our dream?"

"You'll have plenty of time for dreaming after you've put a couple of years into the company. Earn yourself the right."

"The right to dream? But—"

"You've got to learn the value of money before you spend it all."

"Why should I give up my youth to make money in a job I hate when you've got so much of it?"

"It won't last if you don't value it."

"I value what it buys!"

"Sure you do. But suppose the economy goes bust? Suppose I lose it all? What then?"

"Hey, man, lemme live while I can. When the bust comes, I wanna be able to say I enjoyed my life."

"He's right, Dad," Gwyneth broke in. "My dream is to be on the stage. Front and center. That's all I've ever wanted."

"You're disgusting, the two of you," Pandora spat at them. "That my children should move so far from God's wishes..."

"Ma, you're a pill," said Gwyneth. She turned toward Merlin. "You two belong back in the twentieth century!"

"Cut!" Rocky shouted as laughter broke out. "What a bunch of clichés. Crock of shit, gang. Dr. Napoleon, explain to us what's going on. How is our little group evading the truth?"

"Yah yah," Napoleon pulled at an imaginary beard, his on-again, off-again accent booming. "Ze fodder, as I see it, is unhappy vid ze choices he has made in his life. He needs his son to validate them. Ze children are rightly rebellious in zis unloving atmosphere. And ze mudder, unknown to all, is toking to escape from her endless feelings of guilt."

Pandora raised her thumb and forefinger, pretending to hold a butt to her lips. "With kids like these plaguing me, I need to escape." Her voice had dropped down an octave, as if she were mimicking the words of a voice she'd heard before. As she took a shaky puff of imaginary weed, sniggers and snorts filled the room. Her frown turned into a sly smile.

"We've certainly hit on the buzz words," Rocky drawled when the sounds had died down. He held up a fist, a finger popping up with each word. "Dysfunction, rebellion, validation, lack of love, guilt. How about anger, real but unexpressed? Underneath the jokes I sensed a lot of that."

The cast looked anywhere but at each other. *He's hit on something,* Cleo thought. *We'll all be pondering this scene for some time.*

Amid applause and whistles, the actors resumed their seats." Let's get some feedback on the play we've just witnessed," said Rocky. "Perhaps there is some truth underlying it all. The question is, would you have reacted this way if your real names were being used? Expressed your anger more violently? Or would you have found it necessary—safer—to disguise your reactions? Think about it. Your homework assignment will be to analyze the play from both your old point of view and your new persona."

As the class settled into a lively discussion, Cleo noticed Merlin doodling in his notebook. The gold pen he always carried glinted as his hand moved rapidly across the paper. Leaning toward him, she was startled to find she recognized half a dozen faces from the class. With a few strokes he had captured both their looks and their personalities. The man was talented. Was he an artist in his other life?

She had no time to dwell on the thought, for Marzin began to outline the next plot. "A club. Saturday night. The band has just taken a break, so four people are at the bar. One dating couple," he pointed to Butterfly and Dylan—a big guy with a Texas drawl, "and two singles, Cleo and Sigmund"—a black guy who confounded the class with street jargon no one could decipher. The job of narrator was given to a round-faced, heavy young woman who'd chosen the name Cameron.

The play began. As a pickup ploy, Sigmund set about analyzing Cleo, his words so garbled she had a hard time keeping a straight face. She kept attempting to reject him without hurting his feelings. At one point she picked up an imaginary glass and gulped it all down. As he kept trying to psych her into bed, she signaled for another drink and mimed throwing it at him. The watchers snickered.

In the lull between words, Cleo heard the couple at the bar arguing loudly about commitment. She was surprised to hear Butterfly raise her voice. Once she got going, the girl let loose. She pulled a chopstick from her hair, raised it like a weapon. The other students egged her on until her pretend boyfriend was reduced to sputtering. A laughing Rocky called a halt. "We certainly stirred things up," came Cameron's breathy comment. "I think it's great that we can bring these problems out in the open."

"Okay, gang, we've run out of time," said Rocky. "We'll save discussing this psychodrama and performing our third play until the next session. Try to remember your reactions." He looked around the room and applauded. "Good class today."

The students gathered their books and left, still chattering. "That was quite a session," Cleo said as she and Merlin walked over to the deli. "Did your role strike any sparks in you?"

"More than I liked," he answered ruefully. "Dad got me into the business, so he's won round one. I'm supposed to be boss now, but he keeps butting in. Besides, it's not how I want to spend the rest of my life."

"Darn, I wish you could tell me more."

He smiled. "Couple more months, and all will be revealed."

"I couldn't help noticing your doodling. Your sketches are really good, and you're so fast. Just a few strokes and you've captured personalities."

"It's a hobby of mine." Merlin pushed open the deli door. "I grew up on Superman and Ironman. Buffy, too. All the greats."

Cleo wanted to question him further, but Merlin's expression warned her off. She slid into a booth and ordered a burger. "Did you learn anything from the lawyer?" she asked.

"You did the right thing. The bank that issued the card will take over. If any purchase slips by them, you could inform the police, then place a fraud alert. The lawyer didn't think you'd need to."

"I swore I'd never lean on a man again, but in this case it's good to have your support." She placed her hand over his. "I'm not used to problems involving theft and police. As for lawyers, the only ones I know work on divorce cases."

Turning Cleo's hand around, Merlin stroked her palm. His touch made her arm tremble, but he didn't seem to notice. "It's the uncertainty. Wondering what can happen, and when. Leaves you hanging."

"You do understand."

"Been there, done that. But changing the subject, would you like to go out one night? Dinner and a movie? We can meet at the restaurant, so I won't learn your real name."

She hesitated a moment, then beamed at him. "I'd love it! Let you in on a secret. I'm crazy about movies, and a sucker for the old romantic films."

"I'm into movies too. Lots of action and suspense."

"Works for me, as long as you guarantee a happy ending." The tip of her tongue rubbed across her upper lip.

He couldn't stop staring, responding to the tiny motion. She watched him as his eyes moved lower, then with a start, returned to her face.

"Uh…for you, Cleopatra, that's what's on the menu—action, romance, and the good guys win in the end.

"I'll work on it."

Chapter 11

Teetering on stiletto heels, Pandora walked around her bedroom in her new faux alligator boots. Classy. And best of all, she'd gotten away with using Cleo's credit card. Good thing the picture on the card was so small. She'd guessed right. The sales clerks she'd dealt with at Bloomies had both been fooled.

She paraded around the room, getting used to the strange pressure on her toes. Whenever she passed the full-length mirror on the back of her closet door, she looked at herself and smirked. On one pass she pretended to be Cleo, frowning in bewilderment at the reptile skin boots. Cleo couldn't wear them—they weren't her style. It took a tall, slender figure to make them look sexy. One like hers. Pandora tried a little victory dance, but twisted her ankle and ended up stumbling over to the bed.

For a moment, she brooded.

She'd had fun at the cosmetics counter, trying out the different lipsticks, but a particular shade of red had triggered that memory again. She'd flashed to the dark red spill on the wooden floor. A curl lay in it. *Why was Faith sleeping on the floor?* She tried to picture the image more clearly, but a headache started, so she erased it from her mind. Turning the lipstick tube back and forth, up and down, she became conscious of the clerk looking at her oddly.

She'd spun around. A security guard was making his way through the pre-Christmas shoppers. Dropping the lipstick onto the counter, she'd forced a smile and escaped toward the escalators, melting into the milling crowd.

As her heartbeat slowed, footsteps sounded outside Pandora's bedroom. Jerking off the boots, she jumped up and flung them into the closet. She slammed the door shut, rattling the mirror as her mother walked into the room.

Even at a head shorter than her daughter, the skinny woman was imposing. Mrs. Bronski eyed the closed closet door, then peered suspiciously at Pandora. "What are you doing?"

"Just finished my homework, Ma." She leaned down and left a quick kiss on her mother's cheek. "Putting my book bag away."

"Why are your feet bare, Prudence? Where are your shoes?"

"Uh, the heels were worn down. The taps the shoe repair guy added are coming loose. Thought I'd better change into my ballet slippers."

Her mother still looked skeptical. "Hurry up, then, or we'll be late for the prayer meeting. Afterwards, you can drop them off at the shoemaker."

"He just repairs shoes, Ma. Those guys don't make shoes any more. Anyway, there's no hurry. I'll do it on my way to class tomorrow. I won't forget." Pandora bent forward and tilted her head as she gazed wide-eyed at her mother. She'd perfected the innocent look years ago.

"Very well, but be sure you do. We can't afford to waste money on new shoes, not at today's prices. Your old ones are still serviceable."

Prudence nodded, too full of the old resentment to speak.

As soon as her mother left the room she flipped back into Pandora mode, pulled open the closet door and grinned evilly at her face in the mirror.

Close call. Ma would have conniptions if she ever saw those boots. She'd snap off the heels and aim them at me, like poisoned darts.

She swiped her arm across her forehead and waited for the adrenaline rush to fade. Her body began to shake. Falling back on the bed, she wrapped the quilt around her. She'd become a whiz at simulating obedience, but there was always a price to pay.

I'd better not try to use Cleo's card again. Too dangerous. Almost got caught at the cosmetics counter when I had that strange flash. Wonder how long it lasted? She must have appeared guilty for a second— the clerk gave her that look and called the guard.

Shaking off her sudden fear, Pandora threw off the covers, brought her knees up to her chin and hugged herself.

That was a blast. I'll hang onto the card for a while, let the bitch worry about what's going to happen next. Yeah, way to go.

I wonder what was behind Marzin's psychodrama. Why did he cast me in the mother's role? Does he know? No, there's no way he could find out. My records are sealed. Nosy Marzin is poking around where he doesn't belong, but it was fun making Ma take a hit. Too bad it wasn't for real.

I need to get back into his office, read those assignments. There's bound to be something in those descriptions that I can use to rattle Miss Queen of the Fancy Briefcase even more. She's got all the guys ogling her boobs. Cleopatra is due for a comeuppance.

Pandora snorted. *Oh, m'God, I'm actually using one of Ma's words. For shame, Prudence.*

Slapping the back of her hand, Pandora lowered her feet to the floor. She slid into her ballet slippers and checked her Best-Buy watch, sneering at the large numbers in the stainless steel case. That, too, was serviceable.

How she hated the word.

I'll take a peek at Rocky's schedule tomorrow, find out when the office will be empty. Lord knows that's often enough. Men are never there when you want them.

There I go, using Ma's favorite saying. I was glad when Papa started to drink. It serves Ma right. He was no help before—she walked right over him. Now he ignores both of us. Why does he bother to come home at all?

Conjuring up her father's face, Pandora scowled. Once, he had yelled back at Ma, his voice so loud she had been scared. She tried to remember when it had happened, but all that came to mind was the image of that bloody curl, the candies that weren't candy, and her throwing up…

As she stood, trying to fight through the headache that had started again, she became aware of her mother's footsteps returning.

Dropping thoughts of papa, Pandora reopened her closet door. She checked that the boots were way in the back, out of sight. Even her bloodhound of a mother wouldn't find them under all that mess.

Picking up her plain black church-going purse, she slung the strap over her shoulder and took one last look in the mirror.

Ready...set...on with the meek and mild mask.
I could spit.

Chapter 12

"Cynwyd, I hosted my bridge game yesterday, and there was an accident."

"What happened, Mama? Are you hurt?"

"Not really. It wasn't that kind of accident, but I'm terribly upset. My nerves…. I almost had an attack."

"Did you take your medicine?"

"Well, I was drinking wine, and alcohol and medications are deadly, so I took another glass of wine instead."

"I'm sure that helped."

Her mother ignored the sarcasm. "It did calm me down, enough to hostess the rest of my bridge game. I'd bought a delicious rum cake from that Viennese bakery—served it afterwards with tea for me and the Costa Rican coffee you brought back from vacation. The women said I made it just right, though I don't see how. I rarely drink it myself. But it was very hard to concentrate on bridge. I must have lost fifty dollars."

"It didn't break the bank, I'm sure. What actually happened, Mama?"

"You know my partner smokes. Marilyn is the only smoker I'll allow in my home, but we've been partners for years. I can't say no to her."

"What did she do? Set fire to the living room?"

"Close. There is a severe burn in the Oriental rug. What an odor! We had to stamp on the spot, and spilling the chardonnay on it didn't help, either."

"At least it was white wine. The rug's insured, isn't it?"

"I imagine so."

"Then call the insurance company. They'll get someone to reweave the damaged part. It's in the policy."

"I was thinking of writing your father about it."

"Don't bother him with it, Mama. He's too far away to help, and if you tell him, he'll probably think more than the rug got burned. He'll start calling the hospitals."

"He needs to worry more about what's going on at home."

"Not if he's set on getting a divorce. We're not part of his new life. Don't try to stop him—you can handle this on your own. You should feel proud that you can take care of things by yourself."

Her mother sighed. "You grew up in a different world, Cynwyd."

"Are you starting that, again? Remember what the counselor told you when Daddy left? You're stronger than you think. You can cope."

"Well, I wanted to let you know. You can see the damage for yourself when you come over on Sunday."

"Okay," Cyn said. "I'll bring bagels."

Hoping Audrey's emails would erase the residue of her mother's call, Cyn turned to her text messages. There were quite a few.

"Tony just called me," Audrey wrote. "He asked Merry and me out for a day at the zoo. Tell you about it later. I'll clue Merry in to Alice being my secret nickname. I won't forget! ☺"

Cyn read the note with delight. Introducing "Alice" to Tony had been inspired. She clicked on the next message, sent that evening.

"Tony got here so soon he must have been in the neighborhood. He had a kid's car seat in the back—in his large family someone always needs it. And the zoo was great. We saw a baby giraffe, only a week old. Merry was so excited."

Before Cyn could form the next question, her BFF was already answering it.

"Merry took to Tony right away. She skipped along between us to the giraffe compound. Kids were running about, squealing. It was feeding time, and the zookeeper fed the baby giraffe from a bottle. Merry jumped up and down until Tony picked her up and put her on his shoulders. She had the best view in the house."

Smiling, Cyn clicked on the next message.

That image is engraved in my memory. Merry's cheeks rosy from the air's cold bite. Her chubby arms around Tony's neck. Her flasher sneakers in his hands. She kept calling out that she was as tall as the 'jraf.' I've never seen her so happy.

"After the feed we watched gibbon monkeys hanging by their tails from a tree inside their cage. They bounced from branch to branch, and Merry bounced up and down along with them."

"We stood in a long line for lunch, ate at a picnic table. After, we saw the elephants and a lion with two cubs. By then Merry was dragging her feet. Tony picked her up and carried her to the car. She fell asleep in his arms, and he strapped her into the car seat without waking her. What a man!"

As she checked the last message, Cyn licked her lips.

"Tony asked me out again," Audrey wrote. "Next time, I'm getting a sitter...."

Chapter 13

Pandora tried to sleep, but as she tossed and turned, half asleep and half awake, she was suddenly at the beach, playing with her pail and shovel beside a tidal pool. The water in it was different. Bright, tiny tropical fish swam about in the blood red water. They circled around something else in the pool, something with a handle. She couldn't see what, for the rest was buried in the sand. The doctors from the hospital marched by, white coats flapping, carrying Faith. Her mother trailed behind. She turned toward Pandora as she passed, but a big wave crashed on shore and drowned out her words. Pandora started to run after them, but someone pulled her back. Someone was sing-songing, Puker Pru, Puker Pru, and pulling her into the sea. It was Cleopatra….

****

Cyn took her time deciding what to wear. The few dates she'd been on since her divorce had been easily forgettable. Tonight, however, something inside her hummed. Tonight felt special.

And Merlin had everything to do with it.

She gazed at her clothes, daydreaming. Audrey had teased her about having two men in her life. True, but even though she loved attending class and working for the professor, she'd begun to separate her fascination with him from her reactions to Merlin. The only emotions Rocky stirred in her were respect and—face it—a touch of fear.

So far all had gone smoothly, but whenever she was alone with him, the vision of falling backward gave her a start. He didn't mention it, but the connection intruded. Rocky's flirting struck her as surprisingly asexual—a sop for his virile self-image. The vibes she got were not at all like the whispers of dark power that called to her from Merlin.

Now there was a man whose mysteries she'd give a lot to penetrate. He was so secretive about himself, so rarely let his strength show. But underneath his masculine confidence, she sensed a restless spirit. Merlin was searching for something and, whatever it was, she wanted to help him find it. The desire was irrational; she had no idea what the something was, only that it grew brighter when they were together, a shivery current of feeling she shared but couldn't name....

The deep bong of the antique hall clock snapped Cyn out of her reverie. It was getting late. From her closet, she pulled her green silk sheath from its padded hanger. Did the cowl neckline drape too low for a first date? Was it overly suggestive? Nonsense—the dress was her color, and it hugged her figure in the right places. The matching shoes had four-inch heels; she could never wear them with Roger. She'd once wondered why he'd needed to look down on her, but the answer to that, of course, was the key to their failed marriage.

Forget him—tonight was about looking forward, not back. She scanned the dress once more. The short skirt had a longer sheer overskirt that drew a guy's eyes to her legs, and they were her best feature. For this date, her urge to look smart and sexy was strong.

Two silver combs held back her mass of burnished curls, blending with the entwined snake earrings she'd purchased at the fair. She wore no other jewelry, for the dress said it all. Her matching green evening bag held lipstick, comb, money and keys—no room for her cell phone. For once, Mama couldn't interrupt and spoil things.

Giddy with a sense of freedom, Cyn locked up and drove into town.

Merlin was waiting in the lounge at Guido's. She sighed inwardly as her gaze rested on the tall man who so perfectly filled his Armani suit. Power radiated. Thank goodness she'd guessed right and gone with the slinky silk dress.

His eyes lit when she walked in. "This restaurant is the newest rage in Italian cuisine," he told her. "Their pesto is out of this world, and their red sauce is a family secret handed down through the generations."

"I've heard that Guido's bakes a dessert cake using vinegar," Cleo said. "My friends tell me you've gotta taste it to believe it." Pursing her lips, she bunched her fingers toward her mouth, then flicked them away in a gesture she'd picked up from an Italian movie. *"Mama mia!"*

"Hey, you do that finger thing real well! You'll have to teach me how."

"Later," Cleo teased. "Right now I'm starving."

As he took her coat, Merlin's gaze slid over her. His pupils widened. "I like the little green dress. Matches your eyes." He lingered at the deep sweep of her neckline before taking in the whispery, jungle-leaved overskirt that floated as she moved. "You've given me an appetite, too." He licked his lips, led her into the dining room.

"I got tired of New York black," she said as the waiter seated them. "I had high hopes for this dress, but I didn't expect it to make you hungry."

"Are you sure?"

She blushed. "Well, not for food."

He laid his hand on hers. "You've awakened all my appetites."

"Watch it!"

Merlin grinned.

They shared a crisp calamari appetizer, dipping the little circles into a peppery red sauce, and followed it with cups of the chef's renowned wedding soup. The main course, lobster *fra diavolo* over velvety fettucini, was accompanied by a special reserve Chianti.

And they talked—of the class, the assignments, the professor. Both were determined to avoid personal topics that would reveal who they were.

"What about that vinegar cake?" Merlin asked when the last of the wine had been drunk.

"Oh dear, I don't think I have any room left."

"I'll order one slice, so we can each have a taste."

"You're a man after my own heart." She blushed. "That was the wine talking."

He laughed.

Cleo felt so comfortable with Merlin. He seemed to understand her, respect her, and still protect her. That sounded absurd, even to her wine-soaked brain, but there it was. No accounting for feelings.

As they waited for their cake and cappuccino, she couldn't resist testing the boundaries. She really wanted to know more about his clever cartoons. "Are you sure you're not an artist?" she asked, twirling the stem of her empty wine glass.

"Well, I did get some training—my mother's a painter and I took art classes in college. But I don't use it to earn my daily bread. At least, not yet," he mumbled.

Taking the gold pen she recognized from his inside pocket, Merlin pulled out the cloth napkin from the empty breadbasket, shook out the crumbs and drew a quick sketch of Cleo on it. He drew her full length, taking a step forward in her sleek dress, its sheer overskirt billowing around long shapely legs.

Cleo grabbed the napkin and flattened it out on the corner of their table. "That's amazing!" She looked up at him, astonished. "That's me…and you drew it so fast. We'll have to buy the napkin—I'm not giving this up. It may be worth millions one day," she said, fluttering her lashes.

His smile grew wider. "I shouldn't, but…I have to tell you about Oxy Moron."

"Oxymoron? You mean the figure of speech where the second part contradicts the first? Like cold fire, or hot ice?"

"Yep, but it's also the name of my graphic novel hero. He aims for one thing but always gets there by doing the opposite. Accidentally, of course."

"Wow, what fun! Tell me more."

"It's something I've been working on for quite a while, mostly in the middle of the night. Helps me to turn off problems that won't let me sleep. I plot the story lines in the dark and then draw them whenever I can squeeze in a short break."

"Sounds like a plan. What's your premise?"

"Oh ho, so speaks an English major," he teased. All I can say is that Oxy's my man. He stumbles along spouting my ideas and accomplishing my goals."

"Your alter ego?"

"In a way…although he's bigger and clumsier…and much better looking."

Cleo's eyes sparkled. "How far into the book are you? I can't wait to see it."

"Still quite a way to go. It's tricky finding time to work on it."

"Could you bring a page to class and show me?"

"Sorry, but no. I'm keeping it as far away from Rocky as possible. Don't want him to analyze my imaginary world. It gives too much of me away. But I will show it to you one of these days," Merlin promised. "Just not yet."

She pouted. "Fine, arouse my curiosity and then stop."

"Is that all I've aroused?" He peeled her fingers from the wine glass and took her hand. "I'm not doing too well, then, am I?"

Cleo's breath caught in her throat. "There's a most suggestive look in your eye," she murmured. "Better stow it along with Oxy until the time is ripe. End of term, remember?"

Her pulse had speeded up. She dropped her glance, then looked up at him. "You know, although I can barely draw a straight line, we've something in common. When I can't sleep, I escape my worries by writing limericks."

"Really? Are they X-rated? 'There was a young maid from Cape Cod'…?"

"Oh no, not that one," she shuddered. "Roger, the

'lodger' is my ex-husband."

"Ouch."

"It's okay He fit the bill, too." She shook her head and laughed. "You men all have a one-track mind. And a few of my rhymes do get down and dirty. Mostly they're just suggestive."

"How about a sample?"

Cleo thought for a minute. "Okay, here's one about a famous Spanish painter. With your art background, I'm sure you'll recognize the two portraits I'm talking about."

"If I don't, I'll never admit it. There's always Google."

They grinned at each other. Taking a deep breath, Cleo recited.

"The Maja, in clothing or nude
Should never be thought of as lewd.
Thinking Goya's a voyeur
In need of a lawyer
Is so crude it should not be pursued."

"Wow!" Merlin laughed so loudly, the people at the next table turned around. Cleo blushed.

"You've gotta write that down for me. My mother will love it. She told me the story once, when we were looking at an art book. About how Goya was forced to put clothing on the woman he had painted in the nude. She was a duchess, wasn't she?"

"Something like that—it's a legend. I'll text you the lines."

"Fine." His slow grin returned as he watched Cleo fold the napkin containing his drawing and stuff it into her purse. "Check?" he mouthed to the waiter. "You're sure you don't want to hit a club? You're dressed for it." As she shook her head, he said, "We'd better leave if we're going to make the movie."

Merlin paid the bill, adding an extra large tip.

Cleo noticed and smiled. That should cover the loss of a napkin.

"What film are we going to see?" she asked as they left the restaurant.

"You said you like the old classics, right?"

"Mm-hmm."

"The Little Theater is having a Hitchcock festival, and it's right around the corner. There's a cocktail lounge in the basement, so we can have a drink after the movie." Merlin glanced at his watch. "We'll be just in time for 'North by Northwest.'"

"Oh, good. It's one of my favorites. Don't you love the scene of Cary running through the cornfields with that crop dusting plane chasing him?"

"A great moment in film history," Merlin said, eyes twinkling. "Can we pretend we're in high school and make out in the back row?"

"Quit teasing me, Oxy. We have to stick to our plan."

"You mean Rocky's plan. Okay, Madame Queen. And no more calling me Oxy or I'll use your middle name. What was it, Ftatateeta?"

"Truce!" Cleo giggled and put her arm into his.

They walked along in the brisk night air. Between the tall buildings, the winter stars were shining. "It's your turn to tell me something about you before you became Cleopatra."

She thought for a moment. "I did have a great month at work just before I left my job to return to school. Both the publisher and the editor of the magazine took off. They're married, but not to each other. I think they were indulging in a little end-of-summer hanky-panky. They must have very modern marriages to take off for so long."

"You don't approve?"

"I'm a little old-fashioned when it comes to fidelity," she muttered. "With reason."

He squeezed her hand, and she knew he understood.

"Anyway, while they were gone, I ran the entire magazine. Full charge. Stories, ads, the works!"

"I'm impressed."

"It was really exciting to find out I could do it. Seems I have a head for that kind of organizing. Thought the stress would get to me, but I found it exhilarating."

Merlin put his arm around her waist and pulled her close for a quick hug. "Good to know I have an efficient executive in my arms. Might come in handy, one of these days."

At his touch, a tremor slid down her spine. The warmth of his body beside hers, and the glow from the wine she had drunk, combined to make her dizzy. It was a delicious feeling. Cleo was aware of his thigh rubbing alongside hers as they walked. It left her tingling—the first time she'd felt that surge of desire since long before her divorce.

Well, she thought, *well, well, well.* A golden oldie floated through her brain, and she hummed as they walked along. *This could be the start of something good.* Maybe they'd take the back row seats after all....

Chapter 14

Pandora slipped into Professor Marzin's office. Glancing around, she noted the books were gone. His desk had been cleared off, but his computer was still humming.

Perhaps she'd send another cryptic e-mail to Cleopatra from here. Shake her up some more. Wouldn't it come in handy if Ms. Queen traced it back to Rocky's office? What would happen if she grew suspicious of her dear professor? Maybe Cleo would quit the job, and she could take over. That would work.

She started toward the computer but stopped herself, remembering the prof's linguistics class would soon be over. *Dammit. There isn't enough time!*

Where would he put the class folder of personal descriptions? Impatiently, she rifled through his desk drawers. No luck. She turned away, spotted a filing cabinet almost hidden behind the huge green leaves of a dusty rubber plant. She yanked at the top drawer, and it slid open.

Just like the man, she thought. He doesn't lock his door, his desk, or his filing cabinet. So sure of himself. Thinks he's invulnerable…but he'll learn.

She opened the drawer, flicked through the folders. What would Rocky call the papers he'd asked for, the two views of how the students saw themselves? He couldn't have thrown them out; he promised to return the papers at the end of the semester.

Slamming shut the first drawer, she opened the second. These tabs made sense. The folders were labeled—Actors, Rock Stars, Historical Figures, Myths. She thumbed through the file on Historical Figures but didn't find Cleo's paper. What could it be under?

As she tried to guess his code, Pandora noticed the sub-heads—M and F. Of course, male and female. Rocky had separated the descriptions by sex. She hadn't expected him to be so exacting. Was he isolating gender traits, or was that Cleo's idea? The woman seemed so organized. Was Cleo feeding ideas to Rocky for his book? Being treated as a secretary…or a colleague? She had to find out. Might be useful ammunition, later on.

Returning to the file labeled "Historical—F," Pandora pulled it out, shut the drawer and sat down at the big desk. She was flicking through the pages, absorbed in her search, when she heard a slight scrape as the doorknob turned. Responding instantly, she slipped the folder under the desk blotter.

The door opened. Rocky tossed his jacket onto the clothes rack, then turned toward his desk. "Pandora? What are you doing here?"

The girl jumped up, moved swiftly to the center of the room. "You startled me," she said, putting on her innocent face. "I had a couple of questions about our psychodrama. Want to do a good job on the homework assignment."

Am I putting it on too thick? It looks like he doesn't believe me. "Can you spare a few minutes?"

"Not really. Better make it quick."

"A-about the mother toking in our little play—was

it reasonable? I mean, she'd be of another generation. They didn't do things like that back then...." She opened her mouth to go on, but the words stuck in her throat. Her eyes flicked nervously to his desk as he watched her, frowning. She prayed he didn't notice the lump in the blotter.

As usual, her prayers went unanswered. Following her glance, the prof reached under it and pulled out the folder.

"Did you take this out of my cabinet?"

Her face flamed. Unable to come up with a smart excuse, she turned to flee.

Rocky jumped up and grabbed her arm.

"Let go of me!"

Releasing her, he stood between Pandora and the door. "What's going on?" A vein pulsed in his forehead.

As she stood there staring defiantly at him, she rubbed the arm where his fingers had gripped. His eyes narrowed. "I didn't hurt you. Don't pull that sexual harassment stunt on me. You were sneaking into my files."

She didn't reply, just flung her hair back and raised her chin.

Marzin regarded her, his facial muscles rigid, his fingers curled into fists. "There's a penalty for this kind of behavior. It's unacceptable."

He watched her for another minute, grinding his teeth. She stood silently, sweat beads forming above her tight lips. "You'd better leave now," the professor's words snapped out, "before I really lose my temper."

Pandora turned and ran. *Penalty*, the word raced through her mind as she fled. *Unacceptable.*

The buzzwords created a storm inside her. *I didn't take anything. Just wanted a peek. What does he think he can do? Spank me?* At the thought, an image of her father rose but quickly dimmed.

Bet the prof would like to get his hands on my ass! I would have put the folder back if the stupid man hadn't returned too soon. I wasn't going to steal it. That's not grounds for punishment. No way!

She burned with anger. Red bangs lifted off her forehead as if electricity pulled them from her skin.

Rocky treated me like a thief! Who does he think he is? The man is vulnerable too. What if I can prove that he's using his students' work as his own? Plagiarizing!

She flew down the next flight of stairs. *First, I'll find a photo booth, take a picture of my arm showing his finger marks. It's lucky I bruise so easily. I could tweak the incident, work it into a real charge of sexual harassment.*

Another flight to go. Her breaths expelled in little gasps. *This can't get back to Ma. She'll start checking my pills again. I have to stop Rocky from reporting me. Make him think twice about causing me trouble.*

She stepped out the front door into a cold drizzle. Pulling the Yankee ball cap from her pocket, she tucked her hair under and raised the collar of her army jacket. Swiping her sleeve under her dripping nose, she hunched her shoulders and headed for the subway, still talking to herself.

He can't get away with making those threats. I'll find a way to even the score.

Chapter 15

As Merlin waited for Cleo after class the next week, Pandora came out the door dressed all in black, turtleneck sweater and slim pants hugging her body. Her eyes were heavily outlined, the pencil strokes angled upward at the corners to emphasize the cat look of her burglar outfit. Her musky, expensive perfume was wrong for her. It made his nose twitch.

"Hi, Master Magician!" She stopped in front of him and flung her hair over her shoulder.

"What mischief are you up to now, Pandora? Getting ready to rob a bank?"

She raised her eyebrows. "Must I always be up to mischief?"

"No, but I've got a feeling I'm right. That outfit you've got on spells mischief with a capital M."

"Do you like it?" Her smile hinted at other things.

Merlin looked down at her long fingernails, painted a deeper red than her hair. "I can't answer that. You're not retracting your claws."

"Scaredy cat."

He was beginning to get annoyed. "Stop scratching, Pan. I'm not available. And that sexy perfume turns me off."

She pouted. "It's Donna Karan." Pandora waved her arm under his nose, and it twitched again.

"Who's that?"

"Oh, you men. You know nothing." She spotted Cleo turning the corner at the far end of the hall and talked faster. "Thought I'd share some inside info with a classmate."

Because I know nothing?"

"Not about this. How do you like the idea of Cleo working for Rocky?"

"Cuts off a bit of my time with her, but I'm okay with it. She's doing a good job, I'm told."

"No doubt by the prof himself."

"What do you mean?"

"He's got a reason. I stopped off to see him the other day during the hours Cleopatra works there and found the office door locked."

Merlin looked at Pandora. "Are you sure?"

"I rattled the doorknob. No one let me in."

"And you're telling me this…why?"

"Didn't want you taken by surprise. You're too nice a guy."

"Really? That doesn't sound like you."

"You could be mistaken about me." As she flashed another flirtatious smile, Pandora turned to see Cleo merely steps away. "Gotta go. Wave your wand, Sorcerer. Get your own answers."

Puzzled, Merlin watched her slink away. Not her usual military stride. Pandora was hinting at something, but he didn't want to go there.

Cleo arrived bubbling with excitement, and he forgot all about Pandora's catty hints. "You look like you've got some news. What's up?" he asked her.

"An excursion. Alice and I thought it would be fun if we all went out together. What's more, I've found the perfect place to visit," Cleo said. "I've already asked

Tony and he agrees."

"I see you can't wait to tell me." He loved teasing her.

"So what?" Her chin went up. "I'm the enthusiastic type. We've all noticed your doodling, Merlin, and we want to support our local artist. You'll enjoy an exhibit of famous celebrity caricatures that opened at the library on Forty-second Street. It's so cool. Original drawings and interviews with the artists, themselves— you pick up a phone to hear their voices. There's even a room set aside to show the earliest cartoon movies."

"Sounds great, but does this stuff appeal to all of you? I could get really involved in a show like that. You'll have to drag me away, and I wouldn't want everyone else to be bored."

"Are you kidding? There's something at this exhibit for everyone. Alice is even planning to take Merry. They're showing the first Mickey Mouse and Donald Duck cartoons. And there's something special for you, too. You love baseball, right?"

He nodded.

"Well, there's a great drawing of Babe Ruth with his head inside a baseball!"

He broke into a broad smile. "In that case, you're on. When do we go?"

"Meet you at the library Saturday morning, ten o'clock. Fifth Avenue entrance."

"It's a date. Let me walk you back to your car, Highness. Something I want to ask you about."

"Okay, but not that nickname, pul-lease."

Merlin said nothing as they walked along. Pandora's sly comments had gotten under his skin, and they came back to him now. What was the girl hinting at, and why? He wanted to ask Cleo but hesitated, uncertain how to start.

Cleo squeezed his hand. It brought a warm, close feeling, but he was uncomfortable, too, suspecting that she thought he was building up to something romantic. Should have made it clear, he thought briefly, but no, she wouldn't assume that. Not Cleo. When he finally asked, "Does Pandora have a grudge against you?" her look of dismay caught him by surprise.

She swallowed, then turned to him, her expression bland. "I don't think so. What makes you ask that?"

"She hinted at a 'non-academic' attachment between you and Professor Marzin. Something about locked doors."

"Me? Making out with Rocky?" Cleo laughed. "You've gotta be kidding. He jokes around in class and loves dropping innuendos, but when I'm working in his office, he's completely professional. Actually, he pushes me to get things done faster."

"Does he touch you?" Merlin's voice was tight with barely controlled anger.

"What? Oh, you mean when I said *pushes?* Chill, it's just a figure of speech. Marzin's first priority is his book. As for the door, I never noticed it was locked. Maybe it was stuck."

"I guess so." Merlin nodded. "Probably been years since anyone oiled the locks in the building." He took her arm. "Forget I mentioned it. Pandora must have been looking for a way to shock her audience again. In this case, me. She's as bad as Rocky when it comes to provoking reactions in people. Wonder what she gets out of it."

"I think Pandora has a thing for the professor,"

Cleo mused. "She tries to ward off competition, so she imagines things."

"But why cause trouble between you and me?"

"Well, it could keep me busy defending myself, and away from Rocky."

"Perhaps…. I can't get rid of the feeling that she's up to something."

"You've been suspicious of Rocky all along, Merlin, and now Pandora, too. Sure you're not a little paranoid?"

"Maybe. Maybe not. I feel it in my gut."

"Ah, man's intuition!"

"Now you're laughing at me, Cleo."

"No, I'm not. Well, maybe just a little. But I won't discount your feelings. Some persons are more aware of the vibes people give off than others. I'm not going to worry about it. She's barking up the wrong tree if she thinks she can persuade you with that line."

Her trust in him felt so good…so right.

****

The garage ahead was dimly lit. She turned around as they reached her car, and Merlin moved closer, leaning her against the door.

Cleo was conscious of the strength in his arms, the width of his shoulders as he caged her. Her breaths quickened. "So, till Saturday."

"Saturday," he repeated, then bent his head and kissed her, warm and slow. She melted into him. She hadn't guessed wrong—this was a romantic interlude, after all. Her arms came up around his neck, and he tilted his head, took her mouth at a different angle. The kiss turned from gentle to fierce as he pulled her closer.

Cleo clung to Merlin, loving the feel of his lips on

hers, of his roving tongue. His kisses slid down to her chin, to the side of her neck. He nipped her, then licked the spot. She shivered.

His body pressed into hers, and a hand on her hip squeezed. His other hand slid to her breast, flicking her nipple. She moaned and fitted herself to him, rubbing her hips and rocking. This was even better than the movie's back row.

A sudden sound—her eyes flew open. A car engine had started up. Noise and exhaust fumes invaded their shadowed space. Kicking up dust, a sports car roared out of the building.

Reluctantly, Merlin pulled away from Cleo. He took a deep breath, coughed. "We've got to stop meeting in garages."

"Yes." Cleo wrinkled her nose. "They're not the most romantic spots."

He chuckled. "Definitely not. I'll think of someplace better," he promised, running his fingers down her arm as he held the car door for her. "Names can remain a secret, Cleo, but Christmas is too far away to wait for other revelations."

"I'm beginning to feel what you mean." Cleo stepped into the car. She leaned out the door and pulled his head down for a last quick peck. "I'll leave it to you—wave your magic wand and conjure up a magical setting."

"That's twice today my wand has been called into play." His wolf smile followed her out.

****

As Audrey set out cheese, crackers, and the Spanish wine Tony had brought her, Cyn breezed in.

"Sorry I'm late. I dallied after class to set up our

excursion."

"No problem. Mom and Merry left only a few minutes ago." Audrey sipped her wine and got right to the point. "Did you know that I've been seeing a lot of Tony since the zoo trip?"

"Really?" Cyn plunked down on the couch, kicked off her shoes. "Tell me more."

"I don't know where to start," Audrey began. "I guess with the night we watched a DVD of *Saving Private Ryan*. The movie was devastating." She shuddered. "I wept on Tony's shoulder while I told him all about Merry's father being killed in Afghanistan. He listened, stroked my hair, and called me *querida*. That's Spanish for sweetheart." Audrey sighed. "He held me for a long time."

Cyn reached over and hugged her. "I was so right to get you two together."

"Claiming all the credit?"

"Naturally. What happened next?"

"Well, I stayed up all night afterwards, filled with doubts and guilt. Am I betraying Jonathan? He's Merry's father, and he gave his life for his country. I'll never, never forget him—I see him daily in Merry's blue eyes. But although he has a piece of my heart, the rest can mend, can't it? For Merry's sake, as well as my own?

Cyn pressed Audrey's hand. "You've been through a heart-wrenching ordeal, the worst there is. I remember your despair when the news came about Jonathan. But you were strong. Merry never saw your unhappiness, never knew of your struggle to get past the hole in your world. You didn't let your misery spoil your child's chance for a normal life."

Her rush of words slowed. "I know how loyal you've been to Jonathan's memory. But Aud, it's been four long years of grieving."

"Do you think…? Maybe it's time?"

"To put it in the past? Think about the future? Wouldn't Jonathan want that for his family?"

Audrey wiped away a tear. "I'm so relieved to get your take on this. I'd begun to think the time was right to let go a little, to start thinking about a new life, but I needed some encouragement." She leaned over and hugged Cyn once more. "What would I do without you?"

"You'd suffer, of course."

Audrey smacked Cyn's arm. "Merry's gone with Nana to visit her other grandmother. There'll be fresh lemonade with warm gingersnaps, and then a visit to the playground." She smiled. "The two grandmas will sit on a park bench and gossip, while their eyes are on the children shooting down the slide. You know, Cyn, these two women have so much love for their only grandchild. Jonathan's mother will never have another, but now there's a chance that Nana could lavish all that love on more than one."

"It's something to be added to the scales," Cyn said. She cut off a chunk of cheese and put it on a cracker. "I didn't realize it's been so long since we really talked."

"Oh, it's been a while. Several weeks. I had to get the last class reports from Tony."

"Sorry I haven't kept up. My life has been a madhouse. You don't know the trouble my mother is causing."

"You know what she's doing, don't you? Every

time she bothers you, it's a ploy to get her husband back."

"Do you really think so?"

"Honey, for an A student, you're awfully naïve about yourself and the people around you."

"It's always harder close to home. But this time Daddy's got a new love. I think he'll stick to getting the divorce." Cyn studied her friend. "Have you met Tony's family? Mexicans can be clannish."

"I know. There's the religious difference. And my age—I'm five years older than Tony."

"But not too old to have more children. That would be something his family would think about. And you can help his career. You're so smart and sensible, you'll be a real asset."

"Our relationship hasn't gone quite that far yet. I'm probably reading more into it than actually exists."

"I doubt it. Your intuition has always been good, and you've got a generous heart. If you're really falling in love with Tony, the problems can be worked out. You can't let guilt feelings about Jonathan's death color your entire life. It wasn't you who put the bomb in the road."

Audrey winced.

"Oh, Aud, I'm sorry. I shouldn't have blurted it out like that. Me and my big mouth. But there's Merry to consider, too. A father's love and guidance can mean a lot to her. She's really taken to Tony?"

"Oh yes. She crawls all over him. Screams with laughter when he lifts her up and spins her around. Merry knows Jonathan only from his picture, you know."

"I know. When she's ready to ask, you can tell her

stories. Fill her memory book."

The room was quiet as the two sipped their wine.

"Well," Audrey said, "I feel better for having spilled the beans about Tony and me. My mother has been wondering, but I can't talk to her about this. I needed your support."

"You have it. Wholeheartedly. And you'll give me updates?"

"Step by step." They laughed.

Reaching out, Cyn twined her pinky around Audrey's. "Sisters, forever."

"Better than blood."

Raising their glasses, they clinked. Tiny bubbles rose in the pink wine.

"Enough about me. Have you anything to tell me about Merlin?" Audrey asked.

"Something's going on between us, too, although we haven't moved as fast as you and Tony. We've been working on class projects, mostly at the local deli." She paused. "Our feelings go beyond friendship, though. I can sense it. I'm just not sure what I want to do about it."

Audrey sat up straighter. "And when you're not at the deli…what then?"

"Well, we did manage to go out on a movie date. Sat in the back row and…"

"He kissed you!" Audrey guessed. "How was it?"

"Beyond ten…at least a fifteen." Cyn winked, didn't mention the garage kisses. "Of course, I have no intention of getting serious about another man."

"I know. Woman power. Self sufficiency."

"Damn right."

"Still, it doesn't stop you from having fun. I'm so

glad we're going out on a double date. I want to see this for myself."

"Ditto, ditto," Cyn said. "Can't wait to see you and Tony together, now that you've told me. Who knows what Saturday will bring?"

Chapter 16

Cleo was leaving Professsor Marzin's office when he stopped her. "Are you busy tomorrow afternoon?"

She turned back. "Not particularly. Do you need me to put in some extra hours?"

"I'd like you to attend the English Department meeting with me. Take notes. The chair's secretary stopped me this morning and hinted that I'd better show up. She had a malicious gleam in her eyes. I do have a reputation for skipping out, but this time my instincts tell me something's up. I'd better attend this meeting—*and* bring a witness."

Cleo laughed. "Okay, boss. Three o'clock, right? I'll be there."

Teachers drifted into the room, taking their seats around a scratched oak conference table. A bubbling urn sat on a small table off to the side, along with a stack of Styrofoam cups, paper stirrers, sugar packets and coffee creamers. A black carafe with a sticky-note attached reading "decoffinated" stood next to the urn. Was someone hinting that coffee could kill?

Marzin entered, spotted the sign, and chuckled. He usually deplored misspellings as another sign of slipping standards. Today he just laughed, enjoying the irony no doubt. A misspelled word, joke or not, in an English Department faculty meeting. How droll. It probably made his day.

The chatter died down as the meeting was called to order. When the yawning minutiae of the business portion finally ended, the chairman turned his flat glare in Marzin's direction. Cleo watched Professor Haskell closely. He was tall, almost cadaverous, with thinning gray hair and a wart at the corner of his right eyebrow. The bowl of a pipe hung out of his breast pocket. It was rumored that he hadn't lit the pipe in years, yet his clothes still held the musty aroma of stale smoke.

Haskell cleared his throat. "It has come to my attention," he said, his pompous manner reinforced by the slow wiping of his eyeglasses, "that some members of the faculty have been planning to award all A grades to their students. Grade inflation has become a serious problem at this college, and the trustees want it to end. They have decided that if a professor awards only A grades this will, in effect, mean the students are only auditing the course.

"If a range of grades is not turned in for each class, we will have no way of judging whether the students have met our standards for the Master of Arts degree." Haskell stared directly at Marzin. "The trustees feel this would put the school's reputation at stake."

As Cleo watched, all eyes turned to Marzin. He sat with his arms crossed, his face impassive.

Minutes passed. No one commented. *How long can Rocky maintain his composure?* At last, the bell signaling the next class rang. Cleo picked up her notes and returned to the professor's office. He followed her in, slamming the books he was carrying onto his desk.

"That pack of fools is so antiquated," he raged. "They can't see that my teaching methods are a huge step forward in unlocking closed minds. When my students leave here they'll not only read in new ways, but also listen and comprehend as well. Instead of memorizing and spouting back useless ideas, they'll understand the significance of the facts that shape our lives."

He began to pace, crossing the room several times before he calmed down. "Maybe my motives aren't entirely pure. Are anyone's? Of course I want success and fame—they're not dirty words. But I've worked hard to develop a rapport with my students that goes way beyond the classroom. Check out the way they greet me when I show up at our deli beer sessions! I'm their mentor, but still one of the gang. I may use the students in my experiments, but I keep them anonymous. Each one is a real person to me."

Rocky sat down, talking more to himself than to Cleo. "It's disturbing to know someone tattled. Haskell is the one who slipped the juicy gossip to the trustees, but who got to him? Didn't the snitch realize everyone would be caught in the backlash? Grad students aren't usually that stupid. Why mess with a good thing?"

Cleo sat quietly as Rocky brooded. "Hannibal...Napoleon..." he mumbled, "no, they're into grumbling and posturing, not making trouble. Sigmund...he'd looked gleeful at the idea of an easy A. Antonio...not with that wide-open smile. He's too good-natured to harbor a mean thought. Merlin...wouldn't bother to make waves. His out of school life is more important than what takes place here."

She continued to transcribe her notes.

"Butterfly is a stickler for procedure, but she's too timid to do anything so devious. Cleo...you were angry with me for embarrassing you when you couldn't fall backwards, but surely we got past that, didn't we? When you got back at me with that quip, 'I'm not falling for you,' the double meaning brought the class to your side. The laughter that followed was with you, not at you."

She nodded.

"The other women seem less interested in grades than in getting dates and finding the right husband, at least from what they wrote in their papers," he mused.

"What about Pandora?" Cyn interrupted.

Marzin sighed. "Pandora... Yes... Her real name is Prudence, did you know? It's a poor fit for her character. I can see her being vindictive..." His voice trailed off.

She had to let a trouble out of the box, Cleo thought. Will we all be paying for her latest outrage?

Rocky heaved a deep sigh. "No point in dwelling on this problem any longer. I might never discover the answer. Perhaps I can make use of this diversion from my plan. How will the students react....?"

His mind had already drifted elsewhere, so Cleo got up to leave. "I'll see you in class tomorrow."

He nodded, so distracted she doubted he saw her walk out. She'd have to wait to learn the consequences, hoped they wouldn't be too devastating. Her success in returning to school hung in the balance.

Chapter 17

Driving to the dentist after class, Cyn passed a Third Avenue bakery. Bagels were just coming out of the oven, and the steamy aroma of fresh bread seeped into the car. Her stomach growled. If the dentist found no cavities, she'd buy one to munch on during the drive home.

Clouds had rolled in, and winter's chill hung in the air. The weather report had mentioned the possibility of snow. As she parked by the medical building and hurried into the dentist's office, the first drops of icy rain began to fall.

By the time her examination and cleaning were over, the rain had changed to sleet and was falling heavily. With the drop in temperature, a thin layer of slush already covered her windshield. She slid into the car, turned on the ignition and defroster, and sat shivering until the heater began to blow warm air and clear the windshield. Then she headed for home.

The wipers slapped back and forth as she neared the school. Peering out the slush-splattered window, Cyn spotted a familiar figure. A soaking wet Pandora was striding along, the Yankees cap pulled down to cover her ears. She had braided her hair, and the thick red column lay limp as a snake on the back of her olive drab army jacket.

Pulling over to the curb, "Cleo" cracked open the

window. "Pandora," she called. The sleet had turned fully to snow now, and there was little traffic on the street. After the thudding rain, the silence was eerie.

"Pandora!" she raised her voice and called again. "You'll catch your death walking around like this. Let me drive you home."

The girl had stopped when she first heard her name, but had started walking again. This time she turned around. "Cleopatra?"

"Yes," she shouted through the window opening. "Get in the car."

Pandora walked over and glanced inside. "I'll soak the seat."

"It'll dry. Come on, this is pneumonia weather. Get in and let me drive you home."

"I live in Brooklyn."

"So what? The traffic is very light now. It'll be a quick ride."

The girl hesitated, but a shudder overtook her. She reached down and pulled open the door. A puddle of water landed on the seat as she dropped into it.

"Thanks," Pandora said. She gave Cleo the directions to her apartment through chattering teeth.

They were quiet on the ride, too cold to talk. The defroster blew all the heat toward the windshield. By the time they reached Pandora's building, the snow had stopped. It was melting off the street but still covered the sidewalks. Reaching for the door handle, Pandora turned. "Better come in and warm up a little," she said grudgingly. "I'll make some hot tea."

Although she was anxious to get home in this rotten weather, Cleo's curiosity won out. She wanted to see where Pandora lived. "Can I leave the car here?"

"Yeah. It's the wrong side of the street for parking, but the cops won't be out in this muck. It'll be okay for a few minutes."

Taking note of the "few minutes," Cleo got out of the car anyway. She pressed the key, counted on being back before the lock could freeze. In the freaky silence the snow had brought to the city, the beep sounded like a scream.

They walked up three steps and crossed the dingy lobby. The elevator was old; the padded walls stank from generations of crowded bodies. It clanked as they rose to the fourth floor.

"Sometimes it's out of order," Pandora said stiffly, reinforcing Cleo's doubts about the elevator's safety. "Then it's a long climb."

The girl unlocked the door to the apartment. As if she couldn't wait to get past prying eyes, she pulled Cleo inside and moved swiftly along the hall to her bedroom. A low-wattage bulb lit the hallway they passed through, but Cleo didn't miss the religious pictures hanging on the walls. Most of them depicted the crucifixion, bleeding hands and crowns of thorns standing out sharply. One appeared to be of Saint Sebastian in rapturous agony, his body punctured by arrows. The grim images made her squirm.

Pandora switched on her bedroom light, illuminating the cracks in the ceiling. Cleo looked around. An iron bed spotted with rust took up most of the room. A bookcase fashioned of bricks and planks stood underneath the window, and an old pine dresser was missing a drawer pull.

Cutting through the drabness, the shiny purple quilt on the bed gave color to the room, as did an Op Art poster taped to the opposite wall. Its red, green, and blue lines appeared to flip as Cleo moved closer to the window, the quick change of focus leaving her slightly dizzy. What a way to wake up in the morning, she thought, blinking away her vertigo. Especially if you had a hangover.

"I'll make us some tea. Wait here," Pandora said. She walked out of the room, shutting the door behind her. Cleo could hear her talking to a woman. They seemed to be arguing, but she couldn't catch the words. Her stomach growled again, and she hoped they'd offer some cookies.

The closet door was ajar, and Cleo's curiosity got the better of her. She inched it open wider and stared. Colorful clothing crowded the rod, while shoes and boots lay in a jumble on the floor. High on the back of the door, above a mounted mirror, was a movie poster of "Maid in Manhattan." J-Lo and Ralph Fiennes in a clinch. *Well, well, Pandora has a romantic streak.* Cleo closed the door.

She was sitting on the bed when Pandora returned, followed by her mother. The woman's dour face and dark housedress matched the somber apartment.

"Prudence, bring your friend into the parlor. I have tea brewing."

"I'm all wet. I have to change my clothes."

Her mother turned to Cleo. "Follow me, then," and walked out of the room.

As she trailed behind the woman, Cleo held back a shudder at the religious pictures hanging in the hall. This version of Christianity was a punishing one, unfamiliar to her. She had read about it but never before been this close. It left her uneasy, almost frightened.

In a corner of the parlor a tall, bronze-toned statue stood, "The Agony of Christ" stamped into a brass plaque at its base. On the low table in front of the sofa, an enameled icon in a polished silver frame exposed the same tormented face. Next to it, a faded photo of a young girl filled a plain black frame. She wondered who the child was. A sister?

Cleo sat on the sofa's edge, feet braced to rise quickly. Pandora's mother handed her a cup of tea. A lump of sugar and an Oreo sat on the saucer. "Are you and Prudence classmates?" she asked.

"Yes, we are." Cleo took the cup. "Thank you."

"You look too old to be still in school."

Taken aback by the woman's bluntness, Cleo choked on a bite of cookie. "I-I came back after a few years away," she stammered.

Pandora's mother looked as if she were going to probe more deeply, then abruptly changed the subject. "You get projects to do outside of class—work that can't be done at home?"

Cleo stalled for time, stirring the sugar into her tea until Pandora entered the room. The girl's face was stony, but her eyes held a flicker of anxiety.

"Oh, yes, the professor keeps us extremely busy," Cleo said, turning back to the mother. "In graduate school there are lots of involved projects that demand the students' participation." She gulped down her tea and rose. "I really have to be going. It's a long drive home, and there's bound to be ice on the roads. I'd like to be back in my house before it starts to snow again and covers up the slick spots." Putting down her teacup, she grabbed the rest of the cookie and walked with Pandora to the door. It slammed shut behind her.

Cleo sighed with relief when she stepped out of the creaky elevator. She walked across the faded lobby and down the few steps to her car. As she sat inside and waited for the windshield to de-fog, she wondered about the look Pandora had given her at the door. She would have thought the girl would be grateful. Hadn't she driven her all the way back to Brooklyn and covered up for her as well?

Yet the last thing she had seen in Pandora's eyes was anger.

Chapter 18

Marzin picked up his briefcase and walked down the hall. "I have some disquieting news to report," he told his class. "The Administration somehow got wind of my proposal to give everyone an A grade. I've been informed that if I do, you will all be considered auditors, rather than matriculating students."

An unhappy murmur ran around the room.

"Therefore," Prof Rocky continued, "I'm asking for volunteers for a grade of B."

A moment of shocked silence met his statement. A buzz of angry comments followed, the words indistinguishable but the tone loud and clear. Then, "What the hell," came booming from the back of the room. Napoleon raised his hand.

Looking disgusted, Merlin raised his. It was followed after a moment's hesitation by Antonio's. The class quieted down.

"Thank you, gentlemen. We'll need a woman, also," the professor said, glancing around the room. "How about you, Cleopatra?"

Her eyes filled with dismay. She'd had a 3.4 average when she'd enrolled in grad school. That was a lot of A's. She squirmed. He was making her uncomfortable, but his remorse was short-lived. Would her answer reflect her old self, or her new one? This little face-off with the trustees was coming in handy.

Cleo hesitated for only a moment. "Sure," she said. "Who am I going to disappoint? My father, the Pharaoh?"

"Good girl." He nodded. "And I think we should have one C, for the bell curve. Pandora?"

The redhead stared at Rocky, chest heaving. *Payback*...it was in her eyes.

"I'll take that look as an affirmative. Okay, it's settled. This should take care of the matter." Marzin marked the grades in his book, then snapped it shut.

"Now, we had one psychodrama left to perform. This one will take place in a large firm where you're all working hard to make a name for yourselves. Your advancement may call for some devious methods. Let's see how well you handle it."

****

"Rocky is playing us," Merlin said to Cleo as they sampled the micro beers after class. "You were really bothered about taking the B grade, and he knew it."

She sighed. "I guess he did. It was *déjà vu* in a way. I made one of my few B's in college my freshman year—in English, no less."

"How did that happen?"

"I was seventeen when I left for college, on my own for the first time. School wasn't my main interest then." She looked at Merlin with a guilty grin.

"At seventeen? Let me guess. The frat boys were more appealing than Will Shakespeare."

"Any boys, no need to be specific. Mooning over dates for football weekends, real important stuff like that, took up a lot of time."

"So you got a B in English. Forget to hand in your homework?"

"Not exactly. I loved to write, always got A's in comp and lit. Then I saw some of the papers my classmates wrote and decided I could do better without even trying."

"Pride goeth before a fall," Merlin said.

She looked up quickly, searching for sarcasm, but saw only sympathy.

"Truer words and all that. At midterm we had to write an essay analyzing one of the characters in Hamlet. When I got mine back with a B, I was disappointed. But then I traded papers with the girl sitting next to me and saw that mine was so much better—yet she had gotten an A."

"What did you do?"

"Went to see my English prof. I stormed into Dr. Painter's office, waving my paper about. I can still hear his voice. 'Sit down, young lady,' he snapped at me. 'I won't discuss another student's essay, but I will say this.' He looked me right in the eye. '*Your* paper was B work for *you.*'"

"Aha!"

"He didn't add, 'Aren't you ashamed?' the way Daddy would have, but I felt it right in my bones. Best lesson I learned all year. After that, boys were still on my mind, but I straightened out my priorities."

"He was the kind of teacher one never forgets."

"Yes. He died during my senior year. I'm sorry I never got a chance to tell him how he influenced my life."

They sat quietly, drinking their beers. After a few moments Merlin said, "This isn't quite the situation with Rocky, though."

"No, it isn't. I've been doing my best work on

every assignment, except for falling backwards. It doesn't seem fair."

"I'll bet that's the prof's point. Do you think it was any easier to accept the B as Cleopatra than it would have been with your real name?"

"Maybe…. Say, you're right! That could have been his idea. It's easier to change automatic reactions when you start fresh. My old response would have been to refuse, or if I couldn't, to be really angry and resentful down deep. This time I rolled with it." She sipped her beer. "Still, it's not fair."

"Out in the real world, things often aren't fair. He probably wanted to see how we'd react to that shocking reminder."

"Sounds plausible. But, 'shocking'? Pretty strong word."

"Unfairness can do that."

"Mmm…perhaps. You were one of the volunteers for a B. Why?"

Merlin shrugged. "I've never cared much about grades. Flaunted the bad ones when I was a kid. Loved to get my father riled. It was a challenge to see how far he'd let me go before I crossed the line. Damn!" He smacked his beer stein down, spilling foam onto the table. "I fell into the old pattern, too. I hate it when Rocky brings back these childish responses."

"So he got to you, too. All for his book, I'll bet."

"The B couldn't matter less to me, but I resent his disturbing you so much. Didn't the trust experiment cause you enough trauma?"

"Are you protecting me now?" Cleo lifted her stein to hide her tiny smile. "You know, Merlin, I was—and maybe I still am—disturbed by it, but at the same time...."

"Yes?"

"It gives me a good feeling to know I was able to accept that B. I'm finally beginning to realize how unimportant the grade is to my self-image. I'm not pleasing Daddy any more."

Merlin nodded thoughtfully, then winked at her. "Now, if he had chosen you for the C," he teased, and she burst out laughing.

"You've got a point. Got to absorb these new insights gradually." Cleo started to rise. "Time I headed home. There's a load of dirty laundry calling my name."

"You're leaving me for that? Unfair competition!" Merlin grinned, reached across the booth, and took her hand. "Who knows? We may well be different people when the semester ends."

Cleo picked up her mug for one last swallow, clinked it with his. "We might, indeed. I can hardly wait to find out. *Skoal.*"

Chapter 19

Saturday arrived, sunny and brisk. Merlin and Tony waited beside a stone lion at the base of the library steps, their jackets zipped against the cold wind that blew around the corner. Cleo caught their startled look as a tiny, dark-haired whirlwind came barreling into Tony.

"We're here!" Merry shouted. "I rode on the subway, Uncle Tony. It bounced me up and down."

Tony picked her up and seated her on the statue's back. "Did it roar like this lion?"

"Oh, yes," Merry let out a squeaky, high-pitched roar and giggled. "Just like that."

"Hold it a sec," Alice came up with her camera phone. "Let me get a picture of Merry up there."

The child posed, crinkling her eyes and pasting on a fake five-year-old smile. A wisp of memory wafted through Cleo's mind. Before she could bring it into focus, Tony had picked up Merry and climbed the steps to the library's massive front doors.

The exhibit's clever, exaggerated portraits enchanted them all—the writer Ernest Hemingway, clad only in a leopard-skin loincloth, holding a bottle of booze; the actor Clark Gable, handsome head dwarfed by huge ears and shoulders; and Cleo's favorite— psychiatrist Sigmund Freud sitting in his chair leering at the gorgeous patient on his couch, the blonde bombshell of her day, Jean Harlow.

Personalities were caught, characters revealed. No celebrity of the early twentieth century escaped. Nearby panels offered short biographies and amusing anecdotes about the famous—and notorious—men and women pictured.

In a child's chair, Merry sat absorbed by the display of animated films running without pause on a large TV screen. She clapped her hands and squealed at their brilliant color and bouncy movement.

"She's forgotten all about us," Cleo whispered to Alice. "I'll stay in the movie room with Merry. Go ahead and explore the main room with the others."

Alice squeezed her arm in thanks and tiptoed out. Through telephones, Cleo listened to the celebrities being interviewed, then spent some time reading the panels. The material was fascinating and she read slowly, wanting to give Tony and Alice as much time alone as possible. Merlin would be wrapped up in his own world, she was sure. When she finally glanced at her watch it was nearly noon—time to meet the others.

Cleo tapped the child's shoulder. "We have to go now, Sweetums."

No response, so she lifted her from the little chair and into her arms.

"I was havin' fun," Merry said, trying to wriggle free.

"Yes, but you must be getting hungry."

That was the magic word. Merry stopped squirming. "We're gonna have tacos," she told Cleo, grabbing her hand as she was put down.

"I can smell them already. Do you put everything inside the taco shells?"

"Uh huh. Meat 'n cheese, 'n lettuce 'n tomato."

"How about salsa?"

"That burns your lips. Tony says salsa is *peecantay,* but I put on a teeny bit."

"Me, too. Let's go find the others before we starve."

****

Pandora had seen enough. So Cleo had a kid. That intel could come in handy.

She was getting quite good at stalking. No one had an inkling she'd been hiding behind the panel. Now she'd better get back to the prayer meeting. Ma was getting too damn suspicious, and she had no desire to face the consequences.

Merlin didn't pick up on her locked-door hint. Cleopatra had him in blinkers. Does he know about the child? That could put a crimp in his pursuit...but how? Telling him about the kid would keep, for now. She needed to find a new tack, something unexpected.

Pandora hurried down the library steps. Her hair whipped around to sting her face as she fought the wind to reach the subway entrance. Lowering her eyelids against the black soot that blew everywhere, she started down the long flight. Halfway along, her eyes only slitted open, she bumped into a man coming up. He grabbed hold of her shoulder.

She pushed away violently, almost knocking him over.

"What the hell? I'm just trying to help you, miss."

With a mumbled, "Sorry," Pandora stepped back. The rough feel of the man's overcoat hitting her face reminded her of her father. Once again she heard the loud voices...her parents screaming...Papa's hand raised…coming at Ma….

Her head pounding, Pandora clung to the stair rail. She made her way down the rest of the steps and into the station. The fetid smell of wet wool and workmen's sweat lingered in the cavernous space, and she put up her hand to cover her nose. The flash of dreamworld faded, but her mind made a connection, now. That kid in the library had a father, too. Rocky mentioned that Cleo was divorced. Her ex-husband had to be the father.

Pushing through the mass of people heading for the exit, she squeezed onto her train. The guy must still be around to visit the brat, she reasoned as she clung to the pole. Could she use Cleo's credit card to find him? She'd make a few phone calls. With a little manipulation, she knew she could get the ex to interfere and gum up the works….

****

Cyn had trouble falling asleep that night. Although she'd loved the exhibit of caricatures, once or twice she'd been filled with a strange sensation that someone was watching her. She'd turned quickly, but none of the other visitors was paying her any attention. During the day she had shaken off her apprehension, but now it returned.

That wasn't the only problem keeping her awake. What was it about Merry posing on the stone lion's back that still bugged her? When she finally fell asleep, the disturbing picture of Merry's eyes and fake smile as she waited for the photo to be taken was the last image in her mind….

Sun sparkles danced on the pretty blue water. The kiddie pool was crowded, but Daddy held her close in the deep part, beyond the rope.

"Kick your feet, Crinkly Eyes," Daddy turned her so that her tummy lay just below the water, resting on his arm.

Giggling, she kicked.

"Harder! Make a big splash. Now, move your arms."

Skinny arms slapped the water, throwing some in her face. "Aaghh." It tasted funny and she spat it out. She kicked out wildly, her eyes stinging now.

"It's just a little chlorine. Hush." Daddy's other hand gave her fanny a whack.

She opened her mouth to cry and sputtered, swallowing more water.

"That was a love pat. Be a big girl, Cynwydie-pie. You can float, just like a fish. Spread your arms. There, see? I'm going to let go of you now."

"Davis!" she heard her mother call. "What did you do with my suntan lotion? You know how I burn."

Daddy turned away, and Cynwydie went under.

She came up twice, gasping, flailing, too panicked to scream. The third time she went under, the lifeguard pulled her from the pool. He slapped her back, and water dribbled out of her mouth.

Daddy wrapped her in a beach towel. He sat her at the bar under the big straw umbrella and bought her a chocolate Dixie Cup. It didn't help. He took her to the toy store and let her pick out a new outfit for her Barbie. She hugged the box and stopped sniffling.

"All better now? Let me see those crinkly eyes," he said, so she smiled.

But she never forgot.

****

"Hello?"

"Cyn, I've gotta tell you about a phone call I just received."

"Is this Audrey I'm speaking to, or Alice?"

A chuckle came through the line. "I think it's Alice."

"Aha. So the call was from Tony?"

"Yeah. You'll never guess what."

"He's passionately in love with you."

"Well, you're close. He invited me home to try his mother's tamales."

"Oh, Aud…Alice. That's so great!" Cyn gushed. Then she paused. "Isn't it?"

"I guess so. Although it does seem a little soon."

"Meeting his parents is just a first step. Do they know about Merry?"

"I don't think so, but if I go, I'll bring her with me. Nothing may come of this, but I don't want to start out by being dishonest."

"So what did you tell Tony?"

"I hesitated. Said I thought I should stick with your rule and wait till the semester ends."

"Why? You're not registered in the class."

"I know. But I told him it's a girl thing. Loyalty to my best friend. The term will be over in another month. Gives me a little longer to make up my mind."

"I don't know, Aud. The time may be right just now. He's only asked you for dinner. 'He who hesitates is lost,' and all that cliché garbage."

"He did sound awfully disappointed. Maybe I should change my mind and accept?"

"It's a thought, girlfriend. Sleep on it. In the meantime, Merlin has an idea for another excursion for us."

"Sounds good. Where?"

"He's keeping the place a secret for now. When he's got the deal worked out, he'll tell us."

"I'm all for it, wherever it is."

"Me, too. The last trip turned out real well."

"It did. Merry couldn't stop talking about it, afterwards. She wants a Betty Boop doll." Audrey laughed. "They went out of existence ages ago."

"You could check eBay."

"If there are any, they'll be collectibles. *Mucho dinero.* She'll want something else after the next trip."

"Well, I'll see if I can coax Merlin into telling me where. Meanwhile, think some more about Tony's invitation."

"I'm already on that."

Chapter 20

With a snort, Pandora took in the sophisticated modern décor of the physicians' waiting room. All glass and burnished steel—a far cry from the Victorian "parlor" she'd grown accustomed to in the hospital annex. Obviously, plastic surgery had a lot more prestige than institutional psychiatry.

Faking the information on the questionnaire the receptionist had asked her to fill out, she handed it in with a lack of concern. She knew how to pull this off. An attractive nurse added it to her clipboard and led Pandora briskly along a corridor. Its walls were hung with watercolor seascapes so dreamy she could almost smell the ocean.

They came to a pair of glass doors etched with swans. Ugly ducklings stop here, Pandora thought as the nurse pushed them open.

"Your patient, doctor." With a practiced smile, the nurse handed him Pandora's file and retreated.

The man who rose from behind the desk to shake her hand was slim and narrow-shouldered, but carried himself with considerable confidence. A silk suit and polished Italian loafers were visible beneath his hand-tailored white lab coat.

Pandora straightened, gripped his hand too tightly. "How do you do, Dr. Shiff."

"Ms.—

"Brown," she hurried to say.

Gesturing to a chair, he extracted his hand from hers and returned to his seat. His reassuring glance didn't fool her.

Pandora looked around the office, taking in the pale peach walls, the molded plexiglass desk with its crystal vase holding a single tea rose. A decorator's dream. She sat back in a gray leather chair, her gaze focused on the man with the boyish face and thinning hair.

She wondered if the doctor had any idea what the impersonal room revealed about him—flaunting wealth but lacking a single intimate touch. Evidently, his patients didn't mind footing the bill. There was no framed picture of a new wife on his desk, so perhaps he still carried a torch for Cleo. That would help.

Forcing herself to restrain a sneer, Pandora watched the surgeon's eyes slide down her body with an assessing glance. He was studying her like a specimen. Most of his mind, she knew, was elsewhere. She'd had enough experience with the medical fraternity to sense the coldness in Dr. Roger Shiff. How she hated it!

...So this is Cleo's ex. Smart of her to get rid of him. He may be raking it in at the office, but he'd be disappointing in bed. Too calculating. Lovers, like patients, can sense when they aren't the doctor's chief concern. Of course, this one promises to make them beautiful. That would wash away a lot of dissatisfaction.

Shiff smiled reassuringly. "What is it you'd like me to do for you, Ms. Brown?"

Pandora caught herself squirming and grew still.

She had dared to do this and would get away with it as long as she was careful. From her purse, she removed a photo taken with her cell phone at the library exhibit. It showed Cleo's face clearly.

"I'd like my nose to be more like this one," she said, getting up and handing it to the doctor.

He looked at the photo, then turned and glared at Pandora. "This is Cynwyd, my ex-wife," he said, handing it back to her. "What are you doing with it?"

"Oh, good," she gushed, "I found the right surgeon. Actually, I don't want a nose job. It was my way of getting in to see you so I could tell you about her."

Eyes narrowed, he scrutinized Pandora once more. "You're not implying that you're a friend of Cynwyd's? You're too young."

"Oh, no." She jumped up and leaned over the desk, her ankh pendant swinging perilously close to the crystal vase. He snatched it, moved the delicate object farther away as she talked faster. "You're wrong to assume that, Dr. Shiff. We're in a class together. It's experimental, asking for unaccustomed responses from the students. Age doesn't matter there. Cynwyd and I have become good friends, and I'm worried about how she's adjusting to the challenge. You know, she's been out of school for a long time."

Shiff's mouth grew tight. "This is inappropriate. You shouldn't be here." He rose.

She couldn't let him get away.

"Please," she said, reaching across and clutching at his sleeve. "Give me a chance to explain. This is important!" Her tone grew shrill.

Flicking off her fingers, Shiff waited until Pandora had backed off and returned to her chair. "I'll give you a minute. Be specific. And brief."

She'd been shredding the tissue in her hand. Pandora stuffed it into her pocket and began again. "The class started with an experiment in trust. On the first day, the students stood in a circle with the professor behind us. Cl-Cynwyd was unable to fall backward—even though the professor caught each of us without any difficulty. But she couldn't let go." Pandora's voice took on a sympathetic tone. "It distressed her enormously to feel she failed on her first day back in school."

The doctor said nothing, but he was still listening.

Sure of herself now, Pandora began to relax. "Cynwyd seems increasingly disturbed with each experiment. She's taken to spending a lot of time in the professor's office. I don't know what goes on in there— perhaps he's tutoring her. He's quite handsome." She tossed off the *non sequitur* and continued. "She won't tell me about it, even though we've formed a friendship."

Pausing, she watched him closely. "I just thought...if you still cared for her...that you might want to know about this." She offered a tentative smile. "I'm a worrier."

Pandora directed the same earnest gaze she used on her mother. She caught a flicker of anxiety surface, but a second later the doctor's eyes were shuttered, the professional mask pulled down.

"I'm surprised you sought me out here, in my office, *Ms.* Brown," Shiff said, emphasizing the Ms.

"Well, Cynwyd did mention you—said you taught her all about drinking beer."

The doctor's laugh was hollow. "Thank you for

your concern. I'm pleased to learn my ex-wife has made new friends in school, but she is quite capable of taking care of herself. Her plans to quit her job and get a graduate degree have made that clear. I'm sure Cynwyd would not appreciate any interference from me." Pushing back his chair, he stood once more. "You're wasting valuable time."

"Well, if you'd like me to keep an eye on her and report back to you?"—but Shiff was already ushering her out the glass doors.

Damn. A pulse began to beat in Pandora's temple. *I should have been more frantic. A little drama, and it might have worked. Get him to worry a lot more. Force him to take some action. He must still have feelings for her—they haven't been divorced that long. And look how angry he got.*

Muttering to herself, she made her way back down the empty hall. She should have played the doctor with more finesse. She'd been too nervous. A few more minutes, and he would have come around, agreed to her spying. It wasn't her fault she failed. He hadn't given her enough time.

So, the plan for the ex didn't work out, but now she was on a family kick.

Maybe she'd have better luck with Cleo's mother. If the woman were anything like Ma, she'd be easier to deal with. Perhaps she could ferret out some personal stuff from Mrs. Westland, something Cleo didn't want exposed.

It was worth a try.

Cleo's ex was a pompous ass. And slimy. Just thinking about him made Pandora want to wash out her mouth. Scraping her teeth over her tongue, she pushed through the double doors to the waiting room.

"Do you want to make another appointment?" the receptionist asked.

Glaring at her, Pandora pulled her hat down and stomped out of the building.

Chapter 21

Try as he might, Merlin couldn't wipe out Pandora's insinuations about that infernal locked door. Why had the girl made up that tale? Even knowing Pandora got her kicks from making mischief, he was disturbed. His niggling doubt felt suspiciously like jealousy, but of course that conclusion was ridiculous.

Still, he couldn't leave it alone.

A chilly wind had risen as they headed back to their cars after class. Clouds drifted over the weak winter sun.

Walking beside Cleo, Merlin brought up the subject again. "So, what *were* you doing locked in with the prof?" he asked, punching her arm lightly to make it a joke.

Cleo looked at him. "Are we back to that?" She shook her head. "We were making passionate love on top of the filing cabinet, of course."

"Wasn't the metal cold?"

The visual of her bare bottom on the metal made her shiver, then laugh. "I really didn't know the door was locked, Merlin." She glared at him. "Do you doubt my word?"

"Of course not! It's just so strange…."

"When I came to work, Rocky unlocked the door and hurried me right over to the computer. I didn't hear any click, but I wasn't listening for one. It must have locked automatically."

"Makes sense, I guess. Pandora could be spreading rumors out of spite. Some people thrive on causing trouble. I suspect she's one of them."

"I know she hoped to get my job." Cleo grew thoughtful. "She's had it in for me since that first class when I captured the prof's attention because I couldn't fall backwards. Pandora expects all the attention to be on her, but it seems a strange way to get even."

"No, it wouldn't be your way." His smile was warm. "That would be beneath you."

"Better than me beneath the professor?" She returned his arm punch.

"Definitely," he chuckled. "What kind of office work are you doing for Rocky?"

"Different things. After the prof received permission to use personal statistics—without real names—I set up a computer program to correlate his chosen names with age, sex, education, marital status and cultural background. Then I Googled sources for related studies. Set up a Twitter account so he can be in contact with others in the field. Rocky has very ambitious plans for his book."

"Wow, so it seems. What is he trying to prove with all the facts he's collecting?"

"He's keeping the actual subject close to his vest, but I get clues from the research he's asking for. It's turning out to be a fascinating study. And just think," she added, her voice full of mischief, "we'll all be in there—cross-referenced!"

"I'd like to cross-reference him, one of these days," Merlin muttered.

"He won't be using our real names. Why are you

so resentful of him?"

"The man rubs me the wrong way. It's more important for him to make a name for himself than it is to be concerned about his students. Look at the way he manipulated you into taking that B grade."

"That's pretty harsh."

"What's the other students' take on this stuff they're revealing about themselves?"

"I'd guess we're all pretty careful about what we tell him. We didn't get this far by being dummies."

"Will you get any credit for the extra-curricular help you're giving him?"

"From what I know about how things work in academia, I'm not counting on his sharing the glory." She laughed. "Maybe I'll get into a footnote. I'm a source."

"Student aides get the minimum wage, right?"

She nodded.

"You're doing a lot of professional stuff for a meager payoff."

"I know he's taking advantage, but I don't mind. It's an intriguing study. The job's got similar challenges to the ones I faced the month I was in charge of my magazine. Different problems, of course, but both with a need for creative solutions—and a chance to use my skills. I wouldn't want them to get rusty."

"How do you mean?"

"Do you really want to hear about it?"

"Absolutely. I want to learn everything about you."

Warmth crept over Cleo at Merlin's words. The look he gave her…. She could get lost in those misty gray eyes.

She pulled herself together. "Okay, you asked for

it. During that last month at my old job, I moved pretty far from proofreading. I did the ad layouts, placing them in the right spots for the right colors of ink, while at the same time fulfilling all the advertisers' demands."

His eyes held a questioning look, so she elaborated. "Some wanted their ads in outside columns. Others asked for right-hand pages, or the inside back cover—that kind of stuff. It was like putting together a big jigsaw puzzle, and I love doing those."

"I'm sure that wasn't all you did. What else?"

"After copy editing the stories, there was some grunt work. I fit run-over articles around the ads and wrote photo captions. When the pix came in without sufficient documentation, I grew very creative." She winked. "Facts can be like rubber bands—flexible."

"Is that all?"

"No need to be sarcastic."

"Sorry. Go on."

"The big job was keeping everyone happy. Meeting deadlines. Coping with interruptions. Fielding all the questions no one else was around to answer. My days were so full, they flew by."

"And you loved it?"

"I did," she grinned. "I hadn't realized how natural it would feel to be in charge while the boss was away. It was great to have the opportunity—I may never have one like it again. Rocky's work isn't that complicated, but at least he does listen to my ideas, even incorporates some of my suggestions."

"I'll bet." Merlin gritted his teeth, then relaxed. "So you're a born executive?"

"Is that how you see me?"

He nodded, smiling. "Now I do." Her words

sparked an idea….

"Well, that's my strong side, but some things really bug me, Merlin. I almost fell apart when my credit card went missing. I have a problem coping with that kind of personal hassle."

"Glad to know you're human!"

She swatted him with her briefcase. He ducked and laughed. "Have you heard any more about your credit card?"

"A couple of items were bought before it was closed out, but I wasn't held responsible, thank goodness. One purchase was for a pair of designer boots. You wouldn't believe how much they cost. I didn't spend that much when I was married to a doctor!"

"Were they your size?"

"No, a size and a half bigger. Hey, maybe that's a clue?"

"I wouldn't waste time dwelling on it. All you learned is that whoever used your card is a female with big feet!"

"The Abominable Credit Card Thief? Bigfoot prints in the snow?" She giggled. "I'll buy that."

****

The phone rang as Cyn was getting ready for bed. She fumbled for her cell. "Hello?"

"Cynwyd?"

"Roger? Is that you? Is anything wrong? My mother…?"

"No, no. I'm not at the hospital, and nothing is wrong. I'm just calling to find out how you're getting on."

"At this hour? I haven't heard from you since the

divorce."

"Yes, I know. How are you, Cyn?"

"I'm fine. Reveling in my new life." She forced her voice to remain neutral. "How are Phyllis and the new baby?"

"Doing very well. Danny got his first tooth."

A pause followed. Cyn waited, disturbed by her ex's unexpected call but unwilling to give him the satisfaction of asking why.

Roger cleared his throat. "I'm phoning because a new patient spoke to me about you."

"Oh? Who was it?"

"I can't give out that information."

"Balls. I'm not asking for medical secrets."

"That was crude, Cynwyd. How unlike you."

"You never knew the real me, Roger."

"Perhaps I didn't." His voice was flat. "Forget the name. She seemed concerned about problems you were having in school."

"Nice of her—and you, of course—to care, but there must be some mistake. I'm enjoying my classes immensely."

"Well, I'm glad to hear it. Just thought I'd check."

"You have nothing to feel responsible for, Roger. Not anymore," she added. "That was over a long time ago." Her silent anger flowed along the wires. "I'm sure your practice is doing well, and you're delighting in your new life as much as I am in mine. Goodbye."

"If you're certain—" but Cyn had already clicked off.

Pandora again? Or is Mama meddling? Who else could it be? The e-mails, the midnight phone calls, and now this. Why would Pandora get involved in my life?

What's going on in that peculiar brain of hers?

The call had unnerved her. She needed to talk to someone, or she wouldn't be able to sleep tonight. Cyn looked at the clock. It was too late to call Audrey, but perhaps Merlin was still awake.

Getting into bed, she rubbed her toes against the sheet to warm them. Then she pulled up the covers, picked up her cell phone and punched in his number.

He answered on the first ring. "Cleo?"

"Hi. Did I wake you?"

"No, I've been lying here working out my next cartoon clip. What's up?"

"If I've interrupted genius at work, it can wait."

"I can use the break. My plot was turning stale from over-thinking. Has something upset you?"

"I just hung up from speaking to my ex. First time since the divorce. He said one of his patients had been telling him about me. Hinted that it was someone in our class."

"Pandora?"

"Sounds like she's trying out a new dirty trick. What does she hope to gain by this?"

"Maybe she wants you to get involved with him again and make me jealous," Merlin joked.

"You think it's funny, don't you? But perhaps you've hit on the truth."

"Hmm. It seems ludicrous, but if she is trying to drive a wedge between you and me, she isn't succeeding. How did it feel talking to him?"

"Roger sounded just like Roger. I admit he still irritates me, but that was the extent of it."

"I'm glad to hear that. You handled it well, I'm sure. Forget Pandora. Whatever her agenda is, her words can't hurt you. It's nice to hear your voice—" his own grew husky, "especially at this hour, in the dark."

"You sound good, too." Cyn sighed.

"Where are you now?"

"In bed. I was getting ready to go to sleep when the phone rang."

"I'm in bed, too." *That suggestive tone again.* "Could I interest you in a little phone sex?"

"Oh God, yes." Cyn's heart began to race. She'd heard of phone sex, wondered what it would be like.

"What are you wearing?" he asked.

A giggle came through the phone. "I'd like to describe a sexy, silk gown with a long slit up the side, but actually, I'm in PJ's for a cold night. They're red flannel with tiny Christmas trees and romping reindeer."

He chuckled. "Good visual. I can see you by a roaring fire."

"Please, no bearskin rug!"

"Too cliché?" He laughed aloud. "Okay. We're in your bed. King size?"

"Yes."

"Now, slowly unbutton the top of your pajamas, and then wriggle out of the bottoms."

Her rapid breathing was audible. "Wh-what have you got on?"

"I sleep in the raw."

"I like that visual too." *Too bad we don't have picture phones.*

As if he read her mind, he said, "It's sexier using our imagination. Snuggle into your pillow and get real comfortable." His low rumbling tone was hypnotic. "Then slip one hand inside your open shirt and place it on your breast. Close your eyes. Touch your nipple and imagine it's my hand there, getting ready to arouse you…"

Her breaths were coming faster.

"The nipple is getting hard, longing for my mouth. Tweak it, and caress your other breast. Can you feel my hands there? And my lips?"

"Yes," she whispered, panting.

"Your breasts are heavy, the nipples jutting forward, and your hand slides slowly down your stomach. It's my hand you're feeling, my fingers playing in your curls. They're parting you. Can you feel my tongue caressing that secret spot? Making you wet and longing for more? And now my finger is sliding inside…."

His mesmerizing voice tantalized her. She moaned with sensual delight. She could tell from his quickened words and the rhythmic sounds coming through the phone that he was pleasuring himself, too. Sensations inside her built higher, tighter.

They were apart, yet together—touching one another on a magical level. Her excitement mounted and mounted until she buried her head in the pillow and screamed her release.

The phone had fallen from her hand and lay beside her. At last, she picked it up again.

"That was incredible," she murmured.

"Yes, it was," came the sleepy, satisfied reply. "Think of it as an appetizer. An early Christmas present. Good night, love."

She smiled lazily at the endearment. "Good night, my sorcerer."

Chapter 22

With a grunt, Anwyn pulled herself up from the couch and answered the door. "Yes?"

"Hi, Mrs. Westland, it's Pandora. I called last night. You told me I could come over and talk to you about your daughter."

"Come in. I was just having a glass of wine. Will you join me?"

"Thanks, I'd love to." Pandora stepped into the penthouse apartment and gazed at the lush furnishings that filled the salon. The rear wall consisted of huge windows overlooking Central Park. Its trees were bare now. She could see all the way through to the Metropolitan Museum on Fifth Avenue. Cleo's father must have paid a fortune for this place. She forced her expression to conceal her intense envy.

On the coffee table in front of the couch, a wine bottle sat, already half empty. Mrs. Westland led her to the couch, wobbling on needle-thin heels. The woman was on her way to being plastered—how convenient!

"Be careful, the floor is shl-slippery." Cleo's mother grimaced. "The Oriental rug is at the weavers' being repaired—a cigarette burn. You don't mind if I ask you not to smoke?"

"No problem." Pandora slipped off her coat and laid it on a chair. "I don't smoke. It costs too much."

"That, too, I suppose. I always think it'sh bad for

your health," the woman slurred. "Frankly," she added with a tipsy smile, "I detest the odor. It gets in your clothes and your hair. My father always came home reeking of smoke—from the coal mines, you know. It clung to him."

"Your father worked in a coal mine?" Pandora couldn't believe what she was hearing.

"No, silly." Cleo's mother patted her knee. "He *owns* the coal mines. His wedding present was this lovely apartment." She waved her arm to encompass it all. As she turned her head from side to side, Pandora watched her gleeful smile fade and morph into despair. Tears filled her eyes.

"I'm so sorry." Pandora reached into the tissue box on the table and handed her one. "I didn't realize I was bringing up a painful subject."

"No, no. That's all right." Mrs. Westland blew her nose. "You didn't come here to listen to my problems. Would you like another glass of wine? I see you still have some, so I'll just top off my own. Help yourself to some peanuts." She nodded toward an exquisite crystal dish.

The peanuts filling the stemmed bowl looked out of place. Something more exotic belonged there— macadamia nuts or dark chocolate truffles, perhaps— but Pandora was hungry. She took a handful and stuffed them in her mouth.

"What did you want to tell me about Cynwyd, dear?"

The girl swallowed, coughed. "Cynwyd...that's such an unusual name," she hedged.

"It's Welsh. All the women in my family have Welsh names. I'm Anwyn—that means fair. My sister is Cadi, meaning pure. Cynwyd isn't a typical girl's name, however. It's a saint's name, but my husband liked it. He called her Cynwyddie when she was little."

"I see," Pandora murmured. "How...cute. I'm in her class at the university. She's called Cleopatra there."

"Cleopatra? Whatever for?"

"Oh, we've all chosen other names for that class. I'm not really Pandora, but I like it so much better than Prudence."

"Yes, I can see how you would."

Sarcasm? Cleo's mother didn't seem quite so drunk. Hastily, Pandora changed the subject. "Cleo...Cynwyd is having some problems in class. We did an experiment where we had to fall backward, and she couldn't do it. I'm afraid her failure upset her."

"She's never liked being off balance. We took her to a carnival once when she was five, and it was a big mistake. She refused to get on any ride that shook her up; even screamed when we mounted her on a sweet little carousel pony. Our lovely excursion turned into a disaster...."

"Is that so? I'm afraid the incident in class has left her fearing failure. Perhaps it brought back unpleasant memories?"

"Nonsense. Cynwyd was always an A student. Her father wouldn't stand for anything less."

"Well, I just wanted to let you know, in case she needed a shoulder to cry on...."

"Are you sure you're talking about my daughter?" Mrs. Westland started to laugh, hiccupped instead. "That's not how she handles situations." The woman started to rise.

163

"Could I have another glass of wine?" Pandora blurted. She had to slow things down.

Cleo's mother brightened. "Good idea. It'll help keep you warm in this cold weather. Excuse me while I get another bottle." Leaning on the sofa's arm, she got unsteadily to her feet. "I'll be glad when that rug is back," she muttered. "Much easier on my shoes."

Shoes—so that's what you call it….

As Mrs. W. stepped into the kitchen, Pandora rose and gazed out the window. The wind was gusting out there. People hurried by on the sidewalk far below, their scarves flying about like insects' antennas. Bugs scurrying to and fro….

She looked away, her thoughts turning inward. How would she get Cleo's mother to unburden herself? Something was bothering the woman. Given the right encouragement she looked willing, even eager to confess. Unhappy people longed to reveal their secrets—Pandora had learned that in her therapy sessions. She'd try winding her up with a show of sympathy. A little more wine wouldn't hurt, either.

How many glasses had the woman downed? Good thing she'd had a head start, or Pandora would never be able to keep up with her. She watched Cleo's mother pour from the newly opened bottle.

"This is a lovely Shiraz," Mrs. Westland said. "Cool and dry."

Pandora tried not to wince as she took a small swallow. The taste was not at all like the sweeter wine she was accustomed to. "You've been so kind." She set her glass down. "I know my coming here is a bother to you."

"No, no. It's good to have company. I don't feel

like being alone today."

"Is something the matter? Anything I can help you with?"

"You're a sweet girl, going to all this trouble to tell me about a classmate and trying to help her poor mother, even though we've never met before." She sniffled. "Cynwyd can be unfeeling. She'd only react if she thought I was drowning."

The woman was whining now, but that was an odd remark. Pandora put on her most sympathetic face. "Do you fear the water, Mrs. W?"

"No, but I'd rather lie on a beach chair getting a tan and keeping my hair dry. Cynwyd thought she was drowning once, silly child, just because she was left alone in the pool. There was a lifeguard, of course."

Pandora hid her excitement. This was the stuff she'd hoped to find. She'd keep the old bag spilling the beans. "Sometimes it helps to talk over problems with a stranger. Someone who can never reveal what you tell her to anyone you know…." Pandora radiated sympathy. She was eager to leave now, but didn't want to stop the flow. There might be more to come.

The woman grew quiet, however, kept on drinking. Pandora rose, was reaching for her coat when Cleo's mother spoke again.

"You may be right." She gulped down the rest of the wine, poured herself another glass. "It's my husband. He wants a divorsh…divorce." Tears filled her eyes.

"You poor thing!" Pandora reached over, patted her arm. "Was it sudden…Anwyn?"

"No. He walked out three years ago, but…." She began to blubber. "He knew everything, then. Well, almost everything…all I could tell him." She sniffled again. "He never demanded his freedom before. I think he wants to marry someone else."

"Who?" Pandora asked, then mentally kicked herself. She shouldn't have shown her hand so soon. But Cleo's mother didn't even notice. She was on a roll now.

"It's that Israeli bitch on his team—that so-called 'soil expert,' I'm sure. She must be really good at digging up the dirt."

Pandora stopped listening. Her mind returned to the drowning remark. She began to plan the ways she could get Cleo out to the beach in December, or onto the popular walk across the Brooklyn Bridge. She almost missed the most interesting revelation of all….

"I know we didn't have much in common when we married," the woman wailed, "but I was so beautiful. And rich. I could have anyone I wanted. And I wanted to come to the USA. Get far away from the coal dust. Look, look!" She reached back to the long table behind the couch, grabbed a photograph album. "See how beautiful I was at our wedding." She gestured for Pandora to sit down again and laid the album on the girl's knees. "Go on, open it."

Gingerly, Pandora turned the pages. The laughing woman in the pictures did resemble the drink-sodden woman sitting beside her, but the deterioration was noticeable. "Oh my," she said. "You were lovely, indeed."

"All the men wanted m-me. My debut was the talk of London…." She looked away from the photos and back at Pandora. "I was naughty back then," she whispered, holding a finger to the side of her nose. "I never told Davis how naughty. Not even my father knew."

Pay dirt! Inwardly, Pandora leaped. "Ooh, you have a delicious secret," she cooed. "Can you tell me? I'll never breathe it to a soul."

"Can't tell the secret," the woman mumbled. "Don't know it myself. Still not sure who the father is...." Her eyes started to close. She swayed on the couch.

Holy Mother! Was she really hearing this? "Why don't you lie down for a bit, Anwyn? Rest. You'll feel so much better." Pandora put a sofa cushion behind the woman's head and raised her legs so that she sprawled on the couch. "Does Cl-Cynwyd know who her real father is?" She gambled on asking the right question.

"Never!" The woman's eyes flew open, and she raised her head. "You musht never, never tell." Her eyes closed. "And I never got pregnant again," her voice trailed away. She fell back onto the pillow and began to snore.

"Never, never," Pandora echoed gleefully as she grabbed her coat and crept over to the door. "Well, hardly ever."

She'd forego the beach and the bridge—for now. They would have been only scare tactics. This was ever so much better. It would do real damage. She'd take her time, figure out the perfect moment to let the axe fall.

****

The syllabus for this week's class specified a session on body language and subtext—all the ways people communicate information without using words. It promised to be fascinating.

In body language, they would deal with

unconscious gestures—tightening the thighs, widening the pupils, clutching the chair arm, etc. Subtext fell into the realm of conscious moves, such as seductive voice tones, unfinished sentences, significant pauses, irony. For their end-of-term paper, the students were asked to write their own psychodrama, using all the subtle examples of body language and subtext they could fit into the play. "Be ready," the prof told them, "to perform it on the last day of exam week." The room was buzzing with excitement when the bell rang ending the class.

"That lesson was a blast," Cleo said to Merlin as they left the building. "I've never taken a course that generated as much enthusiasm as this one."

"I have to hand it to Marzin." His tone was rueful. "He's a manipulator all right, but some manipulators make damn good teachers. I'm still concerned, though, about the use he's going to make of all his data."

"You're too suspicious. I'm willing to give him the benefit of the doubt. Anyway, it won't be long before we're not part of the big experiment any more. Semester ends in three weeks."

"Speaking of end of the term," he said, "it's getting harder and harder to wait—no innuendos implied." He searched her face for a reaction.

Cleo began to laugh. The look he gave her was so hot she pretended to fan herself. "Don't go putting ideas into my head."

"I'm not making it up."

She giggled again and he swatted her hand in exasperation. "Aren't there any words without a subtext?"

"Depends on your frame of mind." Cleo chuckled.

"When you have sex on the brain...."

"Okay, I surrender. Try to be serious for a moment. Do you have any questions about the excursion I'm planning for the weekend after classes end?"

"Must we keep it a secret?"

"More fun that way."

"I promised Alice I'd ask if Merry could come along, too."

"I guess so, if we all keep an eye on her. There's stuff she shouldn't touch; it could be dangerous. But as long as we're careful, she'll enjoy the day."

"You've got me concerned now. Maybe keeping it a secret isn't such a good idea. Perhaps you and I could check out this place beforehand?"

"Excellent suggestion." Merlin grinned. "We'll check it out by ourselves first. Make sure it's suitable for a family trip. Our preview has to be next Monday, though—is that okay?"

"Sure, but why Monday?"

"That's the day the building is closed. I can give you a private tour." He winked. "Very private."

"Oh ho! More subtext. What is this place?"

"I'm not telling. Just going with me is apt to give you clues to my real name."

"And we can't have that."

They had reached the garage. Merlin turned Cleo around to lean her against the car. "If you do figure it out, the timing is close enough to semester's end," he whispered in her ear. "We can cheat just a little bit."

Taking her hands, he pulled her arms around his waist. He leaned in, scraped his teeth along her earlobe, nibbled his way around to her lips. She trembled and clung to him. In a flash, the kiss deepened. He slid his arms more tightly around her, hands dropping lower as he pressed her into him.

Cleo couldn't get close enough. She responded to the feel of his arousal with a wriggle of her hips. His tongue darted into her mouth, thrusting in and out. She felt the rhythm building inside her. Holding him tighter, she sank into the sensation.

Before they both lost their balance and fell, Merlin inched back, breathed deeply, and, straightened. His hands fell, but his lips returned. He moved his kiss to the corner of her mouth, licked it, then captured the other corner and nuzzled there.

Cleo barely found the strength to stand alone. "I'll never...see a garage...in the same way again," she panted.

"As for me," he groaned. "I'll forever associate the smell of exhaust fumes with sex."

"Phew. A fate worse than death!"

"Well, I can think of worse!" He watched as she found her keys and unlocked the car. "Let's get an early start on Monday," he eyed her hungrily, "although I'll have to get back to the office afterwards. We can meet at the Glen Cove diner, unless you'd rather I pick you up at home?"

"Not yet. I'll stick to Rocky's rules—as long as I can." They gazed at each other and smiled.

"Okay, be masochistic. Until then...." Merlin kissed her on the nose, grabbed her once more for a quick lip smack. "Drive carefully."

Cleo got into the car, reached out the open window and caressed his cheek. "You, too." She glanced down, smirked. "Give yourself a minute to straighten your pants before you drive anywhere. You'll be more comfortable."

"Siren!" He choked back a laugh.

Cyn drove home, singing along with a Spanish radio station. Making up nonsense words, she bounced with the beat. When the sound faded out in the Midtown Tunnel, she was too lost in happy thoughts to cringe at the tons of water overhead.

Something special would happen on Monday, she was sure. Their body language said it all.

And she could hardly wait.

Chapter 23

"Roger called me the other night." Cyn handed Audrey the pretzels. "First time since the divorce."

"That was out of the blue. What did he want?"

"A patient he wouldn't name told him that I was having trouble in school."

"Weird. Do you have any idea who's been gossiping, and why?"

"It's only a guess, but I suspect Pandora."

"The tall skinny redhead in your class?"

"Yeah. I knew she was angry when I got the job as Rocky's assistant, but I can't imagine why she's carrying the grudge so far. This isn't the first incident."

"What else has she done?"

"The other day she hinted to Merlin that I was screwing around with my esteemed professor."

"The bitch!"

"That's not all. I've been getting strange e-mails and mysterious phone calls. Probably from her, too." Cyn paused, licked the salt from her lips and sipped her wine. "I think she's the one who snitched on Rocky to the dean. Remember, when I had to accept a B for the course? She got stuck with a C, so if she was the one who squealed, she deserved it."

"But why would she report the professor?" Audrey asked. "Didn't you imply that she had a thing for him?"

"Yeah, it doesn't make sense—unless she made a

move on him and he rejected her...."

"Hmm. She didn't get anywhere with Merlin, I assume?"

"No, although he did question me. The prof has a powerful personality, almost hypnotic. I can see why even a self-assured guy like Merlin could have a rumble of doubt. Thank goodness he's too confident to be taken in by a conniving woman. Merlin trusts me."

"From what you've told me, the professor does get under his skin. Competing males and all that."

"Over me? Surely not."

"Come off it, Cyn. You're not that naïve—or unaware of your allure. You don't wave it at people, but you're so vibrant, so enthusiastic. Everything interests you, and that's sexy in itself."

Cyn leaned over and gave Audrey a quick hug. "You wouldn't be my best friend if you weren't my cheering section. When I'm Cleopatra, I have a much more positive attitude."

"Hear hear! I don't blame you for being upset. Pandora has gone to a lot of trouble to find your ex and contact him."

"She's up to something. Merlin says Pandora has an agenda, but no one gets to read the minutes. Anyway, I had to tell you."

"Of course you did." Audrey patted her hand. "I'm bothered, too. This has gone beyond vindictiveness."

Cyn shrugged. "Maybe I'm blowing it way out of proportion."

"Well, let me know if anything else occurs. Don't wait. Call me right away."

"Okay. But enough about these bizarre happenings. What's going on in your life, Aud?"

"Well…" Audrey gave her cat-in-the-cream grin. "You'll never guess where I had dinner last night."

"A new gourmet restaurant?"

"Not exactly, although the food was scrumptious." Audrey swallowed some wine. "How do you like this vintage? It's Spanish—Tony's family introduced me to it."

"His family?" Cyn's voice rose in delight. "So you took up his offer, after all?"

"Mm-hmm. Merry and I had dinner at his *casa* last night." Audrey raised her glass to clink it with Cyn's.

"Wow! I'm pleased you grabbed the opportunity. I've a sneaking suspicion you and Tony were made for each other. How did Tony's folks take to his dating a non-Mexican?"

"They were formal, at first. Stiff. But Tony hadn't prepared them for Merry. When she came out from behind my skirts, I thought their eyes would pop. She curtsied and said, '*banos nuches,*' just like Tony taught her…or close to it, anyway." Audrey chuckled. "Then she ran over to show them her doll. Cleo-patta was dressed in the little Mexican fiesta costume you'd bought for her. By the time Merry wound down from telling her dolly story, they'd turned into doting grandparents."

Cyn chuckled. "That child could charm a Rottweiler into smiling."

"Don't remind me." Audrey shuddered. "I'll never forget that incident. Scared me to death."

"You should get her a puppy."

"When she's old enough to take care of it. A child and a mother are enough on my plate."

"True. A husband would help."

Audrey looked exasperated. "In time, Cyn. Don't rush me."

"So, did you find out Tony's real name?"

"His folks call him Tayo, short for Mateo. That's Mathew in English." Audrey sipped her wine. "It's musical and sounds like Tony, so it's easy to switch. Reminds me of that old Calypso song, the one that starts 'Tay-o....Tay-o.'" She set her glass down, chagrined. "You weaseled that out of me. I shouldn't have told you."

"Don't worry, I won't breathe a word," Cyn said. "I'm delighted that things are working out so well."

"How are you and Merlin getting on?"

"I've got a date with him on Monday, but not to meet his parents. Seems to me he agrees too readily when I remind him about waiting till semester's end before exchanging real names. Is he using it as an excuse for not introducing me?"

"Maybe he wants to be sure you're over the divorce. And bringing you home is a kind of commitment. Merlin may not be ready to take things to the next level. It's not anything you said, so don't go getting defensive."

"I'm trying not to. You know, even though he scoffs at Rocky's ideas, I think he gets a kick out of being 'Merlin the Magician.' The persona fits him, too."

Audrey nodded. "I see what you mean...the mystery fascinates."

"Yeah, why not make it last?" Cyn reached for another pretzel. "Anyway, I thought I should check out the place he's taking us to on our next excursion— make sure there's nothing there that could harm Merry.

He was all for the idea when I mentioned it. I think he wants to take me somewhere we can be alone." Cyn winked.

"At last!" Audrey slapped hands in a high five. "Go for it, Cleopatra—and leave the doubts behind."

****

Cyn stared in dismay at the long e-mail from her father. It began with, *What is going on?* Daddy never did waste time on unnecessary words.

A friend of your mother's wrote me about a fire in the apartment. Was Anwyn hurt? How much damage was done? Why didn't you tell me about it? And what's this I hear of her falling down drunk? I know she tipples a bit, but how much has it accelerated? Who is watching over her? Where are the maids I've been paying for? And where are you?

Scowling, Cyn picked up her coffee mug and read on.

Why doesn't she answer me about making our separation final? She's had enough time to get used to the idea, and she's still an attractive woman. I'm eager to get on with my life, and she should be, too. Concentrating on my job is no longer enough.

Is there any truth to the rumor that you're having problems in graduate school? That isn't like you. I know your divorce upset you, but that is no reason to slacken your efforts.

Heaving a sigh, Cyn sipped her coffee.

All this news from home is disturbing my concentration at work. If things have really gone this far, I'll have to straighten the mess out myself. I'm disappointed in you, Cynwyd.

Her stomach tightened at the old familiar word.

I've booked a flight for this Friday but can remain in the States for only a few days. Since you're alone in that big house, it will be simplest if we stay with you.

How like Daddy to invite himself. Scanning the line, Cyn read the "we" again. She wasn't puzzled for long.

Tirah has chosen to come with me. She has relatives in the U.S. she can visit while I'm clearing up matters. You'll like her—she's outspoken and brilliant. You two should get along splendidly. With her there, I won't succumb to your mother's machinations.

I'll rent a car at the airport, so you don't have to upset your schedule to meet us. We'll be sick of airplane food by then, however, so perhaps you can prepare a late night snack—no baba au rhum, please!

Your anxious father,

Davis

Cyn leaned her head against the computer screen. It would have been nice if he had ended with "missed you," or "I'm looking forward to seeing you," or even the little word, "Love." Why did she keep expecting him to have the emotions normal people had? Not Daddy. He had made a joke about her cooking, though. Of course, it was her failure that he remembered, but at least he recognized that she existed. With a new woman for him to focus on, she'd have to content herself with crumbs.

Putting down the letter, Cyn rose and moved to her walk-in closet. She'd think about it later. Right now, she had other things on her mind. As she slid the padded hangars along the rod trying to decide on the perfect outfit for Monday's date, the phone rang. It was late for a Friday night call, but too early for the hang-up ones she'd been receiving.

She couldn't prevent a rush of fear. At this hour it could be serious. Her mother was alone.

Cyn hurried to the phone. Thank goodness it wasn't Mama or the hospital. She glanced again at the Caller I.D. and read N.C.P.D. Why were the police calling her?

Biting her knuckle, Cyn picked up the receiver.

"Mrs. Westland?"

"It's Mz," she said automatically. "Who's calling?"

"Sergeant Nathaniel Casey, Nassau County Police."

Cyn's heart skipped a beat. She'd been right to worry. "What's wrong?"

"We picked up a woman trying to use your credit card at one of the stores on the Miracle Mile. Claims she's a friend of yours, says you lent it to her. The shopkeeper didn't believe her."

"My credit card went missing some weeks ago. Who is this woman?"

"A Prudence Bronski."

Bronski.... Sounded familiar, but she couldn't think clearly now.... "I don't recall anyone by that name, Sergeant."

"Tall redhead. Says your nickname for her is Pandora."

She should have known! Pandora—and with her credit card. She must have found it that day at the fair.

"Prudence, you said? Yes, I know her." She should let the girl rot in jail tonight, but her mother would be frantic. "Does she need to post bail?"

"Not if you don't press charges. She asked me to call you rather than her parents."

"I'm not surprised. I wouldn't want to face her mother at the police station."

"So, I'll let her go?"

"Well, she's over 18, though not by much. I'd better come down to the station. Make sure she is my 'friend.' And I'd like to dispose of that canceled card personally. It's caused me enough grief."

"No problem. We're at the Central branch in Mineola."

"I know where it is." Cyn looked out the window. Rain again. Damn the woman. She had to pick a miserable night to get caught. And with Daddy and his new woman due any minute. Well, she'd leave them a key and a note. She didn't want to miss the opportunity to get some answers from Pandora. This time, the girl was cornered.

"Keep her there, Sergeant. Please. I can make it in twenty minutes."

Chapter 24

The suspicions Pandora had planted still lurked in Merlin's mind. He trusted Cleo, but not Rocky. Could the professor have made a pass, but she'd been afraid to mention it? Maybe she didn't want to cause any trouble. Or, was it possible she really had a thing for him and was trying to hide it?

None of that sounded like Cleo. Of course not. Damn Pandora for putting the idea into his head.

Switching to "Mac" mode, he left his apartment in back of his parents' mini-mansion and walked around to the front. He entered quietly, walked down the hall to his father's study and poked his head in. "You busy?"

Morgan Sr. looked up. "Just going over some bills. Got a problem?"

His question made Mac grin. *Good old Dad.* "I want to borrow the museum keys. Taking a friend there on Monday."

"Oh? That's a first."

Mac squirmed, unwilling to be baited by his father's sarcasm. "I know I haven't been there since the opening, but my work keeps me quite busy." *As you damn well know.* "She and I want to check out the place without a crowd, see if it's okay to bring another couple with a five-year-old."

"Is this the friend who had her credit card stolen?"

"Yes, it is."

"How did she make out? Did you call my lawyer?"

"Jerry was helpful, but it turned out there wasn't any problem. The company issued a new credit card as soon as she called."

"Then that's the end of it?"

"I guess so. A purchase was made, but she wasn't responsible."

"She's fortunate. There could have been a nasty hassle." His father leaned back in his chair. "I take it this woman is someone special. Why don't you bring her home some evening? I'll drag your mother away from her easel and take you all out to dinner."

She was special, all right. She reached in and touched something inside him no one else had come near. "One of these days, Dad...when the semester ends."

"Don't wait too long. We'll be heading for the Islands."

"I won't. I can hear the steel drums calling you Snowbirds. About those keys...?"

Morgan Sr. opened his desk drawer. "Why don't you have a duplicate set made?" He tossed the bunch to Mac. "The museum is your responsibility from here on."

Catching them, Mac stared at the keys for a moment, looking uncomfortable. "You bought the building, Big M. Redesigned the inside to fit your ideas of a print and publishing museum. I've always thought of it as your monument."

His father chuckled. "Oh, it is that. But it's your baby now, too."

"If that's so, I might get around to putting in a new security system. These keys came with the old house.

They're old-fashioned now."

"Never say so!" Morgan's eyes twinkled. "You make me feel old."

But Mac was earnest. "I know you didn't want any security measures that could detract from the building's design, but you've got collectors' items in there. A scanner can be inconspicuous."

"Hmm. Will I have to put my thumb on the device to get inside?"

His son grinned. "More likely your eyeball!"

****

Cleo pulled into the police station parking lot. The rain had turned colder, and the weather report warned of a hailstorm. The dark street was deserted—not her favorite neighborhood to be alone in at night. She stepped out of the car, clicked the key button, listened for the beep that locked it. Reassured, she turned and hurried into the building.

The room smelled of damp, sweat, and the sharp odor of industrial paint. She forced her breathing back to normal as she passed through the metal detectors. "I'm looking for Sergeant Casey," she told the woman at the desk. "He's with a perp named Prudence Bronski."

The officer scowled at her, and she offered a guilty grin. "I couldn't resist saying the word. Too many cop TV shows."

Shaking her head, the policewoman picked up the phone.

As Cleo waited for Sergeant Casey, she chided herself for the delight she felt in using the real name of that plaguey female. After all the trouble Pandora had caused, it served her right to be saddled with a name like that…. Imagine growing up being called Prudence. Cyn wouldn't be surprised if it was one of the reasons for the girl's peculiar behavior.

A young policeman entered, sandy-haired and freckle-faced. She looked into his watchful, knowing eyes and changed her mind about his youth. This man had seen the world's darker side. He introduced himself, led her down the hall and pushed open a steel door. Sitting at a table in the center of the room, Pandora looked up. As she spotted Cleo, her sullen expression switched to a smirk.

Cleo ignored her, turning instead to the sergeant.

"Is this your friend?" he asked, his tone noncommittal.

Deliberately, she hesitated. *Let the girl sweat.* But she'd already given away her interest by driving here so swiftly in this lousy weather. Heaving a sigh, Cleo grimaced. "I know her."

"Do you want to press charges?"

"No. I guess not. I'm tempted, but she needs a spanking more than a police record." Noticing Pandora's exultant grin, she added, "Or maybe a psychiatrist." Good. At least that brought on a frown. Maybe she'd hit on a weak spot.

"Is she free to go?" Cleo asked.

"Yep. She's your problem now," the sergeant said. He held open the door. "She can pick up her purse at the desk."

"Do I have to sign any papers?"

"No. She hasn't been charged, only detained."

"Thank you, Sergeant Casey."

They walked down the corridor, and the girl retrieved her purse. As they reached the front of the station, the door opened, driving in the pounding rain. A man entered, looked them over, and licked his lips. They hastily backed away.

Cleo turned to Pandora. "How are you getting home?"

"Taking the train," she replied. "Same way I got to the Island."

"Do you know what time it is? The LIRR doesn't run this late on weekends. Didn't you even bother to check?"

Pandora remained silent, glowering.

"What am I going to do with you? I should never have taken the trouble to come down. You don't deserve it."

"Drop me off at the station. I'll sleep on a bench."

"Still defiant, I see. The station is out in the open. Much as I'd like to leave you there, I don't want you to catch pneumonia."

"Yeah," Pandora smart-mouthed. "My ma would never forgive you."

Cleo glared at her. She started to push open the door, then stopped. "There won't be any nearby motels open this late now. It's winter. I guess I'll have to take you home with me. We're in Rocky's class together. It's a shame the connection the rest of us feel didn't spread to you. A little loyalty would help your image."

"I'd like to go home with you," Pandora said.

"Well, that's a change of attitude." Cleo looked at her suspiciously. *I'll bet you would!* She'd be looking around for more mischief, but Cyn felt trapped. What else could she do? She had a dozen years on the girl.

"You'll have to sleep on the sofa bed in the TV room. I'm expecting my father and a friend. They'll probably be there by the time we return."

A strange gleam lit Pandora's eyes at her words, but the girl said nothing. As Cleo started to question her, the station door was pushed open again, scattering her attention. A patrolman let in two of the homeless persons she'd seen hanging around this neighborhood. It was good to see a little compassion among those who serve and protect, she reflected. Even a police station was better than a doorway on a night like this.

An unpleasant odor lingered as they passed by. "Phew," Pandora said. Reaching up, she squeezed her nose closed.

"Stop that." Cleo slapped at her arm. "You could be sleeping out there in the rain. Give them a little dignity." She blew out the breath she'd been holding. "God, what a night, the rain feels like icy needles. Come on, we might as well run for it. You can spend what's left of the night at my house. I'll get you on the first train in the morning."

They sprinted across the lot and skidded to a stop in front of the Camry. For a moment, Pandora glanced wildly about, as if she'd changed her mind and wanted to run. Cleo was tempted to shove the girl into the car, but at last Pandora got into the passenger seat.

Taking her cell phone from her purse, Cleo held it out. "Call your mother, she'll be worried."

Pandora stared straight ahead. "She won't hear the phone ringing this late."

"Nonsense. Your mom's probably waiting up for you. If she isn't, leave a message."

"She's always worrying. Doesn't matter what I do. This time won't be any different."

Cleo gaped at her.

"Oh, very well." Raising her chin, Pandora took the cell and punched in her home number. When the recording machine picked up, she turned her back and spoke sullenly. "It's Prudence. I'm at my classmate's for the night—the one you met that day when it snowed the first time. I'll see you in the morning." She hung up, tossed the cell onto the dashboard.

Cleo grabbed for the phone, returned it to her purse. "Short but sweet," she said sarcastically. "Behave yourself when we get to my home. My father isn't like my ex." She looked for a response to her hint, but there was none.

They drove along in the chill night, Pandora back in her zipped-lip mode. Still furious, Cleo was glad of the tap-tap-tap of the hailstones falling on the windshield. That sound was distraction enough. She concentrated on the road, determined to ignore Pandora.

There were no lights showing when they reached her house. Her father had not yet arrived. Cleo pulled into the garage and led Pandora through the laundry room into the living room. She took her jacket, watching with narrowed eyes as Pandora's gaze roved all around. The girl seemed to be assessing the value of everything.

Cleo shivered, but not from the cold. Was it a mistake to bring her here? Pandora's eyes began to glaze, and once more Cleo felt as if she were disappearing—right here in her own home. How did the girl do it?

Poking Pandora hard, she pointed to the couch. "Sit. I'll make you a cup of tea, then we'll open up the sofa bed in the TV room. Get some sleep. I'll be busy with my father, but we *will* talk in the morning." Cleo stared at the girl until Pandora's eyes returned to normal. As she sat down, Cleo left and put the kettle on to boil.

A few minutes later, she brought in a mug of peppermint tea and handed it to Pandora. "Come. You can drink it in bed." She led her into the den.

Pulling open the sofa bed, Cleo took sheets, pillow and blanket from a closet. "There's a bathroom through that door in back. Good night."

She shut the door firmly behind her as the doorbell chimed.

Chapter 25

Cyn's father stood in the doorway, his pale blue eyes underlined by dark pouches. His clothes had obviously been slept in. The lines on his face emphasized his haggard appearance, but his wheat-blond hair was as wavy and abundant as ever. Despite his weariness he stood tall, no sign of a paunch evident on his athletic figure. It was no wonder females still fell for his Nordic good looks.

The woman standing beside him was as different from Mama as a member of the same species could be. She was tall and lean, big bosomed but firm, and only half a head shorter than Cyn's 6-ft.3-in. father. Despite what must have been a grueling flight, she didn't lean on the man at her side. Instead, she mimicked his erect posture—or perhaps, Cyn thought, he copied hers. Her hair was black and long, pulled into a knot on top of her head from which some strands had come loose. Her dark eyes loomed large in her tanned skin as she scrutinized Cyn with interest. Below her long nose with a bump at the bridge, her lips were lush. Even with lipstick half eaten off, Cyn could see how provocative her mouth was.

With two pairs of eyes on her, Cyn grew conscious of her wet, messy state. "I-I'm just in out of the rain," she stuttered. "Had to pick up a classmate who was caught in the storm. Come in." She stepped away from the door.

Her father made no comment, stating instead, "This is Tirah." With his hand on the small of her back, he followed the woman in.

"Happy to meet you," Cyn mumbled. "You must both be hungry as well as tired. I've lasagna in the warming oven and a salad in the refrigerator. Your rooms are made up. There's a bathroom adjoining them if you'd like to freshen up first."

"Thank you." The woman's voice was deep, with a slight trace of accent as she spoke English. "Davis?" she turned to him.

"Yes, let's wash first. I'll show you to our rooms. Raise the oven temperature, Cynwyd. We'll be back in a few minutes."

Cyn nodded. She watched as he led Tirah to the rear of the sprawling ranch-style home, turning without pause in the right direction. More than three years had passed since his last visit, but the map in her father's brain was as active as ever.

With a shrug, Cyn returned to the kitchen, turned up the oven and set the salad in the center of the dinette table. It had already been set, the Pinot Noir uncorked, an apricot tablecloth highlighting the sparkling white dishes with tiny green leaves around the edges. Then she hurried out to comb her hair and change into dry jeans. As she passed the TV room she paused to glance at the door, but it remained closed.

****

"The flight must have been tedious," Cyn began as she served the lasagna and salad.

"Tirah and I have no time for small talk," her father cut in, despite the scowls both women directed his way.

"How is your mother, Cynwyd? Is Anwyn in any condition to speak rationally? Or is a scene unavoidable?"

The question took away her appetite. She put down her fork, sipped her wine instead. Setting down her glass, Cyn looked directly at her father. "You know how she is, Daddy—that's why you left, isn't it? What did you expect me to do?"

From the corner of her eye, Cyn could see Tirah turn from watching her face to her father's. Did she imagine those luscious lips turning up at the corners? She might get to like this woman, after all.

"I see I shall have to find out for myself." Her father finished his lasagna and started on his salad. "But before I leave," he frowned at her, "we're going to have a long talk about you, your schoolwork and your future."

"Yes, sir," she answered out of habit, then poured herself another glass of wine.

"Oh," she glanced up, her face flushing with embarrassment. "I'm forgetting to be a hostess." She refilled their glasses.

"It is late and everyone is tired," Tirah said in her deep voice. "Perhaps, Cynwyd, we can get to know each other better tomorrow, while Davis is seeing Anwyn?"

"I'd like that," Cyn said, turning to her. "But I have to get rid of my other house guest first. I'll be taking her to the station to catch an early train, so just sleep late."

"Oh, I will. I sleep like the dead." Tirah's rich laughter rolled out, causing her father to look up and finally smile. Cyn watched the intimacy of that smile and was struck by envy.

"I'll see you tomorrow, then." She got up abruptly, put her dishes in the sink, and dragged herself to bed.

****

Saturday morning dawned brisk and clear. Freezing rain had washed away the exhaust-fueled air. Although snowbanks still lined the roads, frigid air blowing from the Arctic had kept the snow from melting. Sunlight sparkled on the frozen masses, and translucent ice glazed every branch and bush. Cyn looked out the window onto fairyland.

It was time to take Pandora to the station. The Manhattan train left at 7:30 a.m., and she wanted the Bad Fairy on it. She carried the coffee mugs and two cinnamon rolls to the dinette table. The cloth was gone, replaced by bamboo mats. As she set the mugs down and sat facing Pandora, the air reeked of hostility.

Cleo once more, she spoke first. "Why did you do it?" she demanded.

No reply.

"Why, *Prudence?*"

"Don't call me that!"

"Well, it certainly doesn't fit your imprudent acts. What have you got against me? Why am I a target?"

With a sneer, Pandora waved her hand toward the living room. "You've got it all. Money. Freedom. Men."

"What the hell are you talking about?"

"I see the way guys ogle you. Merlin, Rocky...."

"That's ridiculous. What you call freedom came after a painful divorce. As for men, I'm hardly a *femme fatale*. You could fit that bill better than I if you wanted to. You've got a model's body, but you carry yourself like a teenage hood."

Pandora snorted. "Don't make me laugh."

"Would anything make you laugh? You've made up your mind to disbelieve me when I tell you that Merlin is my friend, and I work for Professor Marzin—that's all."

"Yeah, behind locked doors!"

"You're being ridiculous. Rocky is my teacher! Any carrying on is all in your nasty imagination. Do you think he'd chance being accused of sexual harassment? I'm untouchable."

"Don't you believe it. I see the way he looks at you."

"Pandora, Rocky's a tease. It gratifies his ego if a female falls for his games. I don't, and he knows it. If you want to make a play for him, as far as I'm concerned, he's all yours."

Pandora tugged at the hem of her sweater. Cleared her throat. "You remind me of my sister," she muttered, her voice fading out on the final word. Before a startled Cleo could get in a question, the girl's tone switched to low and cunning. "You were in my home. You saw the miserable way I live." She spat. "The only way to get anything I want is to lie. And cheat. I have needs, too…."

Suddenly reaching over, she covered Cleo's hand with her own. "Haven't you figured it out, yet?"

Cleo looked down. Watched in amazement as Pandora's thumb tickled her palm, then slid back and forth over her wrist. Her fingers crept upward, dipped under her sleeve, nails slowly scratching.

My God! Pandora is coming on to me.

She saw the girl's eyes flare and pulled her hand

away. What did she want? Impossible that she coveted more than this home and Rocky's affection. Why, Pandora didn't even like her.

Turning away, Cleo forced her mind to forget the leap of insight. She couldn't cope with this—not now. She was being manipulated again.

"This conversation is going nowhere." Gulping down the last of her coffee, Cleo started to rise. For an instant, she sensed another feeling in Pandora's drooping posture—rejection. It was one she knew only too well.

Her steps faltered...but she was too emotional today, too exhausted since her father's arrival to figure out what Pandora was up to. The girl flipped moods so fast, she could be reading the signs wrong.

Pandora's army jacket had dried. Cleo handed it to her, then hustled the girl into the car.

They arrived at the railroad station just as the train pulled in.

"Remember to change at Jamaica if you want to go to Brooklyn," Cleo said. "Do you have the fare?" Pandora shook her head, and she thrust some bills into her hand. "This will cover it. Hurry!"

Getting out herself, Cleo watched from the station platform. Pandora stepped onto the end car and stood in the open vestibule. As the train slowly began to move, she turned and stared at Cleo. Her voice barely carried over the chugging of the engine when she called out, "HAVEN'T YOU CAUGHT ON YET? I'M 'BI.'"

With a chew-on-that-for-awhile smirk, Pandora turned and walked unsteadily down the aisle to her seat.

Shocked, Cleo stood motionless, her eyes following the train until it disappeared from view.

Chapter 26

Had she heard the girl correctly? Did Pandora really call out that she was bisexual? Cyn stood on the station platform, shaking her head in disbelief. She had left her little bombshell for the last minute…quite the exit line.

Could Pandora's feelings for her be some kind of twisted lust? That sly glance seemed deliberately perverse. Provoking her was just another of her nasty little tricks, wasn't it?

Reentering her car, Cyn sat and fidgeted. She tapped her fingernail against the steering wheel. Could she have been too friendly? Impossible. Pandora was trying to throw her off-balance. What a way to start the day—right before she had to face Daddy.

What was that line about good deeds never going unpunished? This was her reward for being helpful. Whatever the truth of the matter was, it was Pandora's problem. What could she do?

Cyn wanted to tell someone about the incident. It was too disturbing to be left unresolved. She could call Audrey, but her friend had never met Pandora. Anyway, it was Merlin she really wanted to talk to. This was Saturday—he might be home working on his graphic novel. She couldn't wait until their date on Monday. She needed Merlin now!

Forgetting for the moment that her father and Tirah

were waiting for her at home, Cyn gave in to the urge to hear his take on Pandora's confession.

The noise of the train had faded away. Settling into her Cleo persona, she took out her cell phone and punched in Merlin's number. He sounded sleepy.

"Did I wake you?"

"No, just haven't had my first cup of coffee yet. What's up?"

"I know I'll be seeing you on Monday," she rushed to say, "but there's something I must talk to you about, and it won't keep."

"Has something happened?" His tone grew sharp. "Are you okay?"

"Physically, I'm fine," she hastened to assure him. "I'm at the Roslyn train station, but can't explain why over the phone. Oh damn. I just remembered I can't stay here. My father and his, uh, female colleague flew in last night. I'd better get back and make a stab at putting breakfast together. Then I'll be showing Tirah around for a bit. I should be free by four—can you meet me at the diner then?"

"No problem. I've some odds and ends to clear up at the office but was planning to be home by noon. Four will work out fine. Don't fret. I'll buy a paper and get some coffee if you're late."

"You're an angel." She blew a kiss over the phone and hurried home to face the inquisition.

****

The house was still quiet when she arrived. Cyn found half a dozen stale croissants and started them soaking in a mixture of eggs and cream for French toast. Then she slapped a pound of bacon into the broiler pan and set it in the oven. There was no way of knowing how hungry her guests would be.

The coffee left over from her breakfast with Pandora would serve. While it reheated, she squeezed fresh orange juice and warmed the maple syrup she'd brought back from Canada. Finally, Cyn filled her mug and collapsed onto a chair. What a morning!

The day didn't improve. During breakfast her father lectured. Cyn half listened while watching Tirah pile her plate with French toast and slather it with butter and syrup. She should be starving after not being able to eat last night, but her father's scolding kept her stomach in knots. So many "yes sirs" were giving her indigestion.

When the lecture was finished he departed, promising Tirah to stand firm with Anwyn. At last she could settle down to some tepid toast and a whole lot of leftover bacon. When she was finally sated, Cyn turned to her guest. "What would you like to do this morning?"

"I wish to sit out back on your lovely patio and talk," Tirah said. "The ice limning the bushes and trees paints a beautiful scene. It is not something I see in my country."

Cyn had never thought of sitting outside at this time of year, but the chairs were still on the patio. She had only to pull off the plastic covers. The house walls would protect them from the wind. With a shrug, Cyn put on her down jacket, earmuffs, and fur-lined gloves, then grabbed two woolen throw rugs and joined her equally bundled Israeli guest outdoors.

Tirah settled on a lounge chair with a throw draped around her legs. She surprised Cyn with her first words. "Why do you allow him to do that to you?"

Cyn shrugged. "Habit, I guess. Daddy's always treated me like that."

"Perhaps because you do not fight back. How old are you, thirty?"

"Thirty-two."

"You are past the age to be treated like a child. Davis has a great many wonderful qualities, but his authoritative persona has its place, and that is not here. Nor should it be allowed to slip over into his private life. I stopped him the first time we met."

Cyn stared at Tirah, then slowly smiled. "In no uncertain terms, I'll bet."

Tirah's rich, throaty laugh rang out. "I see we understand each other. I know Davis was forced into the protective hero role by your mother, but you should not let him extend it to you. Not any longer. Women have rights, and educated women have a duty as well, to teach men the respect we deserve."

"I hear you, Sister," Cyn murmured. "While I was growing up, Mama completely absorbed Daddy's affection. I felt he had no room left for me, except for instruction and scolding."

"You are wrong to think your father has no love for you. Davis talks about you often. He is quite proud of your accomplishments. Do you know he remained in an unsatisfactory marriage because of you? All those years he chose not to leave until you were safely in the care of another man. If he had known you were going to divorce, he might be still here, living an unproductive and unhappy life."

"I never saw it that way...." Cyn looked troubled.

"How could you? You were a child. Dependent on whatever your parents could give you—food, shelter, *and* affection."

"Do you think my father will escape Anwyn's hold on him now?"

"He will not find it easy. Habits are hard to break, but I am a firm believer in man's ability to change, or I would not be in my profession."

"Yes. You're the agricultural expert. And you truly believe you can help the farmers of those backward countries to better themselves?"

"I do. Even for peasants, the uneducated workers of the soil, there is some hope. As for the educated people, I have great faith. But it will not be easy." As she grew quiet, Tirah's face lost its benevolent expression. Her enthusiasm died. "The problem for Davis is different. I believe Anwyn has some hold over him—some secret that affects you. Otherwise, why has he not fought back before? You are the catalyst here, Cynwyd."

"A secret? I can't imagine what you mean."

Tirah searched her face, then looked away. "Whatever it is, I have a strong feeling that this visit will bring it into the light."

****

Cleo arrived at the diner early, chose a booth and picked up the *Times*. She started to fill in the crossword puzzle. When Merlin arrived, her spirits rose. "Hi," she said. "What's an eight-letter word meaning water wings?"

He sat down beside her. "Seaplane?"

"Damn, it fits. Why didn't I think of that?"

He reached over, took a sip of her coffee, made a face. "This is why. Drinking this sludge will poison your mind."

"I should have asked for a fresh pot. It's probably left over from lunch hour."

Merlin waved to the waitress. He pointed to the mug and held up two fingers. She came over with the pot and another mug. "Is it fresh?" he asked.

"Just brewed." She turned to Cleo. "Sorry about the first cup, but you looked like you needed a hit right away."

Startled, Cleo looked up. What had the waitress seen on her face?

"Anything to go with it? I just got in a lemon meringue pie."

They shook their heads and Merlin turned to Cleo. "Tell me what happened. You look upset."

"Apparently everyone noticed," she said in disgust. How to start? Stalling, Cleo nervously folded the napkin into accordion pleats. She might as well blurt it out. "Pandora spent the night at my house."

"What? You let that girl into your home? After what's she's done?" He scowled at her.

She could see his temper rising, tried to down-peddle her response. "The county police called me. They were holding her for trying to pass off a bad credit card as her own, but she soon changed her tune. Said a friend had lent it to her."

"Was it your missing card?"

"Mm-hmm."

"But why did the cops call *you*?"

"She asked them to."

"Odd…. What did you do?"

"Drove down there and sprang her, of course. I couldn't let her spend the night in jail."

"Some people would—and they'd be the smart

ones." Merlin gritted his teeth. "Cleo, it was dark, and the station isn't in the best neighborhood. You could have been mugged!"

"Come on! I drove right into the police parking lot."

"That wouldn't have stopped the druggies. What saved you was probably the freezing rain. Why did you bring Pandora back home with you after all the trouble she's caused? The girl strikes me as unstable. She'll do anything to harm you."

"We weren't alone for long. I knew my father would be arriving shortly. And it was so nasty out. Too late for her to get a train back to Brooklyn."

Merlin stared, his anger growing. "Your actions were unbelievably foolish," he blurted. "Driving alone through that seedy neighborhood. Believing Pandora wouldn't harm you. Putting yourself in such danger. I thought you knew better than that!"

Cleo blinked, surprised to see him lose control. She had never heard him raise his voice before. Perhaps she had acted foolishly, but she wasn't going to admit it. Who was he to shout at her like this? And in public!

A cold rage overtook her. Today had been too much. She wouldn't tolerate another person scolding her. Every man she knew thought he had the right to tell her what to do. First her father, then Roger the Rat. Even Rocky in his wheedling way, and now Merlin! How could he? She had thought her sorcerer knew her so well, understood that she was capable of making her own decisions.

She wanted to scream, but cut off the sound before it left her throat. Blind anger had never gotten her anywhere. Yet underneath her icy fury lay a huge sense of disappointment…again. Merlin had turned out to be another overbearing male, and she'd had all the protective crap she could stomach. Tirah was right. Enough was enough—to hell with the Y chromosome. She was through with men. She would concentrate on a career.

"You're making a scene," she told Merlin coldly. Grabbing her coat and purse, she stood up and marched out of the diner.

****

Slumping in the booth, Merlin leaned his elbows on the table. He dropped his head into his hands. What had gotten into him? He'd never been that frightened for someone else before, not even with Tiffany. But he'd been a kid emotionally during his brief marriage. Maybe one had to grow into protectiveness. Till now, all those instincts had gone into Oxy—the problems faced by his imaginary figure were always solved the easy way, with pen and ink. He hated losing his cool. The class, and his growing desire for Cleo, had changed him—and he didn't like it.

But what could he do? Flummoxed, Merlin slammed his fist onto the table, making the mug bounce. How on earth was he going to mend this rip in their relationship? Just when he was getting ready to make his move, Cleo pushed a button he didn't know he had, and he'd messed up. He'd better think fast.

****

Cyn ran to her car and drove away. The tears she refused to shed filled her eyes. She could barely see where she was going. Merlin had listened to her, but he hadn't heard. Hadn't understood. He was too ready to play Big Daddy, tell her how badly she'd behaved. As if she hadn't had a bellyful of that this morning.

Foolish, hah. She'd show them all! With each sniffle she grew angrier. Still concentrating on her bitter thoughts, she came to the steep hill that led down to Searingtown Road. Perhaps she and Pandora had something in common after all. Men were the pits.

Suddenly, the Camry skidded across one of the ice-filled potholes. She slammed on the brake. Lost control. The car skewed halfway around and plowed into a snow bank.

Cyn sat still, fingers frozen to the wheel. *Damn, damn, damn.* This was not her day. She knew enough to steer into a skid, not hit the brake. She was an excellent driver. This is what happened when she let herself get rattled. Look where it had landed her.

She waited for her heartbeat to slow, then tapped the accelerator. For several minutes, she tried rocking the car back and forth, without success. The hill was too steep and slippery to back out of the snow bank. She waited for a few moments, hoping another car would pass by and stop, but none did. It was growing dark.

Spying her purse in the far corner of the other seat, she unbuckled her seat belt and stretched across to reach it. She could phone Audrey, but that wouldn't help. Maybe it was sexist, but her BFF couldn't do any better than she had done. Much as she hated to, the logical thing was to check if Merlin were still at the diner. He could figure out what to do.

The weather report had predicted that tonight's low would be in the teens. She'd have to eat her words if she didn't want to freeze to death. Still nursing her anger, Cyn punched in Merlin's number. She was barely conscious that somewhere deep inside her, a tiny part was smiling.

****

Mac sat at the table sipping his third mug of coffee. He stared into space. Another train rumbled into the station, and the noise finally penetrated his consciousness. What was he doing sitting here? Time to go home and talk the whole thing over with Oxy. Drawing his frustrations into the panels usually cleared his mind.

He signaled the waitress for his check. As he paid his bill at the register, Mac's phone began to vibrate. To his great relief, it was Cleo. "Hi," he said into the phone. "I'm glad you called. I wanted to tell you how sorry—"

"Merlin," she interrupted. "Stow it for now. I skidded on Roslyn Hill and ended up in a snow bank."

His tone changed instantly. "You aren't hurt, are you?"

"I'm fine. Just shaken up a bit. But I can't get the car out. I've tried rocking it, but…"

"I know that hill. It has a reputation. Where exactly are you?"

"About a third of the way down."

"I'll be right there. Wait for me."

"I'm not going anywhere."

As he snapped the phone shut, Cleo's words caught up with him. A wide grin spread across his face. At last he had her where he wanted.

This would all work out.

Chapter 27

Merlin arrived moments after her phone call. Taking a shovel and a couple of planks from his car trunk, he chiseled away at the ice, then laid one board next to the front wheels and the other behind the back ones.

Scraping the ice crystals off her side window, he motioned for Cleo to roll it down. "Can you climb over the gear shift into the other seat?"

"Sure. Give me a moment to stop shivering."

He grinned as she maneuvered into the passenger seat, making no attempt to be graceful. The driver's door opened, and he slid inside.

"Do you always travel equipped for emergencies?" she asked as he rocked the car back and forth.

"In the winter I do. We have a long, steep driveway. I've needed the shovel and boards more than once."

In a few minutes, he'd worked Cleo's car out of the snow bank and onto the road. He turned to her. "We need to talk."

"Yes," she said stiffly. "I owe you that much, Macho Man."

"Don't know if that name praises or condemns me."

She wasn't sure, either. "Back to the diner?"

"Why not? I sat there for so long after you left, I'm

getting to be a fixture."

The waitress recognized them. "Returned for the lemon meringue pie?"

"No," Cleo said. "Is any of your special clam chowder available?"

"New batch just coming up."

She turned and Merlin nodded. "Make that two, please. Steaming hot. We're frozen."

As soon as they were seated, Cleo rushed to speak first. "I never finished telling you what happened at my house last night."

He lifted an eyebrow. "Go on."

"Well, besides examining my house as if she coveted everything in it, Pandora made a play for me."

"She did WHAT?"

At his raised voice Cleo looked around, but no one was watching them. "You heard me," she whispered. "The girl dropped hints this morning. Played with my hand. Let her fingers trail up my arm, creep under my sweater. Then just as the train was leaving the station, Pandora called out that she was 'bi.'"

"As in bisexual?"

"As far as I can tell, that's what she meant."

Merlin had been doodling on his napkin while she told him the story. "Now that I think about it," his pen tapped as he looked thoughtfully at her, "I'm not surprised. Pandora is a pendulum. I can see her swinging back and forth between sexual identities. She's a disturbed young woman."

"My feelings, too. I can't believe any actions on my part misled her."

"Definitely not. She spoke of sensitivity sessions once. I wonder if that was a euphemism, and that a psychiatrist was in charge of the group."

"Seems possible, but is her mother aware of Pandora's problems? I met her briefly, and Mrs. Bronski didn't strike me as the understanding type. In fact, her strict religious attitude may be adding to Pandora's confusion."

"Well, there's not much we can do about it. Neither of us has the training. But there might be someone we could talk to at the Student Health Center."

Cleo hesitated. "It's a delicate situation. If we say the wrong thing, we could cause real damage."

"That's true."

The waitress brought their chowder. They ate in silence, both deep in thought. Finally Merlin spoke, his tone decisive. "Let's put it out of our minds, at least until the semester ends. Just keep away from her." Dropping some bills on the table, he helped Cleo with her coat. "Want me to follow you home?"

"Nope. Still playing by the rules. I'll pay attention to my driving now."

"I really am sorry, Cleo. I rarely lose my temper, but I was frightened for you."

"I…I guess I understand. But don't do it again."

"Don't give me cause." Merlin's smile softened his words. He dropped a light kiss on her cheek. "Take it easy tomorrow. Relax. Read a book." Holding up his hands, he grinned. "Only a suggestion. We've got a big day ahead of us on Monday."

Her eyes lit up at the reminder.

Once home, Cleo was informed that her guests would stay a few days longer. "Anwyn is being recalcitrant," her father told her. "She's deliberately prolonging my stay. I don't know what she hopes to gain by it. Despite her veiled threats, I won't change my mind this time."

"Threats?"

Daddy looked uncomfortable, but he ignored her question. "We'll try to leave by Wednesday. Tomorrow Tirah plans to visit her relatives. The Ben-Aarons are intelligent and hospitable. I'll join her there after I deal with your mother. On Monday I have an appointment with my lawyer to discuss strategy. This time the threats will come from me, and they'll be financial."

"That might work...." Cyn wasn't so sure.

"So for the rest of our stay you won't have to bother about us. We'll take care of ourselves."

"Good. I have plans for Monday and class on Tuesday, but I'll cook us a farewell breakfast on Wednesday morning. Tonight, I'll order in Chinese, if that's all right with you."

Tirah smiled and nodded. "It will be fine."

The woman was very quiet this evening. Was it still jet lag, or was Tirah more troubled than she admitted at the outcome of their trip? Difficult as it had been when she'd first heard of the divorce, Cyn now believed it was the right thing for Daddy to do—just as her own divorce had been the necessary next step in her life. She looked at her father with more compassion. Living was all about change, wasn't it?

****

When she awoke Monday morning, Cleo was surprised to see the awesome ice still coated every tree branch. Leaving a note for her sleeping guests, she met Merlin at the diner. As they drove past the North Shore mansions, the crystalline magic of the ice-coated trees came back into view, driving out the last of her resentment.

Cleo peppered Merlin with rave reviews of the gorgeous landscape. "Look, Sorcerer, there's glitter everywhere—it's the background to an ice ballet. See that tree? Isn't it perfect?" She cracked her window open. "It's tinkling like wind chimes. Reminds me of feather-dusting my grandmother's crystal chandelier." Her smile grew dreamy. "Such a delicate sound. I haven't thought about it in years."

"Spectacular sight," Merlin agreed. "I must've waved my wand in my sleep."

"Oh, yes, yes!"

He took his eyes off the road and glanced at Cleo. The corners of his mouth twitched.

She blushed. "Am I gushing?"

"A bit." Merlin laughed. "But this scenery deserves it. We don't get a glimpse of fairyland very often."

"I tried to photograph it the last time we had a storm like this. Made a pretty picture, but it couldn't capture the ambience. You've got to be inside the spell to believe."

"You *are* a romantic."

"And you aren't?" she challenged.

He arched an eyebrow. "The difference between male and female romanticism is that the female's comes from the heart, whereas the male's is located farther down his anatomy."

"Is that so?"

"Male orientation, from eight to eighty. Trust me."

"Words of Wisdom 101?"

"You bet."

She chuckled. "I can work around that."

Soon they were driving on narrower and narrower roads. Cleo put her nose to the cracked-open window and sniffed. "Do I smell the sea?"

"Long Island Sound is just over the horizon." Merlin turned onto a graveled drive, rounded a curve, and the trees parted. "Look ahead."

In front of them, on a slight rise, a pure white Art Deco mansion sparkled in the sun. At different levels, short smokestack towers, like those on a ship, rose above room-sized cubes. Cantilevered decks spread out in all directions. A Greek key trim zigzagged around the structure, uniting the various parts.

Cleo gaped. "Oh my...it's stunning! Like a giant child's building blocks creating an enchanted castle."

Displayed against the cloudless blue sky, the mansion was breathtaking. "I feel like I'm dreaming, Merlin. It's the most intriguing house I've ever seen. Does someone live here?"

"Not any longer. My father bought it from the previous owner and turned it into a museum."

"How could anyone part with such a magnificent place?"

Merlin shrugged. "The usual reasons—kids grew up and the stock market went down."

"How did your father find it? I've lived on the Island for years, and I never saw it before."

"It's well camouflaged by all the trees."

"I'll say. Yet it fits into the landscape beautifully."

"They had a super architect, and my mother designed the interior. That's how we knew about the place. When it came on the market, she was tempted to buy it but decided it was too big for our small family."

Cleo sighed. "I'll bet she found it hard to give up."

"Yeah, but in the end we bought it after all, though not to live in. Dad had a dream. He found a sympathetic contractor and worked with him ever since his retirement. Turned it into a museum of printing and publishing. They tried to alter the building as little as possible and still get the presses in. Managed that by converting the four-car garages, but it took a long, frustrating time."

"Amazing that they were able to do it so well. The graceful proportions are still there."

"It's Dad's monument now." He parked in front, and they stepped out of the car.

"Wow." She continued to stare. "I'm having a problem taking this all in. How large are the grounds?"

"Twenty acres, going right down to the Sound. That's a lot of waterfront property. In the spring I'll show you around outside. The gardens are spectacular, and the owner's sculptures are still there."

"Must need a large staff to keep it going."

"The museum's been set up in a trust. Should be here for our children." He smiled at Cleo, and she felt her heart speed up.

"Can we go in now?"

"Sure can. I have the keys."

Laughing with delight, she hurried up the polished granite stairs. Inside, the many windows offered spectacular views of snow-covered lawns rolling down to the gray waters of Long Island Sound. Merlin hung her coat on a hook and led her to a room fitted out as a newspaper workplace of Ben Franklin's day. There was a screw press, various tools, samples of hand-made rag paper.

Glass display cases along one wall revealed other

artifacts of the Colonial period. Spinning around to take them all in, Cleo spotted a doll in one. "Merry will love this," she said. "She's a little young, but I think she'll have fun and learn something, too."

In the next room, an etching of the Gutenberg press hung on the wall above a facsimile of the first printed Bible. Another room displayed two linotype machines of her grandparents' day. And in the converted garages, huge presses silently evoked bygone days.

From the doorway, Cleo gazed at them. "I saw these working in some old movies on TV. Remember 'Libeled Lady?' And 'His Girl Friday?' Must have been fun to be in the news game then—racing after scoops, typing madly in the clatter. STOP THE PRESSES!" she shouted, grinning at Merlin as her voice echoed in the cavernous space. "It makes me nostalgic for a time I never knew."

"It hits me, too," Merlin said. He pointed to the yellowed print of famous news events hanging on the walls. She paused to read the gory details of President Lincoln being shot in Ford's Theater in Washington, D.C. and grimaced. "Reporters haven't changed much. This paper describes the President's brains leaking out."

Another headline screamed, "Titanic Sinks!" A third used the entire front page to reveal the mushroom cloud of the first atomic bomb. "I'm flabbergasted," Cleo said. "I could spend hours here reading what's on the walls alone."

"Save some of your enthusiasm for the next visit." Merlin put his arm around her waist and turned her around. "I've got more to show you."

A wave of warmth rolled over her where he touched. She blinked, then gave in and shut her eyes for a second. The man could distract her so easily.

"Let's go upstairs. I want to show you the publisher's office—still with its original Art Deco furniture."

The handsome office brought forth another cry of delight from Cleo. In the center of the room, an off-white carpet formed the background for an abstract pattern of red triangles, green circles and blue squares. Behind the rug, a magnificent desk of walnut and brass stood, its staggered shelves resembling surfboards. On the desktop, a brass lamp with a tall, triangular stem and spiraling shade echoed the shapes in the rug.

Cleo turned around. A weaving of Manhattan's dark skyscrapers hung above a sleek couch, curved like an apostrophe lying on its side. Its plump cushions of nubby raw silk matched the rich red in the carpet.

"It's perfect," Cleo murmured, reaching out to touch. She regarded the room with a tactile pleasure.

"Mom's an expert on Art Deco—a little sideline she indulges in when she isn't painting."

"She was inspired. I'd like to meet her someday."

"You will," Merlin promised. "Come, take a look at the view from here." Moving his arm from her waist to curve around her shoulders, he led Cleo to the picture window. Steel and bronze sculptures dotted the snow-covered lawn, slivers of ice hiding in their crevices. Beyond, she could see the waters of Long Island Sound stretching across to the Connecticut shore. Tiny waves lapped at the sandy beach. A lone seagull rested on the dock, fluffing its feathers against the winter wind.

As she gazed out the window, Cleo felt the heat of Merlin's body behind her. Its warmth slipped under her skin. She wriggled her hips against him, and a new awareness assailed her. She was affecting him, too.

His hand began to move up and down, massaging her back in a teasing caress.

With a sigh, she turned and met his eyes. The fire in them blazed. A streak of sunlight landing on his face transmuted their mysterious smoky gray into an intense silvery gold. He pulled her closer and kissed her, sliding his tongue along her lips as he invaded her mouth. Cleo melted into him. She slid her arms around his neck and lost herself in the kiss.

This was what she wanted. Their relationship had moved beyond friendship. Beyond an affair. Way beyond phone sex. Despite their recent blowup, something about this man ignited a spark within her...and the spark was starting to glow.

Merlin's fingers slid up under her sweater, under her bra, and around to the sides of her breasts. His palms rubbed slowly back and forth until her flesh strained against him. As she let out a soft moan, his hands dropped down to pull her tight against him.

Cleo's fingers reached up his neck into his hair, her nails scratching his scalp in slow suggestive circles. Merlin leaned into her hand. "So good," he murmured. "You're driving me crazy."

She echoed his words as her hand slid around to explore his ear. Turning, he nipped at her palm, then suckled a finger. "You know," he said, "there's something about Art Deco design. All these suggestive shapes—the squares and triangles, and especially your circling fingers—have made me horny."

"Is that what's causing it?" She snickered. "It's affecting me, too. I never figured on lust having a geometric side."

He kissed her jaw, the tender spot below her ear. "Have you ever pictured yourself lying languidly on an apostrophe-shaped couch?"

"Can't say that I have." Her breaths were coming faster now. She could barely get the words out as he kissed the little hollow at the base of her neck, then licked a trail to her breasts.

He lifted his head. "Makes me hot to think about making love to you on a red couch. I can see you with a teasing smile on your face. Your head is leaning back on your raised arms, and a leg is swinging to the floor, its shoe dangling from your toe. That pose is a favorite fantasy of mine."

"I can visualize it, too," she mumbled, "only with a not-so-languid sorcerer draped over me."

Laughing, Merlin pulled her sweater up, bent and planted a kiss on her bare midriff. His hands rose beneath the soft cashmere to cradle her breasts.

She let out a little gasp as he tweaked a nipple, then rolled his palm around it. His other hand snaked around to open her bra clasp.

"I like the way you dress," he murmured, pushing her miniskirt even higher and tickling her stomach as he reached under the elastic to roll down her tights. "But except for the one shoe, my fantasy has you naked."

"Almost like Goya's *Maja*," she whispered, stepping out of her tights and slipping back into her pumps. "The painting shows the duchess lying on her divan, just like in your fantasy."

"It's not every day a man realizes his dream." Merlin's voice grew husky as he carried her to the sofa and removed the rest of her clothes. "Let me look at you, *Maja* Cleopatra."

Leaning back and resting her head on one arm, Cleo smiled—a wicked, witchy smile. She beckoned with her other hand, her index finger curling suggestively.

"Come on down, Sorcerer...."

The couch bounced—and her shoe fell off.

Chapter 28

After three-months' wait, their built-up anticipation came roaring to life. The lovers fought to get closer. Cleo scrambled on top, only to find herself rolled over beneath Merlin. Her laugh was smothered in kisses—kisses that grew more wild, more feral, escalating their pleasure. Aware that she was sucking madly on his tongue, pulling him into her mouth as she flagrantly mimicked the act of love, Cleo exulted.

She didn't know Merlin's real name, nor did he know hers. Within the sensual cloud whirling through her mind, the question drifted—did the anonymity add spice? Yes, it did, but this bout of loving was so much more fulfilling than fantasy sex with an exciting stranger. She trusted this man, and that made all the difference. She let herself go, free to experience every sensation. He was the one she desired—whoever he was.

Wherever it led.

Merlin. No one else.

To be able to admit this feeling was seduction itself. When they broke the kiss to gasp for air, Merlin leaned over her, picked up the leg that dangled over the couch and set it in his lap. He sat back and gazed at her, sprawled and open before him. At his look of pure male satisfaction, she smiled, reveling in her feminine power.

Taking her foot, he nibbled each toe. She trembled.

He raked his teeth across the sole, and she shivered at the delicious sensation. Moving to her heel, Merlin bit the back of it, touching sensitive nerves that made her jump. The thrill rolled through her body. He looked up at Cleo's expression, grinned wickedly, then moved his mouth up her leg, trailing kisses along her calf. When he reached the back of her knee he nipped, then licked the spot. She caught her breath. His tongue slid up her thigh in a snakelike squiggle as she squirmed, giddy with pleasure.

He arrived at the coppery curls between her legs. Dropping kisses, he pulled at a ringlet with his lips and watched, eyes gleaming, as it spiraled back onto her startled flesh. He cupped her, rolled his palm, then lapped at her dewy vulva until her eyes glazed over.

Looking up, Merlin took a deep breath and smiled—the sexiest smile she had ever seen.

In that second's pause, a thought came to Cleo unbidden. *My sorcerer can arouse me with only a look. Nothing Roger ever did brought on the thrills that Merlin creates.* She wanted to touch him, too, but before she could change positions, she felt two fingers move inside her. As she moaned, the fleeting memory of her ex faded and disappeared forever.

With his fingers still causing delicious havoc between her legs, Merlin nibbled his way up her body, stopping at her breasts to glide his teeth along each nipple and follow that with a sucking kiss. It was too much…almost.

"Sorcerer…." She gasped as he entered her, tightened and slid in and out. She wrapped her legs around him. Intoxicated with pleasure, Cyn lost herself in the sensuality Merlin evoked. He quickened his thrusts and she rode the rhythm, faster and harder, until she was carried away in the glory—and shattered. Merlin's shout echoed her scream of release as he exploded long and hot within her.

He collapsed on top of Cleo—and they tumbled off the couch.

At the bump, her eyes flew open. They had landed on a red triangle and a green circle. Even in her blissful state, arms and legs tangled with his, Cleo couldn't restrain a giggle.

With a comical frown, Merlin pulled her on top of him. "Timing wasn't the best," he muttered, holding her securely. "Relax. I'll take the rug burn."

"My hero. God, what a shock."

"Are you all right?"

She was still trying to catch her breath. "Mm-hmm. Talk about unforgettable experiences. This morning is engraved in my memory."

"To infinity." He hugged her. "Next time we'll take it slower."

Cleo swatted at him. "Stop trying to overachieve, Merlin. The lovemaking was perfect—but the bumpy landing could be improved upon."

"I won't let you fall again."

"Too late….." She let her words hang.

He looked up into her laughing eyes. "As you wish, oh mighty Queen. I'm your humble servant."

"Calling me that gives me ideas." She walked her fingernails up his arm. "Watch out, or I'll turn you into my sex slave."

"That's a plan." He stroked her head, played with her hair. "What name would you prefer? *Cherie? Querida? Liebschen?* Cleo doesn't cut it. I want to call you something special, just between us. Not an overused term like darling."

"Show-off. You're awfully good with languages."

"Dad started his career as a diplomat. We traveled a lot, so I remember my favorite words from each country."

"For all your girlfriends?"

"Naturally." He reached around to squeeze her butt. "But this time the words express my true feelings."

"Aah, good to hear. Did you ever get to Wales?"

"No. We missed that one."

"The Welsh word for sweetheart is *cariad*."

"*Cariad*." He rolled his tongue around the word. "That sounds just right."

Cleo's smile was sweet and sad as she remembered her father singing it to her mother.

"Is it okay if I call you that?" Merlin asked. He seemed to pick up on her momentary sadness.

Cleo hugged him tightly, and the long-ago memory drifted away. "Oh, yes, it's our word from here on. I've an important question, Merlin."

At his frown she poked him. "It's not about that dirty word, 'relationship.' This is a more intimate question." Her fingers raked lightly through the golden hairs on his chest as she looked down, not meeting his eyes. "Do you think the sex was fabulous because we don't know each other's real names?"

Puzzled, he reached up and raised her chin until she looked right at him.

"I mean," Cleo said hesitantly, "can we express ourselves more easily, more completely, without fear of doing the wrong thing? Without being so conscious of trying to fulfill the other person's expectations that we can't relax and be ourselves?"

Merlin chuckled. "That's a girl thing," he teased. "I knew I was pleasing you as well as myself. But I admit not knowing your real name added a pinch of spice. Next time, when I use the name you were born with, the loving will be even better—just different."

"You're sure of that?"

"I guarantee it. We'll have today's memories to add to the experience. I'll never forget this crazy apostrophe of a red couch, or the little plop as your shoe fell off."

"And the bigger plop we made falling off the couch," Cleo said, laughing. "I'm definitely going to drop my shoes from now on. Whenever I do, the sound will remind me of this fabulous day." She snuggled a few minutes longer until, at last, he moved her gently off him.

"The door behind you leads to a bathroom. Give me a minute to get rid of the condom, then I'll straighten up in here while you wash and dress."

"Okay. And we'd better clear the air before the museum opens tomorrow."

"I'll run the air conditioning for a bit, but I like the scent of passion."

"Turns me on, too." They smiled at each other.

Soon they were dressed and ready to leave. At the door, Cleo turned to look once more at the exquisite office, restored to its perfection. "I'll dream about this room tonight."

"So will I...and all the things we can do in it."

"Naughty thoughts? I'll join you."

He grinned. "We're soul mates, admit it."

Soul mates. She hugged the words to herself. "And you say you're not a romantic."

He laughed. "Did you think only women are allowed to change their minds? Not in this century."

His arm around her waist, Merlin guided Cleo back to the entrance. As she breathed in the cold, crisp air, she recalled their planned excursion. "Will it be very crowded when we return with the gang on Saturday?"

"No, not too many people know about the museum yet. It's only been open a short while, and it's winter. Come spring, the schools will schedule class trips, but now there'll probably be only a handful besides the five of us. We'll have it practically to ourselves."

"Good. You and I have already seen most of it, so we can keep an eye on Merry and let Alice and Tony enjoy themselves. There's a lot of machinery here. We'll have to watch that she doesn't poke a finger into something and get hurt."

"Don't worry, we will. I gather Alice and Tony are much better acquainted, now."

"Mm-hmm. They'll appreciate our help. It hasn't been easy to find time to be alone together."

Merlin held the door for Cleo, then locked up. As they walked to his car, she glanced back. "I still can't get over this fantastic building. When you round the curve of the drive, the view is startling."

"That's how the architect envisioned it."

"He certainly succeeded. I'm going to Google its history."

"Then you're bound to find out my name."

"True, darn it. I'll have to wait."

Merlin hesitated. He stopped at the car door, his hands still around her waist.

"Now that we've been so intimate, perhaps we can break Marzin's rule. The semester ends in a couple of weeks. I'm willing to exchange names if you are."

She looked into the eyes gazing so intently at her. "I suppose...we could."

"Let's do it. Then I can take you home to meet my family before they head south for the worst winter months. It will give you a chance to say hello. Don't be surprised to get the once-over."

She looked at him, her pulse picking up again. "Are you ready for that?"

"Yeah. I've a plan in mind. I want Dad to meet you before I spring it on you both."

"Oh." His factual reply was unexpected, leaving her uneasy and vaguely disappointed. *Silly girl.* She had to stop jumping to conclusions. Hadn't she decided to live in the moment? No more serious attachments.

Pinching herself to help remember, Cleo took a deep breath. "Okay, I'll do it. How do you do?" Feigning a formal introduction, she held out her hand. "I'm Cynwyd, a Welsh name. "My friends call me Cyn—that's the American pronunciation."

"The double meaning suits you." Lifting her hand to his lips, he kissed her knuckles.

She chuckled. "It's always caused me problems. Who, sir, is behind the magician's mask?"

"Well," Merlin looked embarrassed. "Let's get started and I'll tell you." He held the door for her, then got in the car, turned on the ignition and drove slowly down the gravel drive.

"Quit stalling," Cyn said.

"You'll see why." He turned partly toward her, still keeping his eyes on the road. "I'm cursed with two family names, Morgan and Chase."

"Good grief…as in the banks?"

"Uh huh. Officially, I'm Morgan Jr., but everyone calls me Mac."

"I like it. Not as romantic as Merlin, but it definitely fits your personality. It's more…male."

"That Y chromosome. Does it every time." He grinned at her. "Goes well with 'Cynful.' You're quite a woman."

Cyn and Mac. The two together sounded…spicy. All of a sudden, her teasing name became endearing. Daddy hadn't made such a bad choice, after all.

It took a minute before she realized the irony of recalling her father at a moment like this. With a chuckle, she turned to Merlin. "Let's hit the road, Mac."

"Roger."

Her eyes widened.

"Damn. I've watched too many old WWII movies. They've crept into my speech. Sorry." Mac's apology was cut short by Cyn's laughter.

She whispered in his ear, "Wilco." The touch of her breath was starting to ignite him again. He hit the accelerator—fast.

Chapter 29

By the time they reached the highway, Mac had regained his composure. As they headed for the diner to pick up her car, he apologized for not taking her out to lunch. "I'll make it up to you soon, but I've got to get back to the office today. Work has been piling up."

"Hey, I understand," Cyn patted his arm. "I've had plenty of excitement for today...." Her eyes sparkled. "We can go the gourmet route another time. You know, Mac, I'm still thinking about Pandora. Can't quite get the police station and what followed off my mind."

"How did she act when you showed up?"

"Gave me that 'gotcha' smirk, but seemed relieved not to have to call her mother."

"Did you question her when you brought her home?"

"Mostly the next morning, since I was waiting for my father to arrive. But when I did, she evaded all my accusations. Wouldn't admit to anything besides picking up my credit card. Not even to snitching to the department chair that Rocky planned to give all his students A grades. Yet it had to be her."

"Is she angry at Marzin, too?"

"It's even more complicated. I think she fancies the prof, but her feelings are all mixed up. Some kind of love/hate thing. She's grumbled that her father is seldom around, so maybe it's a kind of transference."

"From Papa to Rocky?"

"Could be. They're both influential figures in a girl's life." Cyn paused. "There's more."

"Go on."

"She claims I've got Rocky in one hand and you in the other."

"Well, that's true."

Cyn smacked his arm. "Rocky appreciates me because I work hard for him, at so little pay, but even the pittance I earn would have helped Pandora. She wanted the job. I feel a bit guilty for taking it, but I won't give it up. I need the challenge Rocky's project offers. Yet that niggling guilt might be what's behind my getting her out of jail and bringing her home."

"You may not need the money, but you're the right person for the job. Don't let Pandora put you in the wrong."

"I'm trying not to," Cyn said ruefully. "Now I'm having trouble believing she was coming on to me."

"No kidding. Did she really feel you up?"

"Just my arm!" Cyn looked affronted. "Tickled my palm, to begin with…then her hands moved up."

"A closet lesbian, do you think?"

"I didn't think so before, but now I'm not so sure. Perhaps that feeling was behind those anonymous e-mails. She wouldn't admit to sending them, but she was even more adamant about not making the midnight phone calls. Insisted she didn't make those."

"You got a series of calls? You never mentioned that to me." He frowned.

Cyn bristled at his accusing tone. "We talked about the e-mails, Merl…Mac, and it got us nowhere. They were so cryptic. I never found out what she was driving at. The poaching bit might have referred to the prof...who knows? And the phone calls were totally meaningless—no way to identify the heavy breathing. They might have been made by my mother, especially if she'd been drinking. When I was talking to you about phone calls, I had a different one in mind."

He grinned. "Okay. You win on that one."

"Besides," she insisted, "I can take care of myself."

Mac didn't mention the lost credit card. Or the car in the snowbank. He could see she was in no mood to acknowledge his help. "Damn," he said instead, "two men and a woman are after you. That's quite a score!"

Cyn smirked. "Are you jealous?"

But Mac grew serious once more. "I don't like it. There's too much anger and frustration in this scenario. Maybe we shouldn't wait until the end of the term. None of Pandora's dirty tricks has worked so far, but who knows what she'll try next? She even threw herself at me once to get you jealous, but you didn't notice!"

"When you're in sight, I see no one else," Cyn teased.

"I'll bet. Have you told me all of her ploys now?"

"There's another. Remember when I reported that my ex called? Pandora set him up for that. She reacted when I mentioned it and must have made up a phony excuse to get in. I wonder if she wanted bigger boobs— that's one of his specialties." At the surprise on Mac's face, Cyn laughed. "He never operated on me."

"I'm relieved to hear it. They sure felt real."

"Har har."

"So she got in to see him?"

"Yeah, told him a fanciful tale, and it bothered him enough to call me. I put him off. He was glad to forget the incident and get back to his new wife and baby—the family he'd started before the divorce."

Mac listened closely. There was more rue than bitterness in her voice. "Then she tried to make us suspicious of each other," he said. "Pandora certainly is devious."

Cyn started to gnaw on a knuckle but stopped herself.

"This has me edgy, Cleo." Mac winced. "Sorry. I still think of you as my Queen Cleopatra."

"I don't mind. You can call me Cleo or Cyn...or *cariad*." She put her hand over his. "I'm sure to slip back into calling you Merlin when you act especially mysterious." She batted her eyelids in mock flirtation, but Mac stayed on point.

"I don't think you should be alone. Pandora has failed in all her efforts. She may try to harm you in a more physical way next. She's obsessed."

"Psychic vibrations coming to you, Magician? Got your protective instincts revved? Surely, being picked up by the police frightened her off. What other dirty tricks can she dream up in the short time left to the semester?"

"I shudder to think."

"You know, Mac, I found Pandora so confrontational in class, it didn't seem normal. But it was stimulating. I was fascinated, even wished I had her nerve."

"She's an original. Obnoxious at times, but she certainly knows how to attract attention."

"That's for sure. I wanted to be her friend, even felt motherly toward her a few times."

"It's your nurturing side coming out."

She glared at Mac but continued. "The girl kept putting me off, so I made no real effort to get past her shell. If she had any lesbian feelings, they must have developed later."

He shrugged.

"Remember that big storm we had? The one that ended up dumping a foot of snow on the city?" When he nodded she said, "I had a dentist's appointment not far from school that day. As I drove past our classroom building, I saw Pru-Pandora walking in the freezing rain. Boy, of all the inappropriate names, Prudence takes the cake."

"I'll say. Having to live with a name like that, it's no wonder she behaves as she does."

"You may be right," she said, "but blaming it all on her name is too simple."

"Sorry. I shouldn't take the situation so lightly."

"No, I'm sure you've hit on a part of the puzzle. I stopped the car and asked if I could take her home. Had to coax her. I don't think Pandora wanted me to see how she lived."

"She gave in?"

"In that weather she would have been mad not to…oops." Cyn gave Mac a wry smile. "Bad choice of words."

"So, you drove her home?"

"Yes, all the way to Park Slope, an old Brooklyn neighborhood. She offered me a cup of tea before I headed back to Long Island. I was consumed with curiosity, so I followed her inside.

"As we walked down the hall to her bedroom, I noticed a gruesome print of St. Sebastian, blood running down his body from all those pierced arrows.

Then her mother invited me into the 'parlor.' On the coffee table by the couch, an enameled icon of Jesus, his eyes rolled back in extreme suffering, was mounted in a silver frame. I tell you, Mac, I was afraid to sully the tableau by putting down my teacup."

"What happened then?"

"Her mother wanted to know how well Prudence was doing in class. What did she expect me to say? I wasn't going to grass on the girl. I drank my tea quickly and got out of there. But I can tell you—in front of her mother, Pandora was all Prudence."

"Probably how she learned to cope. Kinda rough, growing up in a place like that."

"Mm-hmm. Yet she succeeds in being just the opposite of Prudence outside her home."

"It must keep her hopping," Mac's forehead wrinkled, "always alert for the exact second to switch between the two personas. She'd be tense all the time."

"I wonder if she's scared that she might forget— bring the bad girl home—"

"And be punished."

They shared a moment of profound understanding.

Mac took his eyes off the road to glance at Cyn. "We're here." He pulled into the diner parking lot. "I'll be heading back to the office now, but I'll call you when I get home," he promised.

"I'd like that."

"Say, what are you doing next Sunday? Will you have a few hours free?"

"Daddy and Tirah should be gone, but I can't promise. My mother is still holding out, making excuses for not signing the divorce papers."

"Well, if you are free, I'll pick you up at one. Is

229

that okay?"

"Sounds fine, but what did you have in mind?" Leaning over, she rubbed against him, loving the feeling. She must have some cat in her DNA.

"Not that...at least to start with," he grinned. "You've been pestering me to see my comic strip. By the weekend we'll have put all the 'zines to bed for this month, so the pressure will be off for a few days. I'm eager for you to meet Oxy, don't want to wait until after our excursion."

"You're so impetuous." Reaching forward, she planted a kiss on his cheek. "I'm already looking forward to it."

Mac walked her to the Camry, and Cyn rolled down the window. "It's been a wonderful day, Mac." She touched her fingers to her mouth and blew him a kiss.

He grabbed her hand, leaned in, and kissed her quick and hard. Her eyes started to get that faraway look again.

"That's enough magic, Merlin. Go to work, or your father's greeting won't be friendly when we meet."

With a chuckle, he let go of her hand. "Mom and Dad won't be home on Sunday. This trip is only for introducing you to Oxy. Drive safely, now."

"Count on it." She waved and drove off.

****

Mac watched her till she disappeared. The smile that had lit his face after that kiss was gone. Once at work, he looked up her Roslyn address, remembering her last name from the first class, then called a guy he knew in the security business and asked him to keep an eye on a special friend. After giving him the data on

Cyn, he hung up, feeling better.

His great idea was starting to jell. He would hire the efficient Ms. W. and let her take over the office management part of his business. It would free time for him to spend on Oxy Moron's escapades. Saving people—that's what Oxy did. If protectiveness were such a bad thing, they would suffer together.

****

Before class started the following week, Cleo met Pandora in the hall. She opened her mouth to make a scathing remark about their last encounter, then changed her mind. She had agreed with Merlin to wait until semester's end. By then, cooler heads would prevail.

As she reached for the door handle, however, Pandora stopped her. "I met your mother," the girl said.

"Oh? How did that come about?"

"We were both shopping in Bloomies, and I recognized her. She looks so much like you."

Cleo raised an eyebrow. "You don't expect me to buy that. My mother is petite and elegant—not at all like me. The only thing we share are green eyes and, even there, hers are emeralds and mine are peridots."

Pandora smirked.

Damn! She was giving herself away. Now Pandora knew how she felt about her appearance. She had to watch herself around the girl. Pandora was so sly.

"What do you want? Spit it out or we'll be late for class."

"Just to tell you of the encounter, Cleo. We talked about *Anwyn's* problems over some coffee at Starbucks. She was looking for someone to confide in."

"Coffee? My mother seldom drinks it. Were you

trying to sober her up?"

Pandora shrugged. "She ordered tea. I think she doctored it."

"And of course you said nothing?"

"I was only being respectful."

"Yeah. Right."

"She asked me to call her Anwyn. Told me all about her father's coal mines, and her wonderful debut in London. All the young lords were after her, whatever that means these days."

"Yet she picked my father. He was the best looking of the lot," Cleo emphasized.

"That was one of the reasons," Pandora replied evasively. She looked away, but not far enough to miss Cleo's reaction.

"Did she give you others?" Cleo's foot stopped tapping as she waited for the answer.

"Well, not exactly…. She did cry on my shoulder that she had been a very naughty girl that weekend. Her mind seemed a bit hazy about who had shared her hijinks."

"Aren't you being subtle," Cleo said with disgust. "Thanks for alerting me to that piece of news. Better hurry. You'll be late for class."

Head high, she pushed open the door and walked away from Pandora's wicked laugh. No way would she reveal how perturbed she was by the girl's insinuations.

Chapter 30

That evening Mac listened to his parents discussing their plans for a Caribbean cruise. Perhaps he'd take Cyn on one of those luxury yachts one day.... As they rose from the table, he turned to his father. "I need to talk to you."

"Is it about the magazines, Mac? I'm already in my vacation frame of mind."

"This is important, Big M, and should be decided before you leave."

"Come into the library, then."

Mac kissed his mother's cheek. "Spot of blue under your left ear," he whispered, smiling as he watched her casually scratch off the paint.

Following his father, he poured cognac from a crystal decanter into a balloon glass, handed it to him, and got right to the point. "The magazines are all under control, and the e-versions I added are doing even better. But they've taken over my life, and I don't like it."

Morgan Sr. nursed his cognac, saying nothing.

"I want to hire someone to manage the everyday business of publishing," Mac went on. "I'll still be owner and editor, but an executive assistant will shield me from the mundane office details. I need more time for my other projects. You knew I had outside interests when you asked me to take over," Mac reminded him.

"I haven't given them up."

His father studied Mac's determined face. "You've been thinking about this for quite a while, haven't you?"

"Yes, I have. And I believe I've found the right person for the job. She's worked in publishing and is a whiz with computers, as well as a proficient organizer."

"She?"

"Yes, a woman I met in my communications course—the class you asked me to take to meet the movers and shakers." He slipped in the dig.

"Is this the young lady who lost her credit card?"

"It is, but I'm confident that the incident was not an indicator of her ability to perform the job I have in mind."

"I see."

Do you really? Mac's thoughts drifted, but he pulled them back. "I'd like to offer her the job on a six-months-trial basis. If it works out, we can make it permanent."

Big M watched his son for several long moments. Mac's gaze didn't waver.

"Very well." Setting down his cognac, he rose and walked toward the door. "Have a proposal ready for me when I return from the cruise. Be specific. The magazines are your babies now. I accept your judgment." He looked back, his eyes twinkling. "You've got a lot of your mother in you, and I understand why that side needs an outlet. However, I'll have to put this before the board."

Mac grinned. *You have that board wrapped around your little finger,* he thought, but all he said aloud was, "Thanks, Dad. I'll do that."

234

****

How weird her life had become lately! The strain was beginning to tell. While she still kept up with Professor Marzin's assignments, Cyn's enthusiasm was beginning to wane. Pandora's words kept niggling at the back of her mind. It was difficult to concentrate, to fall asleep at night. She was turning cranky, and she didn't like it.

Was there any truth behind Pandora's insinuations? Was it possible her father wasn't her father—and some British lord was? What a ridiculous conclusion. Just because she had chosen the name Cleopatra didn't mean her intuition was telling her that she had any royal blood. The whole idea was becoming more farfetched by the minute.

Daddy and Tirah were leaving at the end of the week, this time for sure. She'd have to take him aside before then and ask him outright if there was any truth behind Pandora's words. She needed answers. Being aware of the medical histories of both parents was important. Someday she might have children; she owed it to them. Allergies could be inherited, as well as features. She had her father's high cheekbones and pale eyes, though hers were more green than blue. And she didn't inherit that soft, wheat-blond hair. Even their noses were different, yet she didn't have her mother's nose either.

Good grief, if she went on like this, she'd end up deciding she was adopted! When Daddy got in this evening, Cyn would confront him.

But when she did, his response surprised her. Instead of denying the allegation outright, his face took on a hard, stubborn look. "More innuendos," he said.

"This isn't the first—I received an anonymous letter recently. It's time you and I put the question directly to your mother."

Cyn was already filled with doubt for having brought up the subject. She dreaded the confrontation to come. By the time she and Daddy drove to Mama's penthouse, however, she had talked herself into a more cheerful frame of mind. The thrilling day with Mac had boosted her spirits.

They left Tirah busily slicing eggplants and browning lamb for *moussaka,* the main course in her promised Mediterranean dinner. As they drew closer, Cyn's glow began to fade. Anxiety took its place. Daddy's face was grim. He hadn't said a word on the drive over. Taking a deep breath, Cyn sat up straighter. Regardless of the repercussions, she, too, was determined to solve this mystery.

The swift elevator ride combined with Cyn's upset stomach to leave her dizzy. She shut her eyes, opened them a moment later to find Anwyn at the door with a drink in her hand. Davis moved past her, grabbed the glass and set it down on the shelf above the fireplace. Hands on hips, her body language radiating resentment, Anwyn watched him.

Davis sat down on the couch, pulled the unsigned letter from an inside pocket and thrust it at her. "Who wrote this?" he demanded.

Leaning heavily on the couch's arm, Anwyn stared down at him, her chin trembling. She ignored the letter. Cyn felt a pang of regret as she watched her mother beginning to fall apart.

The silence that followed was more than she could bear. Cyn rose and plucked the letter from mama's hand. She read it hastily, then looked closer at the handwriting. It reminded her of a paper she had filed for Professor Marzin. As recognition set in, Cyn sent an accusing glance at Anwyn. "This looks like Pandora's handwriting, Mama. How would she know how to correspond with Daddy?"

Anwyn's mouth pursed. Cyn and Davis waited. After a moment Cyn turned to her father. "A classmate of mine wrote this. Pandora has a penchant for making mischief. You were involved as a tool to hurt me. I doubt that she considered the harm it might cause you."

"Abominable meddling." Her father spat the words. "You shouldn't have anything to do with a person like that, Cynwyd. But it doesn't answer my question." He turned back to his wife. "You've been hinting about a secret for years, Anwyn, but you always turn coy when I ask you about it. Now is the time to confess. I tolerated your innuendos for a long time, hoping to spare Cynwyd embarrassment. But it has moved beyond embarrassment, hasn't it?"

Pressing her lips together, Anwyn turned away.

Davis folded his arms across his chest and waited. Another minute passed. "I'm considering cutting off your spa allowance," he said. "Those massages don't seem to be helping you."

Her defiance crumbled at his words. "No, Davis, you mustn't." Anwyn turned to him, grabbed his hand. "I need them to relax, to help me get past my loneliness. I'd be worse without them...much worse." Her entreaty tapered off. She sat down and began to cry. "I should never have mentioned it to that g-girl," she stuttered, "but Pandora was so friendly. She told me she was a g-good friend of Cynwyd's." Her voice grew faint, then picked up again. "I'm so alone!" she wailed.

"And you'd been drinking," Davis pointed out. He seemed unaffected by her tears. "Well, the cat's out of the bag now, so what is your big secret?"

Anwyn looked up at her husband, mascara tracks running down her cheeks to mix with her tears. "Davis, I loved you," she pleaded as she spoke, "b-but I'd had a little too much to drink at my debut. Can you recall that night I had my big coming out party at the Claridge? You left early, said you needed to get ready for a meeting the next morning. That was why I let one of the young lords take me home. When I awoke the next day, I didn't even remember which one. But I vaguely remember being intimate with a man...." Her eyes held a puzzled expression. "I must have drunk a lot of champagne...it was like soda pop, nothing but bubbles!"

Shocked at her mother's words, Cyn turned to her father. She heard only a low "hmmph."

"The following night you and I were together," Anwyn went on. "The moon was full, and we made love in the gazebo. It was so romantic; I imagined we were in a Hollywood film. You were as handsome as a movie star, and I was so beautiful. I wore a floaty chiffon dress in pink, and you called me a blushing rose, do you remember?" she implored.

Oh Daddy, Cyn thought, too shaken to curb her first reaction, *couldn't you come up with something more original?*

If Davis had once had a romantic gene, it was long gone. "I remember," he snapped. "You never said anything about what happened the night before."

"I just wanted to forget! When Cynwyd was born I

convinced myself that you were the father. Why not? We made love every night after that, so the chances were excellent that it was you. I had to believe it!"

The two looked at each other—entreaty in her eyes, slowly dissolving fury in his. Cyn sat there, astounded. She wished she hadn't heard all these intimate details about her parents. It wasn't right. Her heartbeat had speeded up, but her main reaction was disbelief—as if her emotions were in a state of suspended animation.

The room grew silent; her mother's sniffling the only sound. Davis was first to recover. "The thing to do," he said, "is to test my DNA with Cynwyd's. There are a number of private labs in the city. Once we know for certain, we can go on from there. If Cynwyd's and mine match, we'll forget the entire incident. It happened a long time ago."

Anwyn looked up, hopeful.

"And if they don't?" Cyn turned to her father.

"Things will get more complicated, but these problems are solvable. We have to take them one step at a time. You and I will give our samples to a lab tomorrow, Cynwyd. Then you'll have to take it from there. I must return to Cairo."

Cyn turned to her mother. "I wish you hadn't kept this secret for so long, Mama." She started to scold, but the grief on Anwyn's face was more than she could bear. She reached over and hugged her, noticing the gray hairs among the honey brown where Mama's head rested on her shoulder. "Don't worry, it will all work out. I'll call Aunt Cadi and ask her to stay with you for a little while—just so you won't be alone while this gets straightened out. I promise I won't ask her to move in permanently. That's up to you."

Grabbing a tissue from the box on the coffee table, Cyn wiped her mother's cheeks. "Pull yourself together, now, and keep away from the bottle. There's no need for that crutch anymore. We know everything, and no one is going to punish you."

"This has troubled you for a long time, Anwyn." Davis's voice was softer now. "A pity you didn't tell me sooner. I want you to get some counseling—at least try a few visits between now and when the DNA results come through. That could be several weeks, and I know an excellent therapist. Dr. Ben-Aaron is sympathetic. You'll feel better after talking to him. I'll arrange it."

So, the visit to Tirah's relatives had a positive side. Thank goodness for serendipity.

Cyn switched her gaze from mama to her father. "I'll wait for you in the Starbucks across the street, Daddy. Take your time to straighten out the divorce hang-ups and arrange the therapy sessions. Then you and Mama can say your goodbyes."

Impulsively, Cyn leaned over the couch and wrapped her arms around both her parents. Then she stood up and headed for the door. As she left, she took the wine bottle with her. Mama had to do this on her own.

Chapter 31

Sunday arrived. Tirah and Davis were gone, but the DNA lab had yet to report on the test results. Cyn could hardly wait to escape with Mac to his worry-free cartoon world.

"Do you live here with your parents?" she asked as they drove to Oyster Bay.

"Yes and no," Mac said. "The house is a modern version of an Elizabethan manor. You'll see it soon—creamy walls and black shutters. Ah, there it is." He parked. "A wing was added out back that's separate from the main building. Mom and Dad built it to attract me home after a short-lived and disastrous marriage."

"Oh!" she turned, startled. "I didn't know you had been married."

"Come inside, and I'll tell you about it." He escorted her down a flagstone path to the rear.

As they rounded the corner, Cyn saw a wide octagonal door. From a stained glass insert in the center, red, yellow and blue rays glinted in the sunshine. As the light moved with her steps, she caught an image of Superman appearing and disappearing in the glass. She tipped her head, trying to make the figure return.

Mac grinned. "He shows up only when the light hits at exactly the right angle."

"Oh, my. A bit retro, but it suits." She backed up,

tried again and smiled.

Spinning around, she turned to gaze at the wide expanse of lawn bordered by oaks and maples. They were leafless now, but behind them, thickly planted evergreens fenced the property. "It's beautiful. I can see how you'd hate to leave it."

"For now, it's the best of two worlds. Complete privacy and a garden view."

"In the fall, you'll have all the autumn colors splashed against that wall of dark green."

"Yeah, ruby red from the oak, yellow and orange from the maples. The Japanese ones turn a reddish bronze—like your hair. Last October, I looked out the window and found the colors for Oxy's costume."

"Inspiration, of course."

They entered a room filled with comfortable old furniture. A flat TV screen was mounted on the wall facing the couch, while two crushed beer cans and an empty pizza box shared the coffee table with a baseball mitt and a couple of remote control gadgets.

"Be right back," Mac said, grabbing the pizza box and beer cans. He returned with a bottle of wine. Two stemmed glasses clinked as they dangled from his fingers. "I've brought a Prosecco. Goes well with conversation."

Cyn looked intently at Mac. "Perhaps we should save the wine till afterwards. We have a lot to discuss."

"Not necessary. I'll satisfy your curiosity while we drink." He sat down beside her and filled their glasses. "In college I majored in business and minored in art. That really had me racing around campus. I wanted to draw but knew I'd be pitched into the business. Dad can be pretty forceful. When I graduated from Harvard, I took off for an extended surfing holiday in Hawaii. That's where I found Oxy, by the way—the live one."

"Is he a parrot?"

"Nope. You'll just have to wait and see," Mac teased.

"Go on, then."

"I met a bunch of surfing dudes on the Big Island. One day, when the waves weren't right, we hitchhiked up to the volcano. I was staring mesmerized by the heat and stench of sulfur in that hellish landscape when a blonde nearby let out a squeal. We were all far enough away from the edge of the crater to be in no danger, but she sounded scared, so I pulled her back. She latched onto our group, and me in particular. Somewhere along the way that mad summer, we got married." Mac shrugged. "Bringing her home was a big mistake." He gulped his wine, sputtered, looked embarrassed.

"Once we got back East, it didn't take long for Tiffany and me to agree that we had few interests in common. I was unhappy with the way my life was drifting. Too much of Dad in me, I guess. Tiffany hated her job and the cold weather, but the little gold digger got what she wanted before she agreed to a divorce. The settlement gave her enough money to open up a B&B on Maui—and the experience made me swear off commitments for life."

Cyn frowned. "That's a long time."

"I know." He looked at Cyn. "But that life is over. I've been reborn."

"Are you sure?"

"Getting surer by the moment." His look was hot enough to scorch her, but in it she could see vulnerability, too. It had not been easy for him to talk about his divorce.

"Thanks for telling me, Mac."

"I had to, if this relationship is going anywhere."

Her heart skipped a beat as she heard the special word. *Relationship....* Their friendship had just notched up a step. He was watching her intently. She should figure out how far she wanted this to go, but not now. "Go on with your tale," Cyn said instead.

"Afterward, Dad was eager to get me into the business. Mom liked the idea of having me close, so they built this extension to the house. It's a great space. Mom designed the Superman door as a bonus."

"I understand. And I'm so glad you trusted me with the story." She squeezed Mac's hand. "I'm ready to meet Oxy Moron now."

Taking their empty glasses, Mac led her into the sunny kitchen. "Wait here. I'll be back in a sec."

Cyn took in the long countertop of hand-painted tiles—not the usual hearts and flowers, but tiny Toon Town figures. *Oh, wow!* She laid her hands on the cool tiles. Cooking here would be a blast. With Bugs Bunny for inspiration, her domestic genes might kick in.

In a few minutes Mac returned, minus his jacket. Something on his dark green T-shirt moved. Cyn gulped as she noticed a six-inch-long creature with a curled tail blending into the shirt.

"Meet Oxy," he said, petting the animal with long light strokes.

She stepped closer. "Is that a lizard?"

"Yes. This one's a Jackson chameleon."

"It's not exactly pretty." She stared at the lizard's mottled skin and the three long horns on top of its head.

"No, but he's friendly. And quite remarkable. See

his bulging eyes? They rotate in a complete circle, and each one moves on its own. He can follow two different threats at the same time."

"That's amazing."

"Also, his tongue can shoot out the full length of his body. But, unlike me, he won't find you tasty." Mac winked. "Come here and meet him. Oxy likes to be petted."

"Don't we all?" Cyn murmured. Gingerly, she stroked the creature. "He enjoys it," she said in wonder.

"Most males do."

She snickered. "It's a gender-free pleasure, believe me."

"I'd be glad to oblige. Petting's a specialty."

"You're *so* accommodating." Cyn blushed but ignored his come-on, determined to stick to her reason for being here—at least, the one she would admit to. "Can you show me one of your strips featuring the other Oxy Moron?"

"Sure. In my story, the hero is named Oxy and his pet lizard is called Kami."

Cyn followed him into an airy room with tall windows on three sides. The fourth wall, lined with cork, serving as a bulletin board. Notes attached with pushpins fluttered as they passed it to reach the large easel. There, in black and white, lay several pages of the comic strip.

"I add the color at the end," Mac told her.

Cyn peered at the drawings. In the first panel Oxy Moron, looking like a cross between Superman and the Hulk, stood with legs apart, hands on hips. His pet chameleon clung to him. Kami's head was at Oxy's shoulder, its body and long tail extended across Oxy's chest, so that the stretched-out lizard resembled a bandit's bandoleer. The bubble on the panel above Oxy's head read, "I'm gonna get those two guys who're catchin' all these lizards and shippin' 'em 'round the world."

The succeeding panels showed Oxy stumbling through the underbrush and alerting the thieves. One of them turned a gun on him. "Well, well," his bubble read. "Hello, Moron." In the next panel, Kami lashed out with his tail, entangling the gun in its coils. His other eye watched the second bad guy, tongue flicking in and out to distract him as Oxy dispatched Thief Number One with a left-right jab. "Pow! Smack!"

In the last panel, two curvaceous females in long grass skirts piled string after string of leis around Oxy's neck. Mac's drawing caught the sheepish look on his hero's face perfectly.

"So, Oxy goes after the bad guys?"

"Yeah. He's starting small with lizard thieves, but Oxy's going to work up to drug dealers, arms traders, terrorists, oil barons—and just wait till he gets to Washington! He'll have a bumbling field day with lobbyists and crooked politicians."

"Wow, that's quite an agenda! Will he tackle the Wall Street bankers, too?"

"Absolutely. Just because my name is Morgan Chase doesn't mean they get a free ride."

"My kind of guy!" Cyn's laughter was tinged with appreciation. She bent closer to the drawing board to examine the big hero's face. "Do you know, I think Oxy resembles Prof Rocky."

"So you caught it, huh?" Mac's grin broadened. "It's my little in-joke."

"I thought you didn't like him."

"Well, he brought us together...and the class turned out to be pretty interesting. Some of our projects have helped me—and Oxy—focus on fresh ways to cope with the world. The tricks used to indoctrinate people have gone way beyond what I thought I knew. Learning how pervasive they are has been an eye-opener."

"It's frightening, but this is the twenty-first century. We've got to learn how to deal. Oxy is smart to blend technology with the old one-two punch."

Mac chuckled. "He likes to work with his hands, and he's got his lizard to help him with the brainy stuff."

"But why did you give him the professor's face?"

"I admit I read Marzin wrong at the start. He enjoys manipulating people, but I think he believes in his mission to open students' eyes. Inspire them to work for change. I'll credit him with that, but I couldn't resist having a little fun with him."

"Maybe your graphic novel and his linguistic study will be published at the same time." She clapped her hands, her smile mischievous. "You can do a book signing together."

Startled, Mac laughed aloud. "That visual is positively intoxicating. I love the way your mind works, Cynwyd Cleopatra. You're perfect for me."

She turned away, hiding her pleased reaction.

"Come, let me show you the rest of the place. You haven't seen my bedroom yet."

Cyn felt her pulse leap. "More of your sorcery, Merlin?"

"Count on it." He trailed kisses along her jaw and

under her earlobe. Moving over, he placed a kiss on each temple and a third on the spot between her eyes. Then, with Oxy on his shoulder, Mac pulled Cyn down the hall. By the time they reached his room, she was shivering with anticipation.

Still holding her, Mac slid his other hand down her back to press her close. "You belong in my life," he whispered.

Cyn brought her arms around his neck and leaned in even more. "I can tell." She'd meant only to tease him, but he caught her double meaning. As they shared this intimate moment, her heart sang.

Their lips met in a clinging kiss, tongues entwining. *I've tumbled for this man,* Cyn thought as heat radiated through her body. *Head over heels, and it feels so good....* She grew wet as Mac's thigh wedged between her legs. Digging her nails into his shoulders, she let go only so he could pull the sweater over her head.

He unhooked her bra and slipped it off. Her breasts were taut, heavy, the nipples already firm and pointing. "So beautiful," he murmured.

Cyn couldn't talk at all. Instead, she glowed.

Reaching down, Mac slid a nipple into his mouth, suckled and ran his teeth lightly across the tip. His hand caressed her other breast, his fingernail circling the aureole. She breathed faster.

Mac fell with her onto his bed. Laughing, they untangled their legs, shed the rest of their clothes. He reached for a condom, watching her the whole time. The desire in his eyes scorched her, but she bit back the love words that seemed determined to pop out of her mouth. This moment was for forgetting everything but pleasure.

Sunlight streamed through the window blinds, striping their bodies in gold and shadow. The memory of their lovemaking on the red couch kicked in again, and they writhed with slippery delight. They kissed everywhere, vying to see who could please the other most. Mac slid down Cyn's body to the auburn curls. His mouth moved lower, licking her as she squirmed and bucked, gasping her excitement until the tension burst. She let out a long, long sigh of satisfaction.

Grinning wickedly, Mac thrust inside her at just the right moment. Sliding back out ever so slowly, he thrust again and rocked. In a flash, their hot bodies echoed the rhythm of their pounding pulses. Cyn let go completely, screaming as her climax rose to shatter her. With a shout, Mac thrust one last, overwhelming time and joined her in the blazing blackout....

Afterward, they lay on the bed, Mac still inside her, waiting for their breathing to return to normal. Cyn couldn't wipe the silly, contented smile from her lips. She felt herself beginning to doze off. "Merlin's the right name for you, producer of magic," she murmured before she shut her eyes.

He whispered in her ear, "Only for you Queen Cleopatra. The magic wand is yours to command."

Chapter 32

An air of expectancy filled the classroom as Professor Marzin, muscles rippling under his pale blue shirt, reached up and wrote on the slick white board. The students slouched in their customary seats. Their psychodrama had been successful. They already knew their grades, and on this last day of classes, their mood was jubilant.

Everyone's, except for Cleopatra. Her anxiety and impatience for the DNA results colored all her responses.

Setting down his marker, the Prof pulled a stack of papers from his briefcase. "Today I'm returning the assignment in which you described yourselves. I've kept the page on your outward appearance, but it's time for a follow-up on the one about your inner selves.

"What I want now is your evaluation of our experiment in using different names. Four months have passed. Do you now perceive yourselves differently? Did anything occur while you were using your assumed names that you responded to in a new or unexpected way? Have your feelings about yourself undergone a change? Think carefully—even the slightest impressions will be important to me.

"To get you started and give you something of value to take home from this class, I've written a few lines on the board from a sonnet by Gwendolyn Brooks.

Please follow along with me as I read it."

Marzin turned toward the board, his voice projecting to the back of the room.

Exhaust the little moment. Soon it dies.
And be it gash or gold it will not come
Again in this identical disguise.

The class was silent, drinking in the meaning of the words.

After a moment, he handed back their earlier papers. "When you're done, leave both your old and new versions folded together here on the desk. Please keep your writing private—honor system. Everyone knows the grade you'll be receiving for the course, so let the possibility of anonymous fame in my book goad you into doing the best job you can this afternoon."

Thoughtful glances followed the professor as he walked out the door. Cleo turned to Merlin and shrugged. He winked at her and began to write.

She took a moment to deliberate. The class had turned out to be a grand adventure. It was up to her to let Rocky know.

Blocking out the worries she had brought, Cleo wrote of her delight in making new friends. In this class she'd gotten rid of inhibitions, grown to like who she was, even found she was capable of intimacy. When she didn't limit her options, her dreams had a real chance of coming true.

She told the professor how much she enjoyed using her skills where they were appreciated and applauded rather than judged and found wanting. With the new insights she'd developed in class, she could see hurtful remarks for what they were—recognize they were a reflection of the other person's problems, not flaws in herself.

Her conclusion was heartfelt. "I still can't fall backwards, but I no longer feel the need to be perfect." At the end of this last sentence, Cleo drew a little smiley face.

With a lightness of spirit she hadn't felt in weeks, she folded her pages in half. *I've finally unhooked myself from Daddy's expectations. It started the moment I realized that accepting the B grade didn't crush me. But I don't have to tell that to Rocky.*

She looked over at Merlin, who was twiddling his ever-present pen. Hard to picture him without it, the gold glittering as his fingers raced across a page to sketch a face or a body movement. Of course, there were those times when he didn't have a pocket to clip it to.... She stood grinning a moment longer as she imagined him naked.

When he didn't look up, she lifted the smooth river rock on the desk and added her paper to the pile beneath. As she lowered the heavy stone, she saw that someone had inked a cartoon on it—a stick figure waving a sheaf of papers. Tiny horns had been added to the top of its head.

Chuckling, she floated out of the room. The semester was over.

****

Merlin grudgingly admitted that he had found the class useful. Not only had he learned more about subtle forms of communication and manipulation, but he'd also learned more about himself. The assignments had helped him clear out old prejudices, so he could focus on new approaches to his problems. He crossed out "problems," inking over it until the word was indecipherable, then substituted "concerns." Yes, that was revealing enough.

Poking fun at himself for his early jealousy of Rocky, he drew a tiny wizard in a cone-shaped cap pointing his wand at a series of bubbles labeled "misconceptions," popping them open one by one until they vanished. He ended by informing Rocky that he was also writing a book, speculated on whose book would be published first.

The prof would take notice of that challenge. Maybe give him a scare. He deserved that much payback for the way he manipulated his students, even for their own good. Merlin signed his name with a flourish.

Placing his paper under the rock on the desk, Merlin added a Santa Claus hat to the stick figure, scribbled *"Adios"* above its head and sauntered out, heading for the beer joint.

He arrived to find the others busy exchanging real names and phone numbers. Christmas music played softly underneath the chatter. Swaying to the music, he sat down next to Cleo, brushing his thigh against hers.

She turned swiftly. "I've ordered you a pint. They've got Dos XX on tap today."

"Great." He listened to the happy buzz around him. "Glad it's over?" he asked.

"Yes, and no." She clinked glasses.

"Same goes. On the whole, it was a good four months. And it had super extracurricular benefits."

"It certainly did." She ran her fingernails around his wrists, tickling him, and smiled when she saw his eyes grow dark. "What did you want to talk to me about? I'm eager to hear, but this may not be a good time for you to tell me. New problems have arisen with my mother since my dad left."

"I'm sorry. Is there anything I can do to help?"

"Afraid not. But it should be resolved within a week or two—I hope."

"Then try to put it out of your mind, for now. I'm impatient to implement my idea...and it should take your mind off the other problems."

"Well...Okay."

They moved to a nearby booth for privacy. Mac could wait no longer. "It's about a job," he blurted. He caught a fleeting glimpse of disappointment in Cyn's eyes. *What had she expected?* But he let the question ride, eager to continue. "You know I've been publishing a dozen trade magazines ever since my father retired."

Her fingernails began to tap against the glass. "You told me when we visited the museum."

"It's an energy-consuming job, and I want more time to work on my graphic novel."

"You need that," Cyn agreed. "We can't neglect the adventures of Oxy Moron if he's going to save the world."

Caught up in his presentation, Mac ignored her facetious comment. "I've been thinking of hiring a business manager and assistant who'll gradually take over the day-to-day functions. She can handle the ad revenues, computerize the subscription lists, enforce deadlines, and try anything she can think of to make the office run more smoothly. Got the idea?"

Cyn nodded, impatience battling with nervous expectation inside her.

"This would leave me free to spend my time on

editorial decisions and on creating new magazines. So many fields are opening up—look at the latest flying car, for example! Lots of opportunities."

"Yes, I see." He ignored the tinge of fear in her voice.

"I'd still be publisher, but I'd like to get the routine stuff off my hands."

With an effort, Cyn kept her tone light. "Sounds like an excellent idea, Mac. I know how hassled you are trying to do it all and take care of Oxy, too."

"Now you're teasing me, but I'm serious. Would you be interested in trying out for the job?"

Oh my God. Her heart began to pound.

"I've seen how well you handled all the stuff Rocky threw at you, and you told me about the magazine you managed for a month when the editor took off with the publisher. I'm sure you're capable of making my office run more smoothly."

A frightened look crossed Cyn's face. He shouldn't be telling her this now. The timing was all wrong. She was a nervous wreck holding herself together while waiting for the genetic lab results.

"Mac, no! I haven't enough experience for the job. I couldn't take on so much responsibility. Surely, you know I'm not up to that!"

Her look of dismay bothered him. "I know you can do it, Queen Cleopatra. You shouldn't doubt yourself." He covered her free hand with his. "Why do you do this?"

His question was too much. Setting her beer stein down with a thump, Cyn jerked away. "How could you, Mac? It's not fair!" Her voice squeaked, but she didn't care who heard. "I thought you knew me better than this. I'm not a queen, dammit. I don't command. You need an experienced executive for the position you're offering."

Scowling at him, she grabbed her purse and ran out of the bar.

****

Dumbfounded, Mac watched her go. Had he been so wrong? Did she still have that insecurity albatross hanging around her neck?

He'd handled the situation badly. Shouldn't have blurted out his offer, but built up to it. Laid on a bit of flattery first. He knew how to manage people better than this, but Cyn rattled him as no one else ever had. He'd thought for so long before making his proposal that, to him, her acceptance was obvious. She was perfect for the job.

Mac gulped down the rest of his beer. Should he follow her? If he left Cyn alone she might get over that first scared reaction. But maybe not. Women's brains were a mystery. He'd better not take the chance of being wrong again.

Fishing in his wallet for money, Mac dropped some bills on the table and hurried out.

He looked up and down the street, but Cleopatra was gone.

****

Cyn drove home automatically, oblivious to the honking horns as her speed changed with her thoughts. She was so disappointed. She'd expected Mac's grand idea to be more personal—he *had* used the word "relationship." She wasn't looking for a marriage proposal. Of course not. But she'd wanted to hear words that would bring them closer together.

Something more intimate, maybe cooking together in his cartoon kitchen—well, closer than that. But not an offer of a job just now, when her old life was falling apart. When she wasn't even sure who her own father was.

Typical. Just like a man to put work ahead of everything else. How could he offer her a position so way out of her league? She might be ready for it in three or four years, but not yet. Not now!

Mac shouldn't have put her through this stress. It was wrong. He wasn't thinking of who she was and what they meant to each other. She'd believed he understood her as no one else ever had. Yet here he was, asking too much of her. It was Daddy all over again.

As her anger rose, Cyn began to gasp for breath. Her heart pounded. With a curse, she pulled off the Expressway at the first exit and parked at the side of the road. She had to get hold of herself.

Forcing her mind to block out all thoughts, she concentrated on breathing. In...out. In...out. Gradually, her breaths slowed and grew more even. When at last she felt more in control, Cyn was surprised to find that while she'd been pulling herself together, a part of her mind had turned in a new direction.

What am I doing? her inner voice asked. *Do I hear myself? Only an hour ago I'd been convinced that I'd outgrown Daddy, and here I am, letting Mac push the same old buttons again.*

NO! Mac wasn't pushing them—she was. By not trusting herself. By getting angry and blaming him to hide her fear of failure. She mustn't do this!

She wouldn't allow her old sick response to

destroy what was developing between the two of them. It didn't matter who her father really was. Mac offered her the job because he trusted her, believed in her. Maybe he even loved her a little, and this was his way of showing it.

She had the courage to take on this job. In fact, she'd overwhelm him with her efficiency, amaze him with her ideas. Even though she didn't have that much experience, she had all the other qualifications—ambition, the longing to prove herself, the motivation to wow the publishing world. And there was something else she had going for her—she was in love with the boss!

With a long sigh, Cyn put the car in gear and drove back onto the road. It was time for an apology. She'd call Mac as soon as she got home. But as she pulled into her driveway, she heard another car pull in right behind her.

He was here!

****

Mac got out of his car just as Cyn ran over, nearly bowling him down. He grabbed her and held on tightly.

"I'm sorry," he said. "I wasn't thinking clearly."

She placed her fingers over his mouth. "No, no, it's me. I've been a jerk. Fell into my old pattern without even realizing it. All I needed was a little time alone to get back to my new self—my real self. Can you forgive me?"

He pulled her fingers away, squeezed her hand. "Then you've changed your mind? You'll give it a try?"

"It's a dream job, Mac, you know that. I'm hooked. If you're willing to teach me the ropes, I've got the nerve to try it."

He picked her up and swung her around and around. "You've got more than nerve," he assured her. "You've got talent and tenacity. I know it's a prejudiced gender reference," Mac grinned. "But you've got the balls, Cynwyd Westland. It'll be my pleasure to help you over the initial hurdles."

"There'll be lots. Each job you mentioned has its own specs."

"None too hard for a born executive to handle. We'll work together until you're comfortable. I'm not going to leave you alone and race off to Oxy. The big guy's waited a long time for my attention. He's got a lizard's patience."

Cyn laughed. "My competition! But, Mac, are you quite sure about the job offer? It's such a big responsibility...and your father?"

"Big M's agreed. He believes I know what I'm doing." Mac looked pleased to say the words. "Suppose we try it for six months, at a salary commensurate with the position. And did I mention benefits? Health insurance, pension, sick days, dental plan...the works."

"The works, you say? Just what other benefits do you have in mind?"

"Your own corner office, big desk, couch."

"Any other fringe benefits?"

"Making out with the boss?"

She giggled. "I'll want that written into the contract."

"Deal!" Pressing her close, he ran his fingers down her spine. "I'm sure I can accommodate whatever you want. This is definitely a job with perks."

Cyn clung to him, wriggled her hips, then pulled

away. "Come inside. My driveway is no place to make such a momentous decision. You can keep me company while I consider it—from several different positions."

Oh, yeah.... He nudged her toward the front door.

As Mac stepped over the threshold, he turned back, glanced around. This was not the moment for a chill to creep up the back of his neck. "Dammit," he muttered. "What's wrong now?" The icy feeling shocked him, momentarily wiping out his euphoria.

Someone was watching.

He scanned the area, but no one was in sight.

"Mac," Cyn called. "Is everything all right?"

Shrugging off his discomfort, Mac continued inside. Time to conjure up the thrilling methods a sorcerer would use to rid Cyn of her doubts. She *would* accept his proposal...uh, proposition.

The door locked behind him.

Chapter 33

Excursion day! Merlin entered the museum first. Cleo, Tony, and Alice, with Merry clutching Cleo-patta, trailed behind. A dozen visitors followed them in. One, in a high-collared army jacket and a dark woolen hat with a pompom on top, was the last to push through the turnstile.

The DNA lab had not yet contacted her, but Cleo was determined to banish worry from her thoughts. She would enjoy today's excursion to the fullest.

As the group entered a room devoted to the origins of printing, from the corner of his eye Merlin glimpsed a shadow pass the door. He was too busy playing guide to let it distract him.

"Say," Tony called out, "this machine looks a lot like my *abuelito's* wine press." He walked over to it and peered at the metal frame holding the type.

Alice read the placard. "It *was* a wine press, and Gutenberg converted it for printing. How delicious— our first printed Bible came from a device built to make wine!"

"*In vino veritas.*" Tony nodded. "Nice bit of irony."

Merry looked around the room. "I don't see anyone ironing."

"Tony's iron is a different kind." Cleo struggled not to laugh. "But the words iron and press do go together, don't they?"

"I never made that connection before." Merlin sounded surprised.

"You learn—"

"Don't say it!" He held up his hand, stopping Tony. The others groaned. "I thought my friends were too intellectual to resort to clichés."

"Guess you're associating with lowlifes," said Cleo. "Tsk tsk."

Merry looked up at the adults, confused by their tone, but Tony picked her up and bumped heads with her. "It's just grownups' way of playing with words, *chica.* You can start the boring lecture now," he told Merlin. "We're listening."

Merlin raised an eyebrow. "Giving me attitude, are you? Just for that, I'll explain things to Merry, and you can all eavesdrop." He took the child's hand and brought her closer. "That metal plate you're looking at inside the press is filled with words cut into pieces of lead." Picking up a leftover slug, he passed it around. "See the letters here on the edge, Merry? Each line of type is laid into a frame like this one. When all the stories, along with headlines and photos, fill up the frame, it's screwed tight. Then comes the ink. This young man will show you how it was done in the old days."

A teenage boy in a printer's apron walked over. He picked up a half-round leather ball with a wooden handle, dipped it into the bowl of ink and rubbed it along the metal. Spreading a blank sheet of paper over the inked frame, he cranked down the press cover. A moment later he lifted the top, took out the paper and waved it to dry the ink. At Merlin's nod, he handed the page to Merry.

"Look, look!" The excited child showed everyone her newspaper.

"Listen, guys." Alice read from the museum brochure. "The Chinese had type like this way back in the ninth century. And Marco Polo brought a book back to Italy in the eleven hundreds."

"I thought he brought back spaghetti," Cleo said.

"That, too."

"Don't mention food," Tony called out. "I can hear my stomach grumbling."

"Shhh." Alice poked him with her elbow.

Too late. Merry heard. "Is it lunchtime, Mama?"

"Not yet, sweetie. There's a lot more to see."

Merry stood on tiptoe to look at the press. "That's a big screw."

"It is, indeed." Merlin led the chuckling group into the next room. As he herded them next door, he caught sight again of the flitting shadow.

****

In the restroom across the hall, Pandora grabbed a paper cup and filled it from the faucet. She had been following the group since they arrived and had almost been caught twice. She hadn't been recognized, not in this dorky hat with the earflaps down to hide her hair. Something must have caught Merlin's eye, however. Probably the pompom. She should have cut it off, but Ma would have killed her. She couldn't guess what had gotten into Ma to knit something so frivolous.

As Merlin had started to turn the first time, she'd ducked behind a display case—the one holding a copy of the Declaration of Independence. She'd wanted to steal it and shove it at her mother, underlining the bit about the pursuit of happiness. Fat lot of good it would do her until she turned twenty-one. *Fat lot of good...fat lot of good.* The phrase went round and round in her mind. She couldn't shake it out....

****

The group entered a Colonial newspaper office. Cleo walked over for a closer look at an open suitcase leaning against a shelf wall. Capital letters filled partitions in the upper part, small letters in the lower.

"I'll be darned," she said. "So that's what the marks I use in proofreading stand for. I've written U. C. and L. C. dozens of times, but never dreamed upper case and lower case referred to an actual suitcase."

"More trivia." Merlin winked. He watched Merry jump up and down, trying to peer into a display case. "These are toys children owned long ago, Merry," he said, picking her up. "See the dolls in here? Little girls like you played with them when our country was brand new." He pointed to a cornhusk doll.

"I like the other one better." The second doll in the case wore a long white dress and a lace cap over brown curls. Real eyelashes were glued to her bright blue glass eyes. Merry leaned Cleo-patta on the counter. "See, Patta," she cooed. "This dolly wears a nightie like yours. You and she can be friends." She touched her doll's hand to the glass. "Tell her to come out and play."

Cleo overheard. "I'm sure she'd love to, honey, but the case is locked."

The child nodded. "That dolly has a cold, Patta," she explained. "She has to stay inside and take her 'medsin.'" The group looked at each other and grinned.

They left the Colonial room and walked on. As

they turned a corner, Merlin caught a glimpse of something round and black bobbing up and down. This time he twisted around, but it was gone.

****

Pandora looked into the mirror. Her eyes flew open wider. *Oh my God!* She hadn't noticed the urinals. Her refuge was a men's room. She hurried over to the entrance and stood cowering behind the door. It was quiet outside, but behind her she heard a toilet flush. *That's it!* Pulling open the door, she peeked out.

No one was in the hall. With a whooshing breath, Pandora slipped back into the corridor. She'd missed the door sign—a newsboy in a slouched cap holding up a newspaper with "Men" as its headline. Her nerves were shot, her brain a hive of angry bees buzzing in her head. Raising her arms, she pressed her hands over the cap's earflaps and squeezed, trying to stop the noise. If she could only silence that thrumming! She dropped down on a nearby bench and scrunched her eyes tight.

How dare Rocky give me a C for that bullshit course! I'll have to hack into the school computer, change the grade before Ma sees it. Queen Cleopatra settled for a B and even gave Rocky that big smile. All those smiles—doesn't her face ever crack? Miss Royalty, with her rich ex-husband to support her. I hate her and her smarmy friends and her snooty house and her fancy car. She's old, yet she's got two guys sniffing at her. And a kid as well—I saw that hug in the library. It's not fair! Why does she look at me the way she does instead of the way I want her to?

Oh, shut up, Head. Pandora twisted her neck back and forth, from side to side. Then she clamped her hands over her covered ears again.

****

Merlin led the group into the linotype room. The machine's operator, a bald man with a gold tooth among the yellowed ones, smiled at them. "This machine was in use when I was a boy," he said. "If you'd like, I'll make each of you a souvenir lead slug with your name on it."

"Yes," they chorused. Cleo winked at Merlin, delighted with how well their excursion was working out.

Then Merry spoke. "I don't wanna bug," she pouted.

"A bug?"

"That's what a slug is. Nana told me."

"This slug is a different kind," the printer said. "No need to worry." He turned on the machine and put his gnarled fingers on the keys. A loud clatter followed. He turned to Merry. "What's your name, little miss?"

"I'm Merry." She held up her doll. "And this is Cleo-patta. Can her name go on a slug, too?"

"Yes, indeed."

Alice spelled the names for him as he typed, and a lead slug clattered out of the machine. "It has to cool," he warned, then after a few seconds handed it to Merry. "And here comes your doll's." He looked up. "Any of you grownups want a souvenir?"

"Yes," they chorused.

"Which name shall we use?"

"The semester's over," Cyn said. "It's farewell to Alice, Tony, Merlin and Cleopatra. Let's use our real names."

She turned back to the linotype operator. "How about one for each couple? That will be Tayo and

Audrey, Mac and Cyn."

"Do you want me to put 'loves' between the names?" he asked, his eyes twinkling.

The four looked at each other and nodded.

****

The buzzing in her head grew louder. Pandora squeezed her eyes tight. *Cleo knows I'm here. I can feel it. The credit card ploy should have freaked her out, but it didn't. Even the police let me get away with it. Teachers. Cops. All that pompous authority. I can manipulate them all. And I got some great boots out of it!*

A twisted grin spread across her mouth, then faded away.

Cleo's snotty ex-husband should have played into my hands, but he let me down, like all the doctors do. I should have realized it was hopeless after my hospital stay. I lucked out when I tricked her mother, but where's Cleo's reaction? Does she even know? She'll think I'm gone now that class is over, but how wrong she'll be. I'm never going away.

Hunching down, Pandora pressed her arms close, holding her elbows as she rocked on the bench.

Ma was stupid to think she could fix me by carting me off to that retreat. What a farce! All that pious praying on your knees. Good thing I got away before they decided to use me for a human sacrifice. I'm a step ahead of all the dumbwits. Didn't I ace those college scholarships—with only a little help from my computer? Not from God. Who helped Cleopatra get where she is? Her credit card said she's not Cleopatra, she's Cynwyd. Pretty, pretty Cynwyd, Cyn sin SIN.

Saliva dribbled out the corner of Pandora's mouth.

She rubbed it off with the back of her hand, wiped it on her sleeve. *How much longer will they be? I can't keep waiting. Got to find my opportunity before...oops, there they go, heading toward the big presses. Close call number three. They won't escape me—I'm too smart for them.*

Standing up, Pandora stuck her middle finger straight up and waved it at the disappearing group. She shook her head like a rattle, the pompom bouncing. *I'd better get my brain back on track. Mustn't be found out now, when I'm so near my goal. The timing's right. I can feel it. Something's gonna happen, and I have to be there....*

****

"Hey Mac, how much more?" Tayo called out. "The little one is getting tired."

"Am not," Merry piped up.

Tayo looked down at her, his smile tender. "Are, too."

At the head of the group, Mac turned. Merry's doll was dragging on the floor. "One last place to see, and we'll head out for lunch. Come on, I want to show you the big presses."

The acrid smell of ink and metal permeated the vast room. Its gray walls cut the glare from the large windows at back. Four huge presses sat in a row with space to walk around them. Tables had been placed alongside for stacking and baling the bundles before they were carted off.

"These four-color presses were used for top-quality magazines," Mac told them. "Each one prints a different color, and the pages have to align perfectly. No blurry lines allowed on the slicks."

"What's this for?" Tayo asked. A table standing between the second and third press held a stack of tracing paper. Next to the pile were red markers, a razor-edged knife, a glue pot and a brush. A railing surrounded the table to keep visitors from touching.

"It's the make-ready stuff," Mac said. "The folio— that's a four-, eight-, or sixteen-page sheet—goes through each machine. In a trial run, if some of the print comes out a lighter color because the type is worn, the inspector circles the spot. Then thin pieces of paper matching the size of the circles are cut out and glued underneath, layer by layer, until the sheet is raised to make a perfect match."

"It's hard to believe each color needed a different press run," Tayo said. "The process was so primitive back then."

"It wasn't so long ago," Mac pointed out. "Here comes a printer to demonstrate."

A round-shouldered man with a wild mane of white hair emerged from a door to the left. Padded earmuffs dangled from a cord around his neck.

Cyn turned to Mac. "Go on with the demo without me," she whispered. "Have to make a pit stop. I'll be back in time to catch most of the action."

He nodded and she slipped out.

Mac shook hands with the printer. "Everyone, this is John, affectionately known as Einstein—for the obvious reason. He'll show you how the presses work. We've got them set up for a job run, and you'll each get a four-page souvenir to take home."

Mac nodded to the press operator, then turned back to them. "Cover your ears. It gets pretty noisy."

The old man pushed up his earmuffs and flipped a

switch. The sudden shocking racket assaulted the eardrums. Dropping her Cleopatra doll, Merry covered her ears.

In an instant, the first press started moving sheets rapidly through the machine. Fascinated, the group gathered close to see the pages come out. For just a second, Merry was left alone.

Audrey turned around. "Where's Merry?"

Before she could take a step, Pandora came running out from between the huge presses, passing the make-ready table. She had shed her hat, and her blood-red hair flowed around her shoulders. Her eyes were wild. Reaching out, she grabbed hold of the child's sweater.

In her other hand, raised high, she gripped the lethal knife.

Chapter 34

Audrey screamed.

Mac turned, saw, stepped forward. Tayo followed suit.

"Stay where you are!" Pandora shrieked. The huge machines clattered away as she brought the knife down near the child's face.

The men stopped moving. Mac didn't take his eyes off the knife.

Tayo's fist clenched. "*Madre de Dios*! Is she loco?"

"My fault," Mac muttered. "The bitch isn't harmless." His face remained set, his mind working rapidly. Cyn mustn't be allowed to walk back into this. He had to get Einstein's attention. Slim chance, but the printer might be able to slip away while Pandora focused on them.

Audrey stretched out her arms. "My baby—she's got my baby!" Again Tayo started toward her, but Pandora shouted once more.

"I mean what I say!" The point of the knife nicked Merry's neck. Her whimpers turned into screams.

Mac knocked over the pile of newspapers on the table beside him. It caught the printer's attention. His hand fumbled for the emergency button near the switch. He couldn't reach it, seemed afraid to turn around. As his hand scrambled for it in vain, Mac moved again, forcing Pandora to concentrate on him.

"Stay back!" she roared. "I'm in charge here. And you, kid, shut up!" Scooping up Merry with one arm, Pandora shook the child. "Quit kicking, brat." Her glance darted around the room. "Where's Cleo? She's the one I want."

No one answered. The presses continued to roar. Mac caught Tayo's eye. They began to move in tandem.

Baring her teeth, Pandora slid the knife closer to Merry's ear. "I NEED TO SEE CLEO!"

"What do you want with my baby?" Audrey shouted.

Pandora ignored her. "My mother will handle this kid, just like she took care of my sister, Faith. Cleopatra can't have her!"

"You're raving!" Mac shouted, taking another step closer. "Drop the knife, Pandora."

"Keep away!" She began walking backwards, still holding both the knife and the squirming child.

"No!" Audrey ran toward her, arms held out.

"I'll cut her!" Reaching across the child, she grabbed at a curl that had fallen over Merry's shoulder, caught it by her fingertips. The knife flashed. A lock of hair fell to the floor.

Audrey stopped short, gasped. Everyone stared at the dark spiral lying on the tile.

Pandora's eyes flickered, blinking at the curl that lay in a beam of sunlight. The presses' roar climbed to a murderous cacophony. A canny look spread across her face as her eyes focused on something only she could see. She gripped the child tighter still, dug her nails into the chubby arm, and began to scream.

"You're being punished, Faith!" A shudder ran through her tall frame. "Bad girl!" Her tone grew higher, became childlike. "You made Papa yell at Ma, but Ma's telling Papa it's his fault. If he keeps yelling he'll bust a blud vesl." Staring at the blood oozing from Merry's cut, she began to shake. "All that blood! Now Papa's picking up the knife. He's rushing toward Mama!" With a blood-curdling yell, Pandora raised the blade high.

"Stop! Don't do it," Audrey shrieked. "Give her back to me. She's just a baby!"

Her words finally penetrated. Pandora stared at Audrey. "You lie! She's not yours. I saw her hanging on to Cleo."

"MOMMEEEE!" Merry screeched, her high treble just audible in the din. She began to hiccup as she tried harder to squirm out of Pandora's grip.

Audrey took a step forward. "Merry is *my* daughter," she screamed.

Mac stared at Tayo. His chin jutted forward.

Tayo's thumb rose. Message received.

The printer pointed a gnarled finger at Pandora. "Lady, that knife is honed sharp as a razor. Put it down!"

"Never!" She pulled the blade away from Merry's neck and waved it at the old man.

The moment the knife moved away from the child, Mac and Tayo leaped forward. Before they could reach Pandora, the rear door opened. Cleo walked in.

"Cleo, run! Get help!" Mac shouted.

Pandora turned. The knife stopped its stroke in mid-air. Dropping the child, Pandora lunged for Cleo.

Tayo headed for Merry as Mac ran toward Cyn.

The Pat-a-doll lay in his path. He tripped, started to fall. "Shit!" The word exploded from his mouth. Turning the movement into a skid, he slid across the floor, straight at Pandora.

With a gasp, Cyn tried to move out of Pandora's way. As she swung around, her arm flung out. It caught on the point of the knife. Blood ran down her sleeve. Mac's heartbeat accelerated. In a split second, his anger turned to rage.

Pulling away from the knife, Cyn slung her purse at Pandora. It caught the girl on the chin just as Mac sent his body skidding into Pandora, feet first, and knocked her down.

The knife flew into the air. Mac lunged for it, caught it by the blade and flung it as far as he could. He looked at his hand, startled, as blood began to well up. He hadn't even felt it.

The pressroom was starting to look like a battlefield.

Tayo thrust Merry into her mother's arms, raced over to place his foot firmly on a moaning Pandora's back. Mac stood up and reached for Cyn. He held her close, his good hand pressing above the slash in her arm to staunch the bleeding.

"Nonononono!" Pandora wailed.

Cyn stared at Pandora and shuddered. She buried her face in Mac's chest. "I swear," she mumbled against him, "I can feel the girl's bitterness in my gut, smell her sick fear."

Grim-faced, Mac stroked her back. "Don't go feeling sorry for her," he muttered. "See what she's done. What she almost did. I wanted to plunge the knife into her myself."

The printer hurried to the switch as fast as his old legs would carry him. The presses ground to a stop.

In the shocking silence, Merry's sobs echoed.

They didn't drown out Pandora's moans. She had quit fighting. Her body lay limp on the floor, her head swaying from side to side. "Nooo...noooo...." The eerie sound spewed out of her twisted mouth.

Audrey ran over with Merry in her arms. "Give me your T-shirt," she ordered Tayo. Thrusting the child at him, she found a hole in the shirt, stuck in her finger and ripped the cloth apart. As Mac continued to hold Cyn close, Audrey tied the strips of shirt tightly around her arm above the wound.

"Thank God the blood isn't gushing," Mac muttered. "Pandora missed the artery."

"Your hand!" Cyn cried.

"Hand cuts bleed a lot." He held it high, stopping the flow. "See, it looks worse than it is." He pressed his lips tightly together, hiding the fact that his hand had begun to throb. "Security will be here in a minute with a first aid kit." Mac turned to Tayo. "Pandora's down for the count. Cut a piece of twine from the bale over there and tie her wrists. The knife is under the make-ready table."

Tayo crawled underneath, grabbed the knife. He cut a length of twine and tied her wrists tight, digging into Pandora's skin. He looked toward Mac.

"Good." It was a small revenge.

The horror and dread were over in moments, yet it felt as if they'd been immobilized for hours. Mac felt Cyn wince with pain and loosened his grip. Her face was turning green. "You're not going to throw up?" he asked in concern.

"The adrenaline must be wearing off. I'll be okay. Is everything under control?" Her voice trembled.

"It is," Mac assured her. He pressed a kiss to her cheek. "Tayo has Pandora subdued, and the printer has called security. But you need a doctor."

"It's just a nick," Cyn protested. "Doesn't hurt much, or I would have fainted."

"Security can handle the police, but I'm calling for a paramedic. You've lost too much blood. The wound needs cleaning, and maybe stitches."

"Yours does, too!"

"Don't fret. I'll let them look me over as well." Picking her up to sit on a sorting table, Mac tried to manage his cell phone with one hand.

"Let me do that." Audrey took the phone and punched in 9-1-1.

For a moment Cyn swayed. Her lips moved. "Merlin-Mac. Alice-Audrey. Tony-Tayo. Cleo-Cyn." Her voice echoed the singsong Welsh that always appeared under stress. "Mac, who are we? I'm not sure who anyone is, or what name to call them. What a crazy ending to the day…to the term…." The last words came out in a whisper.

Mac kissed her temple, held her tighter.

Gritting her teeth, Cyn gazed at them all. "My God, we're the walking wounded. Was Merry cut bad? How's her neck?"

"She's fine," Audrey said, retying Cyn's tourniquet. "I always carry Band-Aids in my purse. That's all she needed, but the cut on your arm requires more."

"The paramedic will be here soon." Mac hoisted himself onto the table beside Cyn and cradled her in his arms.

She snuggled into him. "We should have called for Oxy. He would have taken care of the bad guy."

"Oxy?" Mac burst out laughing. "I never thought I'd laugh today, but you've done it, my Queen." He kissed her lightly, eyes, nose and mouth.

"Sorcerer," she mumbled into his shirt. "Do you think the dirty tricks are over?"

"I don't think she'll be released anytime soon," Mac said. "The hospital will keep Pandora, for sure. A psychiatrist will take over from the police."

"Shouldn't I call her mother, Mac?"

"You've done enough for the bitch. I know she's sick, but I still resent all the misery she's caused. Leave her parents to the cops."

"Okay." If Cyn expected more, she didn't show it. With a hesitant smile, she finally closed her eyes.

Chapter 35

The DNA report came by regular mail. Tapping the envelope against her fingernails, Cyn decided to open it in her mother's presence.

Mama seemed greatly improved since her twice-a-week visits with Dr. Ben-Aaron. She called Cyn only every other day, and her demands for help had moderated. If the results of the genetic report were positive, she'd run over to the Viennese bakery and buy that rum cake Mama loved. Come to think of it, she'd bring the cake whatever the results, along with large size lattes from Starbucks. They'd both need the lift…and the caffeine. It would serve as a celebration.

Or a wake.

When she arrived in mid-afternoon the next day, Cyn met a different woman. Mama's hair had been shaped into a daring urban pixie cut. Her deep green designer suit was worn with panache. Her eyes were definitely emerald today, and the defining point—her confident smile—was so far from Cyn's last visit, she was amazed. Despite the anxious flicker that crossed her face, mama looked years younger.

"I haven't opened the letter yet," Cyn said. She handed her mother the cake box and sat down. "Thought it would be better if we heard the news together."

"Hurry up," Anwyn waved toward the envelope.

"Let's find out." Her cheeks were flushed.

Cyn removed the lids from the lattes, took a sip. "First, tell me about your therapy sessions. You look marvelous." She felt like teasing her, just for a moment.

Her mother preened. "That can wait. I do want to talk about them, but the suspense has me jumpy. Let's get it over with."

She examined her mother once more, pleased with what she saw. Nodding, Cyn tore open the envelope. Anwyn sat white-knuckled, gripping the chair arms. The paper rattled as Cyn unfolded the report, read the words. She looked up without expression, got the reaction she hoped for, and grinned. "The match is positive."

Moisture surfaced in her mother's eyes, then spilled over, streaking her cheeks. Cyn reached out and hugged her. "It's good news," she murmured, her eyes filling, too. "No more crying—we have our answer."

Gradually, Anwyn's tears stopped. She blew her nose. "Now I can tell you about my therapy, Cynwyd. Something stupendous happened in my last session. Dr. Ben-Aaron called it a *gestalt*. I suddenly realized that I had been passing on the guilt for my behavior that night of my debut to Davis. Remember what I said?"

Cyn nodded.

"I couldn't face my remorse, so I grew angry and placed all the blame on Davis for leaving early. To cover up my secret anxiety, I punished him; became selfish and demanding. In a way, I punished myself, too—I killed my chance to be happy." Mama sighed. "I was a spoiled child, but I should never have allowed myself to drink to the point of blackout. In those days, I grew petulant if I didn't get my own way."

Cyn raised an eyebrow, and her mother blushed.

"You think I never outgrew it, and I guess you're right. It's a good thing Davis stayed around all those years to watch over you, despite my behavior. I owe him a tremendous apology. And you, too, Cyn dear, for you got the backlash. I'm truly sorry."

Awed by Anwyn's candor, Cyn got up and stared out the window. It took a few moments to come to terms with Mama's revelations. Finally, she took a deep breath and turned back. "It's all in the past, Mama. We can't help who we are, only try to learn from our mistakes. I didn't turn out too badly, did I?"

"Oh, Cynwyddie, my dear. You're wonderful. From here on, I'll to try to live up to what you want in a mother."

"You signed the divorce papers for daddy?"

"Yes. And I'm going to make a new start with my life. I'm barely over fifty. That's still young today."

"The way you look now, you could pass for thirty-five."

"We'd be sisters!"

Cyn bit her lip. "I love you, Mama, but we're not sisters. I'd like to be closer from now on, but it's time we each shaped our own lives."

"Yes, you're right." Cyn's mother gazed at her. "There's no turning back the clock, is there?" She sat up straighter. "But we're stronger now. We can do it."

"My, but you've gotten smart in a hurry!" Cyn laughed and hugged her mother again. "Come on, let's cut into that rum cake before our coffee gets cold."

****

"I didn't know the job offer included traveling," Cyn teased. "That's a perk you forgot to mention."

She and Mac stood on the pier at Key West awaiting the arrival of his parents. She had recovered from her ordeal of last week. The medics had cleaned and placed a butterfly clamp on the cut. They'd bandaged her arm, given her a tetanus shot, and left. It was almost healed.

Mac smiled at her. "I didn't want to let you out of my sight. Besides, I'm eager for you to meet Big Morgan and Stephanie. What better way than by coming to wish them *bon voyage?* By the time they return, you'll be handling your new position with aplomb."

Cyn laughed. "Aplomb...I love that word. I'll be happy if I'm over my nervousness by then."

"Oh, you will be." He winked. "And in the meantime, you can recuperate in the tropics for a weekend."

"Bliss." She grinned. "Odd that the hotel had only one room available with an ocean view."

"It isn't at all odd that only one room was reserved. As you can see, I badly need an executive secretary to handle these arrangements."

"Indeed. Accent on the *executive,* of course."

"Definitely." He patted her butt. "We'll watch the sunset tonight, after the yacht sails. Then dinner under the stars."

"Why, Mac, you're turning into a romantic."

"Moi?" he kidded. "Never let it be said."

Was he blushing? Cyn changed the subject. "Were you able to find out more about Pandora?"

"Yeah, although we'll never know how much is true. Dad has a golfing buddy at the hospital where they admitted her, and he managed to get a version of the story."

"I'll bet it's sordid."

Mac shrugged. "Pandora had a sister who was ten years older. Her own conception was an accident, I gather."

"It's hard to imagine her parents ever getting together, much less after ten years. Her mother is so rigid, so sternly religious."

"Outsiders can never fully understand family dynamics," Mac shrugged. "I gather the sister Faith rebelled, filled up on pharmaceuticals and fell, hitting her head on an iron bedstead."

"Oh my. Pandora still has a bed with an iron frame. I noticed it on my one visit."

"Apparently she witnessed the whole thing, including her sister dropping a handful of pills that young Pandora picked up and ate. Meanwhile, her mother accused her father of being too indulgent, and Papa rose from weeping over the body and went after Ma with a knife. That was when Pandora threw up and was carried from the scene. At least, it's the story the psychiatrists managed to get out of her and Mrs. Bronski."

"How horrible."

"We'll never know how Pandora might have turned out if she hadn't been there watching...." Mac's voice trailed off.

Cyn sighed. "She is getting help now?"

"Yes, but under strict supervision."

"I hope they can save her. Her conniving was always so clever. Despite everything, I liked Pandora."

"The hospital will do its best—they've got good doctors there," Mac said. He spun around as footsteps sounded behind them. "Here come Mom and Dad. Right on time to board."

Cyn started to bite her knuckle, switched to offering her hand instead. Mac's parents made a striking couple. Morgan Sr. was tall, with brown hair streaked like his son's but darker, the gray at his temples hardly noticeable. Mac's mother, an attractive brunette, was slender and lively. Her artist's eyes seemed to take in everything. It was easy to see where Mac's good looks and self-assurance came from.

After the introductions, he handed each of his parents a brightly wrapped best seller. "We thought you'd prefer some light reading as a bon voyage gift. More flowers would be redundant." He waved his arm around the tropical setting and got a laugh. "Here's the story of Steve Jobs and the founding of Apple for you, Dad, and Winspear's new book in the Maisie Dobbs series, Mom. You mentioned waiting for the next one to come out."

Stephanie caressed his cheek. "You know us so well. We couldn't fall asleep without our books."

"Jobs and Dobbs..." Cyn couldn't help mumuring, and Mac chuckled. "Another limerick on the way?"

She punched his arm. Mac's parents watched the little interplay with amusement. Then Morgan Sr. turned to Cynwyd. "So this is our wounded heroine?"

With a wide grin, Cyn shook his hand. "Mac was the real hero. He slid into Pandora like she was third base at Yankee Stadium. Knocked her over and saved the day. But he works too hard. I'm looking forward to assisting him with his office chores."

Mac's father eyed her shrewdly. "I'm counting on you to take some of the burdens from his shoulders."

"That's my plan," she replied. "Mac's very dedicated, but with a little help on the routine stuff, he can go on to build your empire."

Morgan looked amused. "I see you've got my number," he murmured. "It goes with that dazzling smile."

"And I see where Mac inherited his skill with compliments." They laughed.

Stephanie came closer and hugged her. Cyn's sore arm was squeezed, and she winced. Mac moved as if to interrupt, but she shooed him away. "I'm so glad to meet you." Her enthusiasm spilled out as she spoke to Mac's mother. "I've wanted to tell you how beautiful I found your Art Deco office in the museum. It's perfect."

Stephanie smiled. "Thank you. Mac will bring you around after we return, and I'll show you how I've decorated our home." She leaned over to whisper in Cyn's ear. "Take care of him while we're gone."

Oh, I intend to, Cyn thought. Chuckling, she nodded.

The yacht, of gleaming mahogany with shiny brass details, rode high in the water. Cyn and Mac watched the pair board, turn as they stepped off the gangplank, and wave. A steel drum band was playing Calypso, filling the air with bouncy expectation. She breathed deeply of the fresh, salty sea, the perfume of the flowers—all so satisfying.

When the couple had gone below, Cyn and Mac walked along the beach to their hotel, hand in hand. "After lunch, I'll take you to see Ernest Hemingway's house," he said. "One of the sights to see, here in Key West."

"Okay, but leave time to search for shells and driftwood. I packed an extra tote."

"We'll definitely fit it in, then a swim in the pool. The ocean is still too cold."

"Don't know if my arm is up to swimming, but it's up to anything else…."

"Good to hear. I've got lots of activities in mind." Mac gave her a smug grin and she returned it, her heart speeding up with all it implied.

The look did it. Mac picked Cyn up and twirled her around. "I've got contracts to discuss," he whispered in her ear. "The office job isn't the only one I'm offering."

"Oh, yes?" The sea breeze blew her hair about, brushing his nose as he kissed her. Couples were sunbathing nearby, and a parasail soared above them, but at the touch of his lips, their world was a desert island.

Moments later, when they finally drew apart, her dazzled eyes still noted the satisfaction in his gaze.

"There's a bottle of champagne in an ice bucket by our bed," he said softly. "I meant to wait until tonight, but my feelings won't be contained any longer. Do you think you could organize more than my office, dearest *Cariad*? An A student should be able to handle two jobs," he teased. "How about my life as well?"

Cyn's happiness welled up like the ocean waves beside her. She ran her finger across his lips, shivered as he sucked it into his mouth. "Is this a modest proposal, Master Magician?"

"That's the end game." He rubbed her scalp, then ran his fingers through her windswept hair. "Move in with me and Oxy for awhile, try it out. We miss you. I want you in my bed all night long, and there in the morning to make love to again."

Cyn clapped her hands. "Bacon and eggs with Bugs Bunny and Daffy Duck! What a delicious idea!" She rested her hand on his cheek, gazed intently in his eyes. "I've been under your love spell since the first day of classes, my sorcerer."

"The spell works both ways. That fateful day when you told the prof you were backwardly challenged— you had me then." He grabbed her hands, planted kisses on her palms, then twined their fingers. "I wanted to give you enough time to get over your divorce, but my feelings built to overflowing. I needed an outlet, so I've been sneaking your name into all my cartoons." His smile was sheepish, but his eyes burned with love and laughter. "You'll find them if you search. The villain scenes hide Cleo, and the hero scenes mask Cyn."

"You disguised my name like that famous caricaturist, Hirschfeld, did with his daughter, Nina?"

"Mm hmm. A good idea is worth repeating."

"Oh, I agree!" Cyn hugged him tightly.

"And speaking of good ideas, we should return to our room for a pre-lunch rest, Cleopatra." Mac lifted her, pressed close and bit her earlobe, kissing the sensitive spot below. "We wouldn't want to delay your complete recovery."

She shivered in delight. "Doctor's orders?"

"Rx straight from Doc Morgan Chase Price, the second."

She giggled. "Put me down, Merlin, and I'll race you back to the hotel."

"Fine." He slid her slowly down his body. As soon as her toes touched the sand, Cyn sprinted ahead.

"Last one still wearing clothes pays a forfeit!" he

called after her.

Cyn turned, dancing as she ran backward. "I can hardly wait!"

The trade winds blew their joyous laughter round and round as Mac began to run.

Epilogue

One year later....

Professor Richard Marzin sat at his desk relishing the reviews his book had garnered. Its catchy title, *A Girl Named Encyclopedia Britannica,* had caught on. As he tilted his chair back and pictured himself a guest on Oprah, a student aide poked her head into his office. "Package wouldn't fit in your mailbox, sir. The department secretary asked me to deliver it."

Marzin glanced at the package. A square envelope was attached on the outside, and he ripped it open. Well, this was a new one—an invitation to a book signing combined with an engagement party. He read the names, took a moment to connect them to Cleopatra and Merlin, and smiled. His class had turned into a matchmaking service! First Tony's announcement, and now this.

It was a good thing Cleo never found out who had made those late night phone calls. He'd found her so easy to talk to, missed her intuitive understanding when he posed a problem. But he'd been wise not to follow up on his inclination.

Yes, he'd attend this event. It was time he learned the ropes of book-signing parties.

With a satisfied smirk, Marzin picked up his scissors. Cutting the tape from the package, he unwrapped a large, colorful soft-cover book and flipped through the pages. Why, it was a comic book—no, that didn't sound right. Would it be a graphic novel? Laughing at the "novel" idea, he turned it to look more closely at the cover.

WILD ADVENTURES IN HEROIC STUPIDITY
The Tall Tale of Oxy Moron—
Alpha *and* Omega Male
By Mac Price

Mac Price...quite a snappy change from Merlin. Chuckling, Prof Marzin opened the book and looked at the first panel. He did a double take. The face looked like him!

Blood rushed to the professor's head. He would sue! He rose and began to pace, but before he had circled the room, reason reasserted itself. *Who of my colleagues will ever see this? And even if they did, no one would suspect me of being a fictional character. The idea is absurd.*

His rage diminished and died. Already he'd begun thinking of how he could use the idea of a comic strip in the curriculum of his next experimental class.

Resuming his seat, Marzin stared at the drawings for a long time. Come to think of it, the face that resembled his own was the hero's face—and he was solving the problems of the world. *Hmm.* The image was actually a subtle compliment.

He turned back to read the dedication page. Two inch-high stick figures, holding hands, preceded the line, "To my nearest and dearest robber baron relatives, Morgan and Stephanie. You let me make my dreams come true."

Below that, nine tiny stick figures bending with

laughter this way and that ran across the page. The dedication continued. "To the ball team that clued me into some of Oxy's biggest pratfalls—and taught me how to slide."

The last line began with a stick figure wearing a minuscule mortarboard, the tassel falling down to cover one eye like a wink. The dedication read, "And to 'Oxy Moron,' who set the stage for the love of my life to fall for me."

Double meanings and subtext.... *I'll be damned.* Rocky threw back his head and laughed.

A word from the author...

I love to travel—have visited all 50 states and 21 countries to collect super memories and great backgrounds for my stories.

Favorite pursuits are reading, including long walks listening to books on disk or cell phone, writing (from a play about fairies and brownies in second grade through all my life—stories, novels, plays, poems, and limericks), and gourmet cooking when I can find time (I've an herb garden with rosemary, thyme, basil, oregano, and parsley).

I am married to an artist, have a photographer son, and now live in the Southwest. I have been a newspaper editor, a college professor, taught journalism and sci-fi, but love writing romantic suspense best of all.

You can contact me at http://evedewcrook.com.

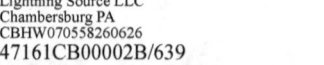